THE BRITISH LOVE PENNY!

"Susan Moody has created a protagonist who strides right into the gallery of memorable amateur sleuths to occupy a position of distinction."

Financial Times

"Penny is black, very. Penny is tall, excessively. Penny is beautiful, demonstrably. Take mighty good care of yourself, Mrs. Moody; we need more from you."

The Standard

"The most exciting detective to appear in a long time."

The Citizen

Fawcett Gold Medal Books
by Susan Moody:

PENNY BLACK

PENNY DREADFUL

PENNY POST

PENNY ROYAL

PENNY ROYAL
Susan Moody

FAWCETT GOLD MEDAL • NEW YORK

For Timothy Bertsch

1

IT WAS SATURDAY MORNING IN CHELSEA. SUNLIGHT squeezed against the windows and buttered the pavement on one side of the quiet road. A streetlamp flickered on and off, its timeswitch gone crazy. Sparrows abused each other. From an empty room, a dachshund watched the action, its nose pressed to the glass like abandoned bubble-gum. Behind a curtained window, someone played Mozart on an out-of-tune piano.

A shabby coat drifted along the road. It paused at cigarette stubs and litter-bins. The shabby gentleman inside it sported a stained moustache, an elderly hat and fingerless mittens. At No 14, he stopped. His hand reached towards the newspaper tucked between two pints of milk on the doorstep. At the same time the door opened.

'I was merely going to glance at the headlines,' he said, in the mellow tones of the Athenaeum.

'Just as well I'm not going to give you the chance,' said the householder. She wore a *hapi* coat of white silk. She had long, long legs and plenty of well-filled skin. The skin was black. 'Besides, you know what the editorial policy of *The Guardian* does to your blood pressure.'

1

'I do wish you would take *The Telegraph*,' said the gentleman.

'Got *my* blood pressure to think about.'

'Ah well,' said the gentleman. 'Beggars can't be choosers.'

'Ain't that the truth.'

'I assure you, Miss Wanawake, I shall make every effort to remain calm, whatever the leader writer says.' There was the merest hint of a wheedle in his cultured voice.

Miss Wanawake laughed. 'Why don't you go over to Dr Lovesey's at No 23?' she said. 'He takes *The Telegraph*.'

The curtains at No 23 were still drawn. Crookedly. A swatch of Sanderson's *Tiger Lily* showed. It was the only sign that Mrs Lovesey was away. Permanently. After twenty-five years, last week she'd cut and run.

'Perhaps I shall do that,' said the gentleman. He paused. He lingered.

'Dr Lovesey won't be up for hours,' said Penny. The doctor had been celebrating his wife's departure by sleeping in at weekends instead of rising with the early worms to paint the woodwork.

'Ah,' said the gentleman.

'Here.' Penny handed him one of the bottles on the step. 'I expect you want this.'

He looked aggrieved. 'I do wish people wouldn't order Gold Top,' he said. 'Skimmed or semi-skimmed is so much healthier. At my age, I really ought to avoid cholesterol as far as possible.' He patted his left side. 'The incidence of heart disease in men over the age of fifty is quite alarming.'

'Especially if they drink other people's milk. However, I'll have a word with the milkman.'

'You're most kind.' He touched the brim of his hat. Penny watched him make himself comfortable on Dr

2

Lovesey's doorstep. He raised the milk bottle in her direction and opened the paper. She went back into the house.

She padded along the thick-carpeted hallway to the kitchen. The black surfaces gleamed like carbon paper. The white ones had the shine of just-squeezed toothpaste. Even the garlic cloves seemed to sparkle in their little wire basket. If you wanted sterile conditions in which to perform an emergency heart-lung implant, it was fine. As a machine for cooking in, it lacked something. That was because Penny had been away for the past three weeks. Lucas, the outrageously handsome cleaning man who came in four times a week, had these *House & Garden* aspirations. It wouldn't take too long to restore some clutter. She scooped Orange Pekoe from the black lacquer tea-caddy into a teapot and added boiling water. She halved a grapefruit and gutted it. From a white pottery container decorated with a delicate Zen design, she took a handful of dried apricots.

She slipped a tape into the deck. Buxtehude expanded into the room. Solemn music for Saturday. Lucas had straightened up the piles of magazines that normally lay around and she leafed through some of Barnaby's old auction catalogues while she ate her breakfast. It was worth remembering that such things still existed in today's bruised world. Sometimes she knew the nuclear threat was an absurdity, that no one would want to wipe out everything, beehives and evening classes, people smelling roses or building snowmen, choirs and bicycles and microscopes. Sometimes she knew it wasn't.

She spread the Saturday paper. The news was the same as last week. And the week before. Riots in Soweto. An upsurge of nationalism in Cairo. A daring art theft in Italy. Half the members of a Yugoslavian trade delegation asking for political asylum. By now, the typesetters could probably make up the front page in their sleep. Judging by the number of typos, they probably had. A small item in heavier type among the news snippets on the right-hand margin caught her eye. When she'd read it, she shook her head. She looked out of the window and watched late daffodils in the flower beds. There was blossom in the back gardens. Buds bulged on the chestnut tree over the wall.

The silence seemed absolute. The Literary Gent in the flat at the top of the house was probably still hideously asleep, dreaming of a long-lost youth. Or the one that replaced him. The Sitting Tenant in the basement flat was almost certainly studying yesterday's racing results and burping genteely while her digestive tract geared itself up for the coming day.

Penny read the item again. It hadn't changed. It informed the reading public that Dr Bruno Ferlinghetti, an Italian archaeologist, and director of the Instituto Ferlinghetti in Rome, had disappeared from his home near Naples. It mentioned that a pair of valuable statuettes had also vanished. You didn't have to be Perry Mason to realise that the doctor and the statuettes were thought to be travelling together.

Anyone else, and Penny could have believed it. But not Bruno Ferlinghetti. Bruno was the sort of guy who wouldn't use one of your nasal tissues without replacing it. Bruno paid parking tickets. Bruno told waiters if they'd added the bill up wrongly in his favour. Bruno was incorruptible. Which was a bit of a waste since no one ever tried to corrupt him. One look, and the potential corruptor moved on to someone with a flashier taste in ties. Someone into drink or drugs or boys. Someone who hadn't inherited a fortune in lire from a doting grandmother and several more from assorted aunts. Bruno wasn't married. He wasn't gay. There was just no leverage.

4

Penny sipped tea from a cup so thin she could have read an insurance policy through it. She thought about Bruno. Incorruptible, yes. But also vague. His mind was sometimes so absent that you wondered if it actually existed. Like on that trip to Venice. She'd arranged to meet him outside Florian's at 10:30 p.m. on Tuesday, 6th June. For once, Bruno had been there on time. The clock on St Mark's had been striking the half hour as he kissed her on both cheeks. Great stuff. Except that he was five days late. It was a good thing she liked gondoliers.

The thing was, could he be so absent-minded that he'd go off with these statuettes, whatever they were, tucked inside his bags? Even for Bruno it seemed unlikely.

She looked at the clock. 7:38. Too early to ring people on a Saturday morning. Especially the sort of people who partied on Friday night. Particularly if they lived in fifteen-roomed flats in Knightsbridge and had a whole bunch of party-loving friends. Even if they were Giulia Torella. Much too early.

She had just put her hand on the telephone when it rang. She knew who it would be.

Giulia Torella's voice was husky. Seductive. Full of ripe promise. Helen of Troy's must have been pretty similar. It lingered over certain syllables, caressed others. Before her marriage, it had driven men wild. Or into sentimental gestures of the diamond-studded kind. It had recently driven her husband into the arms of another woman. Or so you might believe if you listened to the glossy wives of the London-based ex-pat Italian business community, the women who travelled the circuit between beauty parlour, milliner and dressmaker, smooth and hard as Smarties.

Penny sometimes listened. She didn't believe. Oscare Torella hadn't been driven into Mrs Harland Dewey's bed, or anyone else's. Even though, already twice-divorced, she was that sort of woman and he was that sort of man. Virile. Macho. Built like a freshly shaved gorilla. Oscare was in import-export. If Penny had been married to him, she might have ended up in Mrs Harland Dewey's bed herself.

'Penny,' Giulia said with the kind of dying fall that made people order caviare from Harrods to cheer her up.

'Hi,' said Penny.

'You've seen the papers this morning,' stated Giulia.

'Do you bend forks too?'

'What they are saying about Bruno, I am sure it is not true.'

'I absolutely agree.'

'It could not possibly be,' said Giulia. 'I mean. *Bruno*. Stealing some bronze statues.'

'How do you know they're bronze?'

'Marble would be too heavy,' said Giulia. It sounded logical. 'Not that he *has* stolen them, whatever they're made of. Why should he, for heaven's sake? He already has dozens of them.'

'This is true.'

'So why should he steal more?'

'The paper doesn't actually say that he stole them,' Penny said.

'It didn't need to.' Giulia made a forcible spitting noise of scorn. Penny had tried to imitate it for years without success. You had to be Italian. 'My poor Bruno has been judged and found guilty before he's stepped out of his front door.'

'After.'

'After what?'

'Isn't the problem that having stepped out of his front door he then vanished?' said Penny. 'At the same time as some statues.'

'Bruno is not a thief,' Giulia said coldly.

'I'm sure he's not.'

'There has clearly been some mistake. You know what Bruno is like. Perhaps he went somewhere without saying.'

'Like where?'

'I don't know.' Giulia ground her teeth together. She'd done a lot of that sort of thing when she and Penny had been at school together in Switzerland. It indicated that things were not as they should be. It indicated that something must be done. 'But you will find out.'

'Just a minute here.'

'He rang me two nights ago,' Giulia said. The husky voice trembled. 'He told me he was in danger.'

'Where was he calling from?'

'I don't know. We couldn't talk. Oscare was there.'

'Is he still?'

'No. Or I would not be able to talk to you. He flew to Cairo yesterday.'

'Bruno just said he was in danger?'

'Yes. So now you will go and find out what the danger is, yes?'

'No.'

'You must, Penelope.'

'This happens to be the private residence of Miss Penelope Wanawake, just back from a gruelling three weeks in Ethiopia and in need of a rest. Not Scotland Yard. Not 221b Baker Street. Sorry.'

'You must,' Giulia said again.

'Look. I have fifteen billion things to—'

"You will start at the Villa Ferlinghetti.'

'I will not. I've got far too much—'

'I shall send round the keys to you this morning,' said Giulia. She'd always been like that. Persuasive. Or was it bossy? 'Perhaps you will find bloodstains that could furnish us with a clue. Or a severed ear.'

7

'What in hell would I do with a severed ear?'

'It is what they do in Italy,' Giulia said mournfully. 'When someone has been kidnapped.'

'You think Bruno's been kidnapped?'

'It is possible.'

'It's also possible—in fact, it's more than probable—that he went somewhere and forgot to let anyone know.'

'At this time of year it is not crowded. You should be able to fly over this afternoon.'

'Sorry,' Penny said firmly. 'My wings are in for servicing.'

'Penny, do not waste any more time. Go at once. Please.' There was a hint of tears in the throaty voice.

Oh hell. Penny was a sucker for tears. 'I really don't want to do this,' she said. 'I've got enough problems of my own, with Barnaby and all.'

'Please. Please.'

'Give me one good reason.'

Silence.

'You could hire a professional,' Penny said.

Silence.

'Especially if you want fast results.' Penny knew she was being manipulated. 'Pros have contacts with the fuzz, with other pros. I don't. If you want Bruno found quickly, I'm really not your best bet.'

'You will work harder than they,' Giulia said, her voice so hollow she could have been standing at the bottom of a mineshaft.

'Why?'

'Because you love him,' said Giulia. 'As I do.'

Not true. Nobody loved Bruno as Giulia did. Nobody could. They'd got engaged when Giulia was twenty-one, on one of Bruno's trips back to Rome from some far-flung archaeological site. The wedding had been set for the following year. When news had come of Bruno's death in Turkestan or Pakistan, or maybe even Afghanistan, Giulia had refused to accept it. Searches had been made. Embassies had been contacted. Rewards offered. Nothing. After months of hysterical grief, Giulia had subsided into listlessness. Two years ago, she'd yielded to parental pressure and married Bruno's cousin, Oscare Torella. A year later, Bruno had turned up, clutching bags full of old bones and limping from a wound sustained in the fierce hill-fighting that had kept him incommunicado. He was much too late, of course. The Church had been unsympathetic about an annulment. So had Oscare. Having won the prize intended for his rival, he wasn't about to give it up.

Two lives had been shattered. Giulia was trapped for life in a marriage she loathed. Bruno had retreated into a monastery and nearly become a monk. Because of that, Penny knew she'd end up doing as Giulia asked. She didn't want to but she would anyway.

Dammit.

'I'll do it for a cheque,' she said. 'Made out to any charity I care to name.'

'How much?' said Giulia.

'You tell me.'

'Ten thousand pounds,' said Giulia. 'Plus expenses.'

Rats. That didn't give her any choice.

Penny woke suddenly. Outside Bruno's bedroom window, the night was shrill with the whine of cicadas. A bird jarred the still heat with a couple of uncouth eructations. She lifted her arm, watching the luminous green figures on her watch blur and dance across the darkness. Four in the morning. Low ebb time. Giving up time. Dying time.

She'd arrived late the evening before and crashed out almost immediately. Sleeping wasn't usually a problem, but, now she was awake, she'd need help to get back into it. She turned on the bedside lamp. There were books beside the bed and she reached for one, groping among the objects on the table. Something fell, slapping against the pale marble of the floor. A cup and saucer, containing the dregs of one of Bruno's disgusting tisanes. The noise it made was very loud.

A door slammed somewhere below. Footsteps were quick across the gravel outside. Without thinking, she was out of bed and at the window. In the vivid Italian night, a shadow was leaping between the beds of herbs that spread in front of the villa. It floated and bounced across low hedges of lavender and rosemary. It brushed the top of mints and marjorams. The gates on to the road were open. So was the door of the car which waited beside them. With a single movement, the shadow pushed its way into the driving seat and started the engine. The car took off. It disappeared beyond the wall which separated the villa from the rest of Italy.

All Penny had time to register was that the car was dark. And on its windscreen was a silver mark like a star.

2

S HE SLIPPED INTO THE SWIMMING POOL, NAKED AS A knifeblade. The man on the hill watched her. He'd have been crazy not to. Six foot of wet Penny Wanawake wasn't something the average male would want to miss out on. Unless his veins were full of milk. Semi-skimmed.

On the other hand, this was private property. From the way he tried to blend into a bit of ruined stone wall, he knew it. And, since word could hardly have leaked out already that seven kees of salmon-slick black flesh was skinny-dipping up at the Ferlinghetti place, she wondered what he was doing there. He certainly wasn't engaged in the usual occupations of those to be found on Italian hillsides early in the morning, like vine-tending, or olive-gathering. Not unless the average Italian peasant was a good deal more fashion conscious than he'd been last time she paid a visit to Bruno. Besides, among other things that average Italian peasants didn't have were sun-bleached David Bowie haircuts.

She thrashed a few lengths. The sun was hot on her shoulders. She turned over on her back and stared up at the sky. No bigger than an asterisk, a far-off plane dawdled across it. There was a smell of hot pine-resin in the air. She closed her eyes and breathed in deeply. It was intoxicating. Archaic. The kind of smell that reminded you the world had once been young and gods had walked like men.

The man on the hill shifted about a bit. She figured the loose shale he sat on was probably a pain in the ass. She figured if he was still there when she'd finished breakfast, she'd go ask him.

She got out of the pool, went into the house, came out again with a tray. There was a vine-covered gazebo to one side and she sat under its leaves. She drank the juice she'd just squeezed from fruit found lurking in Bruno's fridge. Three oranges and a lemon. Great. She ate a roll from his freezer, spread with Tiptree's wild strawberry preserve, the berries no bigger than matchheads. And another. She didn't bother with butter. In Italy it always tasted like Vaseline. She longed for a pot of tea, something delicate this morning, a pekoe of some kind. Dream on, baby. Bruno only stocked very strong coffee or the tisanes he made himself from plants grown in the herb garden out front. She didn't want to wash breakfast down with an infusion of dried agrimony leaves or fennel root. She peeled a peach.

The man was still there.

Idly she picked up her Hasselblad. She squeezed off a few shots. The hills. The silver grey olives crowding the slopes. The villa from the edge of the pool. The pool from the edge of the villa. Any visitor might do the same. You never knew when an identity mug might come in useful. She went back into the house and put on her white boat moccasins. It wasn't enough. She added cropped sailor pants from J.C. Hook. A hacked-off T-shirt of Barnaby's. Calèche.

She pushed upwards through umbrella pines, the needles scratching her bare arms. Olives began where the ground rose. The man watched her coming, his sunglasses hiding any expression. As she got closer to him she could make out the faint green check on his short-sleeved shirt. The gleam of sweat below his ears. The gun on his belt. He shifted again. Shale dribbled slowly towards her for a moment, then stopped. Below them, the pool glistened green as a lollipop. In the distance, a triangle of sea showed blue between hills. The air was hot and still and full of cicadas doing their Black & Decker number.

The man had both forearms resting on his knees, his back against the stonework of the little wall. His right hand now held the gun. He didn't look as though he planned to pit olives with it. A paperback copy of *What They Don't Teach You at Harvard Business School* was on the ground beside him with a plastic bottle of tanning cream on top. There were binoculars in a leather case. He was thirty-five, going to seed. Loose skin hung beneath his jaw. Somewhere along the line, he'd lost his nerve. It showed in the muscles round his eyes.

And in the way he turned the gun on Penny. There was a slow burn of sunshine along the barrel as he lifted it. He was as strung up as a washing line. She just hoped nobody shouted suddenly in his ear because then she'd be dead.

She stood below him. 'Hi,' she said. She smiled. It wasn't easy with a gun barrel practically in her eye. His finger moved on the trigger. He ducked his chin abruptly towards his breastbone. She guessed he was saying hi. A pulse beat in his jaw.

'You're trespassing,' she said. She kept smiling. Very laid back. Very non-hostile. Nobody in their right mind got hostile with a gun.

'You going to prosecute?' he said.

'This *is* private property,' said Penny.

'Property is theft,' said the man. He must have realised

13

she wasn't a threat. His biceps softened suddenly. Tension flowed off him like sweat.

'That'll earn you some Marx on the barricades.'

'Hope so,' he said. He didn't smile.

'However, until the revolution, this is still private property. So why're you on it?'

He lifted his chin. 'You objectin'?' He sounded like he'd be glad to give her cause if she wasn't.

'Not so much objecting as wondering.'

His lower jaw moved from side to side as he stared at Penny, working something out. Then he reached into the pocket of his shirt and pulled out a wallet. Flipped it open one-handed. Showed her a licence.

'Jack Lavette,' he said. 'Private investigator. Working out of Roanoke, Virginia. We cover most of the southern United States.'

'You must be using a lousy map,' said Penny. 'This is southern Italy.'

Lavette still hadn't released his finger from his gun trigger. 'Who're you, anyway?' he said.

'My name's Penelope Wanawake. I'm a good friend of Dr Ferlinghetti's—the guy who lives down there.' She nodded at the Villa Ferlinghetti spread out below them. 'Also of a good friend of his called Signora Giulia Torella...' she spoke slowly so he could get it down, '...who asked me to see if I could find out where he's got to.' She kept her arms away from her sides and her hands out in the open, where he could see them. After a while, he nodded at her.

'Okay,' he said.

'You still haven't told me why you're here,' said Penny.

'I was hired to keep tabs on the place. See who comes and goes.'

'Who did the hiring?'

'I'm not authorised to divulge such information,' said Lavette. He touched the place on his jawline where the pulse beat.

'Are you authorised to tell me why, if not whom?'

Again his jaw moved while he thought. Finally he shook his head. 'Don't guess so.'

'Wish you'd checked it out, Lavette. How do I know you're telling the truth?'

'Look. The boss tells me to get my ass over to Italy. I don't hand him a test paper to complete before I agree to the assignment. I just pack my bag and git.'

'You afraid of him, or something?'

'In my business, it doesn't pay to ask too many questions.'

'Thought your business *was* asking questions.'

'Not when there's a free all-expenses-paid vacation to sunny Italy I could lose out on, it isn't. I do what I'm told and make sure I don't forget the Hawaiian Tropic.'

'The Savage Tan,' said Penny.

'Right.' Lavette unscrewed the top of the plastic bottle and squeezed cream into his palm. Penny was glad about that. It meant he put the gun down while he did it. Judging by the colour of his skin, what he'd got was not so much a savage tan as a savage sunburn.

After he'd rubbed cream onto his forearms, he pulled a typewritten list from his pocket. 'Who did you say you were?'

'Penny Wanawake.'

He wrote it down. He didn't look like a man who spent a lot of time writing. When he'd finished, the list was covered in greasy prints.

'Basically,' Penny said, 'you've been asked to keep an eye on the place, right?'

'Right.'

15

'What did you see last night?'

Another pause. Another think. 'Nothing,' Lavette finally said.

'What kind of a hawkeye are you, man? After I got here, some dude showed up in the middle of the night. In a car. Didn't you see that?'

'No.'

'What happened? You fall asleep?'

'No. Someone else was doing the rota.'

'Who?'

'I'm not authorised to divulge such information.'

'How many are there of you?'

A longer pause, while Lavette weighed up the consequences of telling her. 'Two,' he said finally.

'And so far you haven't seen anything?'

'Nothing but air.'

'Hmm.'

Did that mean that Bruno's telephone call to Giulia had not come from the villa? Closely questioned, Giulia had insisted that he'd said nothing at all about any statuettes. What *had* he said? That he'd be in England shortly and would take her to see *Ernani* at the ENO. Also that he wished she lived in Rome and not in London. In his only reference to the dig at Toscana al Vesuvio, where he was currently working, he had said that Meg Tarrance was being her usual bitchy self. Then, apparently, Oscare had snatched the phone from Giulia's hand and slammed it back down on the receiver.

That had been on Friday evening. This was Monday. In the interim, Bruno had disappeared. Who had informed the press?

'How long you aiming to be here?' she said.

'Until Steve tells me otherwise.'

'Steve?'

'Littel. The boss of my outfit.'

'Hope you hear from him soon.'

'Why's that?'

'It gets mighty cold up here in winter,' Penny said.

She backed away and then walked on down through the olives. When she reached the belt of pines, she looked back. Lavette was watching her. His forehead was creased. He looked kind of worried. She wondered who'd hired him.

Even more, she wondered why.

3

A SEARCH OF BRUNO'S STUDY YIELDED NOTHING. THE most interesting thing it didn't yield were the current logs of the dig at Toscana. All the ones from previous digs were there. Hard-spined books of fine, squared paper which took up a quarter of the shelves round the small room. Herculaneum. Deir-el-Balah. Ch'in. Nazces. Each written up in brown ink. Each minutely recording how Bruno's expertise had made dead men tell tales. About Toscana al Vesuvio, there was zilch.

No logs. No files. Yet Bruno had spent most of the past three years working on the new excavations there. Even without a sniffer dog, you could tell someone must have been through the filing cabinets. The spare files at the back of each drawer contained inner folders of buff manila. The three empty files that Penny found among the full ones were identical to the spares. Empty. Someone had simply lifted out the buff folders and taken them away.

Last night?

Penny stared at a human skull which sat on Bruno's worktable. The dome was high and polished. Above one ear cavity a small white label said C/3xm/81. She won-

dered about its past. Bruno would have known. He was a
bone man. A physical anthropologist, specialising in classical archaeology. Offer Bruno a femur and he'd tell you if
it had belonged to a soldier or a shopkeeper. Show him a
pelvic bone and from the wear and tear he'd know if it had
been used by a patrician or a prostitute. Wave a discoloured
tooth about, and in no time at all he'd have come up with
its former owner's age, diet and sex.

So where was the stuff about Toscana?

There were three possibilities. Bruno had taken it with
him. He'd left it on-site at Toscana. It was in his office at
the Instituto Ferlinghetti in Rome. She'd have to check all
three.

Searching the rest of the villa took less than an hour. In
Rome, Bruno shared a flat with his mother, Palma, whose
tastes were eclectic and variable and leaned heavily on
clutter. His office at the Instituto was so crowded there
wasn't room to swing a cheese-mite. Here, just north of
Naples, the decoration was mainly light. Wavy light, reflecting from the pool. Green light, pushing through the
vine leaves which swarmed over the house. At one end of
the main room, there were two twenty-foot seating units.
Also an egg-shaped structure on a plinth, with a television
set inside. The other end held six chairs, a slab of polished
amboyna set on brushed-steel trestles and a statue of Venus
Anadyomene dating from the fourth century BC.

Three of the four bedrooms held a bed.

Bruno had gone wild in the fourth. In addition to a bed,
there was a bedside table and a wastepaper basket. On the
table were a telephone and some nail-clippers, two books
and a magazine. There was also a photograph of Giulia on
her wedding day. It didn't include Oscare. Penny hadn't
made it to Rome for what the papers called the Wedding of
the Year. She'd been on her way back from a fruitless at-

19

tempt to find out what had happened to Bruno. Her mother had attended. Lady Helena had said that when Oscare put the ring on his new bride's finger, she distinctly heard Giulia's heart break.

Penny looked at the books. The top one was a much-acclaimed novel by an Italian professor. From its compacted look, Bruno hadn't got round yet to reading it. She checked out the first paragraph. She didn't blame him. The second book was a missal. Limp leather cover, silk marker ribbon, red-edged pages. She picked it up and shook it. It felt like desecrating a grave. Things fell out. Devotional cards from Montserrat. From Rocamadour. From the Vatican. Giulia's first-communion card when she was ten. A dried violet. Romantic, but not the stuff from which clues are made.

She flipped through the magazine. *National Geographic*. On the cover was a beringed skeleton half-buried in mud. It held nothing significant that she could see. No blank pages torn from a notebook of a kind only available in downtown Saigon. No words underlined to form a meaningful message. No telephone numbers scrawled in the margin. Just a lot of stuff about bones. She picked up the telephone and studied its underside, wondering if it was bugged. Trouble was, she wouldn't recognise a bug if it waved its antennae at her.

On arrival the previous evening, she hadn't bothered to take an inventory. So she had no way of knowing whether last night's intruder had got away with anything or not. Around her, the villa was quiet. She took a deep breath. She wished she could just stay, do nothing, see nobody. Preferably for a long time. There was solitude here. Air. No pressures. No problems from Barnaby. Just peace.

Oh well. She got up and went to the window. Wasn't it possible that the whole thing was a mistake? That Bruno had simply dashed off to some important meeting without leaving a forwarding address? The answer to that was not only possible, but very probable. But until she heard otherwise, she'd have to keep looking, for Giulia's sake.

Bruno's room overlooked the pool and the olive groves on the slopes beyond. The room was shadowed, shutters drawn across the windows to keep the heat out. Peering through the slits, light gouged her eyes like a thumb. Squinting, she could see Jack Lavette. He'd taken off his shirt. Even from here, she could see the burn on his shoulders. He'd be screaming tomorrow, when it got to him. He seemed absorbed in Harvard's tutorial omissions but then he put down the book and lifted his binoculars. He stared at something on the other side of the villa.

Penny went into one of the rooms at the front of the house. Through the glare, she could see the road winding down between dusty ridges of parched land. She heard the car Lavette was watching long before she saw it, the noise of its engine ping-ponging between the hills. A red sports car, a Lancia, its top down. The driver wore a white head-scarf with the ends streaming away behind over sunglasses the size of dinner gongs. Penny waited. Except for the car and the crickets, there was no sound. The sun burned the scent off the herbs in the garden below the window. The house was full of it.

After a while, the Lancia appeared at the gates in the high garden wall. Penny had closed them last night, padding barefoot between the herb beds after the intruder had gone. Now, the driver got out and opened them with a key. She drove through, stopped, got out, pushed them closed again. She wore a dress that seemed almost old-fashioned at first sight. A simple flowered silk with a deep V-neck, expensively cut by some Roman couturier. Above the dress

21

there were big pouty lips. Inside it was a truly exceptional bosom.

Oh-ho. Penny raised her eyebrows. She would've known those boobs anywhere. They belonged to Bruno's cousin, Lucia Formaggio. People were seldom stuck for a word to describe Lucia since there were so many monosyllabic ones that summed her up. People often wondered why she wasn't married. They usually stopped wondering after they'd spent five minutes with her. In fact, Lucia had been married once, seven years earlier. Her husband had dropped dead on their honeymoon, smothered, it was rumoured, by Lucia's breasts. As well as a very rich widow, he left her at the head of a large industrial building company. The infighting for lucrative Government contracts filled nearly all the urges in Lucia that her husband no longer could.

Lucia was the sister of Oscare Torella. That made her Giulia's sister-in-law. It had never been an amicable relationship, mostly because Lucia wanted to be Bruno's wife. She'd written many times to tell him so, at the same time uttering endearments of an intimate nature. Bruno had not responded. Lucia had a lot of several things. They included lovers, nerve and hair.

Billows of the latter, salon-streaked and rumpled, fell now to her shoulders as she got out of the car and removed the headscarf. There was a large tapestry-work bag over her shoulder. You could get them in the Portobello Road, though Lucia wouldn't have done. Penny watched as Lucia shook out her hair, the movement causing her head to move from left to right and back again. Behind the big sunglasses, Lucia was studying the rising ground. Was casing the joint, in other words. Almost as if she thought someone might be spying on her. As if she were nervous. Or guilty. It couldn't be. A three-toed sloth would have

22

been able to count on the fingers of one foot the number of times Lucia had ever been either.

She came into the house. High heels clattered. Penny tracked her by ear across the marble floors as she checked the place out. Into the main room. Out again. Into the kitchen. Back to the hall. Pause at the foot of the stairs, then out to the terrace. Back in again and through the hall to the study.

Penny came silently downstairs. Under her bare feet, the floors were cool. Which was why those Italians who could afford it used marble for their interiors. Through the open door of the study, she could see Lucia standing at the filing cabinet. There was a small birthmark on her shoulder. *Quelle surprise*. Last time she'd heard, Lucia had been going to have it removed, just as she'd systematically got rid of every other bodily imperfection. She watched Lucia finger the plastic tabs in the first file-drawer then fling it back into its place and pull out the second. She seemed impatient. Cool as champagne, Penny leaned against the door jamb.

'Well, hi there,' she said.

Lucia screamed. She turned round, her right hand reaching for one of the time-pitted bronzes on Bruno's desk. You had to admire her reflexes, if not the way her mouth hung open after the scream. The lenses of her sunglasses were rose-coloured. It made the skin round her eyes look tender.

'It's only me,' Penny said.

'Oh, for God's sake,' said Lucia. 'Creeping up on me like that.' The muscles in her body relaxed, the frightened mouth regained its fullness. Ungaro, Penny thought, looking at the way Lucia's dress flowed round her hips. The bias-cut was unmistakable. She wondered what Lucia was so afraid of.

23

'Did you find what you were looking for?' she said.

Lucia slid the file-drawer slowly shut. She crossed her arms, then her legs. 'I might have known you'd turn up,' she said. 'I suppose Giulia persuaded you to come.'

'Absolutely spot on.'

'It's no business of hers,' Lucia said crossly.

'What isn't?'

'This nonsense about Bruno disappearing.' Lucia waited a couple of beats. 'That *is* why you're here, isn't it?'

'Yeah.'

'As long as you realise this whole thing is just some ridiculous error,' said Lucia.

'Ridiculous enough for you to drive down from Rome because of it?'

Lucia started to open her mouth to argue, then pulled it in at the corners like a house-mistress instead.

'So what were you looking for?' asked Penny.

'Uh—Oscare rang and asked me to try to find some important papers he left here. Obviously if there's going to be any kind of scandal connected with the family, he doesn't want to run the risk of being involved.'

'Thought you said this was a ridiculous error.'

'Just in case,' Lucia said. 'Surely you can see the harm it could do if Bruno really *has* stolen those statues.' She tossed her hair about. 'Both Oscare and I have business reputations to maintain. Suppose the police came and impounded all Bruno's papers.'

Penny wasn't above telling lies herself though she usually tried to make them sound like truth. What she really admired about Lucia was her ability to tell lies that no one could possibly think were anything else. It was effrontery of such a high order that she often got away with it.

'Sure,' she said.

'You sound doubtful, Penelope.'

'Since when did Oscare start leaving private papers in Bruno's house?'

'Since last time he visited Bruno.'

'What are they, his measles and whooping-cough certificates? Oscare hasn't visited Bruno in years.'

'I don't intend to discuss the matter further with you.'

'Oscare's always been like that, as I recall. Leaving stuff lying around and all.'

'Exactly.'

They both knew Oscare Torella wouldn't leave his shadow lying around if he could help it. Oscare was a skinflint. And paranoid as well. Who was after him and what they'd do if they ever caught up with him, he never explained. Just made sure he didn't give them any unnecessary chances.

Lucia removed her glasses. Under them, her eyes were those of an achiever, protuberant and brown. 'Was it Giulia who called in the press?'

'I doubt it.'

'Because if it was, I'll kill her,' said Lucia. From her, it didn't sound like hyperbole. From her, it probably wasn't.

'She only learned about it yesterday. From the paper,' said Penny.

'Do you realise Carlo and I had to stay home all yesterday in order to avoid the newsmen?'

'Jeez. Certainly didn't realise that.'

'Well, we did.'

'Who's Carlo?'

'A friend.'

Penny knew the kind of friends Lucia had. They were usually blond. They were generally big. They were always male and invariably stupid. Lucia had discovered toy boys long before the term had been invented.

25

'All day?' Penny said. 'My Gaahd. What on earth did you talk about?'

'Luckily, that wasn't a problem.'

'I'll bet.'

'Though I can't say I particularly enjoyed sneaking out of the service entrance this morning,' Lucia said sniffily.

'I don't suppose anyone mistook you for the janitor's wife,' said Penny.

'Of course they didn't. He is not married.'

Sigh.

'When Giulia spoke to you, did she say anything else?' asked Lucia.

'That Bruno told her he was in danger.'

'Who from?'

'He didn't say. They didn't talk much because Oscare was there.'

'Ah.'

'Which does rather suggest that wherever Bruno's gone, he's gone there involuntarily.'

'What do you mean?'

'Giulia wondered about kidnapping.'

'Oh, no.' For a moment the whites of Lucia's eyes showed all round the brown. Her voice shook. Seeing her, you'd never guess that she ran her building company with brutal efficiency, handling union bosses and the like with the ease of a Chinaman handling chopsticks. 'Why would anyone want to kidnap Bruno?'

'That's what I've got to find out.'

'Kidnapped.' Lucia put her sunglasses on again. Under the silver frames her cheeks gleamed. From moisturisers and anti-wrinkle creams rather than from good health. Lucia mulched her skin the way a market gardener mulches his soil. It was a full-time occupation. She was barely

26

thirty-two yet already she'd pulled enough hair out of it to stuff a mattress.

'Looks like I need to find out about these statues that've gone missing. Do you know anything about them?' said Penny.

'Nothing at all.'

'I thought I'd mosey on down to Toscana al Vesuvio,' Penny said. 'The people down there ought to be more clued up.'

'That is a good idea, Penelope. I am sure you will find the answer there.'

'Wish I was.'

'Penelope.' Coming closer, Lucia put her hand on Penny's arm. The hand was covered with thick rings made of gold and assorted precious stones. It closely resembled the skeletal hand on the front of Bruno's bedside magazine. 'Did you know there is a man watching the house?' Her top teeth bit into her lower lip as though it were a doughnut.

'Yes.'

'But why?'

Penny bent the truth a little. 'He wouldn't tell me,' she said.

'If you find anything out,' said Lucia, 'be sure to tell me first.'

'What do you think I'm going to find out?'

'I don't have the faintest idea. But Bruno is my cousin, after all. He may be relying on us, his family, to protect him from any scandal.'

'Bruno doesn't give a damn what people say about him,' Penny said. 'You know that.'

'I mean, if he should need any kind of help, his family should give it. That's what families are for. If he's in trouble, we must all stick together on this.'

27

She made it sound as though she spent her spare time organising family reunions. In actual fact, faced with a relative in trouble she'd have denied him thrice before the cock had so much as cleared its throat. Unless Oscare was concerned. Oscare, the doted-on younger brother that she'd been getting out of trouble since they were both in kindergarten.

It wasn't hard to see why she was pulling this family crap.

Oscare was up to something.

4

TOSCANA AL VESUVIO WAS NARROW STREETS BETWEEN death-smelling doorways. It was broken walls and crumbling flights of steps leading into nowhere. In the distance were industrial chimneys and the shimmer of tower blocks against a sky drained of colour by heat. Beyond loomed the volcano.

The site was new. No more than twelve years old. Unsuspected until a farmer, sinking a concrete post, had fallen into a room decorated with a wall-frieze that would have had the British Board of Film Censors reaching for the cutting shears.

Penny parked on a bit of lumpy blacktop. It terminated abruptly in a square of reddish, grass-tufted mud behind a building made of whitewashed rectangles and flat roofs. Several other cars were parked there, three of them with silver stars on the bottom left-hand corner of the windscreen. She walked over and looked more closely. The silver star authorised the car driver to park on-site.

The air was hot and heavy. Rain had fallen earlier and would soon do so again. Squat as a puffball, a trailer stood beside a crater full of grey mud and bits of history. A decal of the Italian flag was pasted to one window, alongside a sticker advertising Disneyland, USA. Inside, on a table, were a statue of the Blessed Virgin and some faded plastic rosebuds.

A man in a dirty vest was sitting on the steps. A bottle of Coca-Cola rested on a red milk crate in front of him. Tufts of black hair grew aggressively round the edges of the vest. He was playing solitaire and cheating on himself. He looked even less like an archaeologist than Indiana Jones.

Penny asked him if anyone was about. He nodded and turned up a red seven. He put it on a black eight. Penny asked him again. He lifted the black eight and peeked at the card hidden underneath it. He pointed over his shoulder into a heat haze that hung between broken columns of marble some distance away. Overhead, a helicopter clattered across heavy black clouds. There were more clouds on top of Vesuvius. Maybe even coming out of it. Penny hoped not. Last time had been devastating enough. The man turned up a black six. He stared at his layout. Penny pointed out the red seven. He put the black six on it. He didn't seem too grateful. Penny moved off into what had once been a classical landscape.

Here and there, figures wandered about, stooping as though working a paddyfield. One corner of the area had been completely cleared, revealing sunken streets lined with featureless walls studded with the squares and rectangles of long-ago doors and windows.

Distantly, a man in a camouflage jacket fingered his nose. He held a measuring stick in his other hand. Two very young girls sieved wet soil carefully on to large pieces of plywood, searching for clues to a former civilisation.

Leaning against one of the broken columns was a massive stone shard with letters incised on it. An I, a V, an S. Monumental. Beautiful. What would the sequins-and-styrofoam society of the mid-twentieth century leave for its descendants to discover? Dead television sets. Millions of beer-can rings. A few non-biodegradable gantries lettered still in brittle plastic KIWANIS WELCOME YOU. And guns. Rusting, useless, incomprehensible. These fragments I have shored against my ruins.

Face down below another column lay the body of a woman. There were rubber thongs on its feet. A blue diamond on the soles stated they'd been made in Taiwan. A skeleton was stretched alongside it, half-buried, bony fingers scrabbling at the earth. There was a whisk-broom nearby and a screwdriver. Also a non-classical bucket made of orange plastic with TOSC '86 painted on it in drippy black letters.

'Uh,' Penny said.

The body turned over. A well-nourished female, by the look of it, somewhere between the ages of forty and forty-five. When it had eaten its last meal, and how many children it had borne, Penny wasn't prepared to say. It propped itself on its elbows in the mud and looked up at her.

'Yes?' It wasn't what you'd call a warm welcome.

'Hi. I'm Penny Wanawake.' Penny said it slowly. People tended to lose interest after the first two syllables. She liked them to remember all four.

'Should I know you?'

'I'm a friend of Bruno Ferlinghetti's,' Penny said.

The woman got to her knees then hunkered back on her thighs. There was a lot of muscle on them. Flat planes of it ran beneath sunburned skin from rolled-up khaki shorts to dirty knees. There was more muscle under the loose once-

31

pink T-shirt. This was a woman who'd know how to take care of herself in a fracas. Who'd probably caused one or two.

'Are you indeed?' she said. The tone was hostile.

'You make it sound like any friend of Bruno's going to have a hard time being a friend of yours,' said Penny. She hoped the mud would come off her white moccasins.

'I suppose you're another of Bruno's camp followers.' The woman picked a long bone out of the plastic bucket. She held it as though prepared to use it if necessary. There were two deep frown-lines between her eyebrows.

'No one calls me camp and gets away with it,' Penny said.

'No?'

'Not if camp means what I think it means.'

'You don't look as though you get things wrong,' said the woman.

'Bet I'd get it right if I guessed you were Meg Tarrance.'

'A hundred per cent.'

The woman stood up without visible effort. Neither of her knees snapped when she did so. She wasn't very tall. Loose, windblown hair added on an inch that she'd lose when it rained. Her face was weatherbeaten. Tiny white lines whiskered out from the corners of her eyes and round her mouth. She had the kind of fuck-you voice that goes with being English and upper class. Like a man's. Deep and strong. Direct.

'Ms Tarrance, I wondered wh—'

'Professor.'

'What?'

'It's Professor Tarrance. Though I won't insist on the title. Not unless you've come to confer an honorary degree. Or bring me some papers from my ex-husband, the whingeing sod.'

'Neither, actually.' Penny stepped back. She had the feeling that if she touched the woman, she'd get an electric shock.

'Fine. Then call me Meg. Now, what do you want?'

'You're aware that Bruno Ferlinghetti's disappeared, I presume.'

'I most definitely am, the little Eyetie bastard.'

'Dr Ferlinghetti's parents were married in front of a cathedral full of witnesses two years before he was born.'

'The little thief, if you prefer.'

'You mean because he's taken some statues?' Penny said.

'Statuettes,' Meg said loudly. 'Some statuettes. Or figurines. Get the phraseology right, for God's sake. If you're going to disappear with something that doesn't belong to you, you don't do it with statues. Over the years, we've found several of those, along with pieces of mosaic, wall-paintings and small items of furniture. Even some jewelry. All of which are now housed in what the authorities are pleased to call a museum.' She waved contemptuously in the direction of the building behind which Penny had parked. 'If you were going to steal statues, whether of bronze or marble, you'd need trucks and lifting gear. Ropes. That sort of thing. It'd be difficult to sneak off dragging a couple of tons of marble, wouldn't you say?'

'That's what Bruno did? Snuck?'

'Yes.' Meg spoke through clenched teeth, her mouth puckered with fury. The lines on her brow deepened. 'Along with our figurines. They're very easy to sneak with, are figurines. Very easy.'

'And these are—what—some kind of bronze thing, are

33

they?' Penny said. One of her white shoes had almost vanished under the mud.

'No, they are not some kind of bronze thing.' Meg peered at her bare wrist. There was a great deal of mud on it and more under her fingernails. She looked up at the sky. 'Come on. Let's see if that lazy dope of a watchman can produce some coffee.'

She flipflopped towards the trailer. Her buttocks were very neat under the khaki shorts. Like a man's. So was her front. Penny took off her moccasins and followed. Mud squidged up between her toes. Every now and then they crossed deep trenches bridged by planks. Measuring sticks stuck up here and there. Whole sections of the site were quartered off with white marking tape. There were a lot of wheelbarrows.

The lazy dope took some persuading about leaving his cards and producing coffee. It was either the language barrier or the way Meg spoke through her teeth. Eventually, grumbling, he added hot water from a chipped enamel pan to granules he had spooned into polystyrene containers. They'd been used at least twice before and not washed out between usings. Someone had nibbled the edge of Penny's.

Meg perched herself on a bit of Roman ruin. She sipped cautiously from the container. 'Christ,' she said. 'Call that coffee. At least the last one boiled the water first.' She sipped again, grimaced, looked at Penny with her head on one side. 'So you're a friend of Bruno's, are you? You're an improvement, I'll say that much.'

'On what?'

'The last so-called friend he turned up with. Cindy or Sandy or some bunny-girl name like that. God, what a stupid creature. Bruno told us she was shy. Imbecilic would be more like it. Walked away if you came anywhere

34

near her. Wouldn't answer if you spoke to her. Refused to work with anyone but Bruno. No problem guessing what kind of a friend *she* was.'

'You telling me Bruno was fooling around with some woman?'

Meg gave a sharp little laugh. 'Unless it was a man in drag.'

'Here?' Penny asked. 'At Toscana?'

'And all over the rest of bloody Italy, for all I know,' Meg said. She looked down at her mud-caked shirt and moved her shoulders about so that bits of dried earth fell off it. 'Bruno brought her down—Cindy, it was, not Sandy—what, three weeks ago. He said she'd been working on a project with him in Rome.'

'No,' Penny said.

Meg scratched at some mud on the front of her thighs with yellow-tipped fingers. You'd have placed her as a two-pack-a-dayer even if you lived miles from Marlboro Country. 'Look,' she said. 'I don't give a damn what our beloved supervisor does off-site. He can screw the entire staff of his Instituto if he wants. Male *and* female. But on-site, it's a bit bloody much.'

'This *is* Bruno Ferlinghetti we're talking about here.'

'It is.'

The air seemed suddenly colder. Perhaps it always did when a long-held illusion shattered. Penny felt as though she'd just learned that Juliet Capulet not only had herpes but had passed it on to Friar Laurence. Something had to be wrong. Bruno wouldn't screw around. Bruno loved Giulia. Everyone knew that. Knowing that kept one believing in love and all that stuff. Bruno and Giulia were state-of-the-art Romance.

'Shit,' she said.

Rain began slowly to fall. 'If you catch up with him

35

before I do, let me know. I've got things to tell him,' Meg said. She cleaned dirt from under her right thumbnail with her left index finger.

'When did you last see him?' Penny said.

'It's Monday now,' said Meg. 'Three—no, four days ago. On Friday.'

'That's the last time anyone seems to have heard from him.'

'Little double-crossing sod.'

No point in mincing matters with a lady who so obviously didn't go for hamburger. 'He told someone that you were being your usual bitchy self,' Penny said.

'Did he, indeed?' Meg said. 'A female someone, I've no doubt.'

'As it happens.'

'Cherchez la bloody femme, as usual. Trust an Eyetie. One chorus of *La Donna è mobile* and they think they've got to spend the rest of their lives proving it.'

'What exactly were you being bitchy about?'

A twitch developed in Meg's upper lip. 'Security, probably. Or it could have been Bruno's latest trick. Nepotism, for God's sake.'

'I don't believe it.'

'Last Thursday,' Meg said, heavily patient, 'I discovered that he'd leased all the heavy equipment—the mechanical diggers and so forth—from some kind of cousin of his. Thank God we don't use much. Archaeology and JCBs don't mix too well. Even so, once someone gets wind of something a bit dicey, you can kiss any chance of sponsorship goodbye. I told him there were thousands of contractors who could have done the job just as well, so why did he have to go and choose a firm connected to him by family? Do you know what he said?'

'I can guess.'

'Oh.'

'I bet he said he simply chose the first firm that came into his head. I bet he said he had no idea it was owned by his cousin Lucia. He probably didn't even remember her name.'

Meg stared at her. 'How did you know that?'

'I know Bruno.'

'Does he really think the Ministry of Public Works is going to buy that one?'

'Bruno's famous for his lousy memory.'

'It was extremely careless of him. I bloody well told him so, too.'

'And what was wrong with the security?'

'If that's what you call it.' Meg narrowed her eyes. She indicated the rest of the site, with its carefully cut sections peeled away in layers as though the ground were being operated on. 'People round here just wander in whenever they feel like it. It's hard enough to keep even a minimal amount of security going when all we get is an occasional jeep containing three tooth-picking solders. If they remember to turn up. Christ. Don't they realise this is their own heritage we're trying to preserve? But it's always the same. They'd rather have a supermarket or a swimming pool any day.'

There was a deep weariness in the upper-class voice. It was obviously a battle she'd fought many times before, on sites all over the world. 'As for that Coke-swilling slob in the trailer, what the hell kind of protection does he offer, I'd like to know?'

'Against what?' Penny said.

Meg raised her eyes to the clouds. She frowned. 'Thieves, for God's sake. Thieves.' She gestured vigorously at a girl in a wrap-around skirt of Indian cotton who'd been watching them for a while from a shallow pit. The girl had a paintbrush in her hand.

Penny glanced around. Mud. Bits of masonry. Bones. Buckets. She resisted the impulse to look sardonic. *De gustibus* and all that. To each his own. 'What's to steal?' she said.

'What's to stea . . .' Meg poured the remains of her coffee down her throat with a loud gulp. She crunched the polystyrene cup between her hands. At least it saved on the washing-up. 'You obviously don't know about Toscana.'

'Obviously.'

'You've heard of Pompeii, I take it.'

'Rings a bell.'

'And Herculaneum?'

'You're not going to believe this,' Penny said, 'but I can actually do joined-up writing.'

'Toscana lies between the two. So naturally it was hit by the same massive eruption that engulfed Pompeii and Herculaneum,' said Meg.

'Back in AD seventy-nine, you mean.'

'How d'you know that?'

'It's engraved on my heart.'

'Toscana was another of those coastal resorts where wealthy Romans had seaside villas,' Meg said. 'Like everyone else up and down the coast, they ran for the seafront when Vesuvius blew. We're finding dozens of them in the boat-storage chambers where the wharves used to be. Not that it did them much good, poor bastards. Where they managed to escape the ash, they were asphyxiated by fumes from the pyroclastic flow.'

'Pyroclastic doesn't sound like a nice way to go.'

'It wasn't. Very similar to being trapped in a furnace. Mind you, being caught in the ash cloud that came first wasn't much fun, either,' Meg said. 'It would have been like a boiling-hot sand-storm. Hot air, saturated with ash and debris, swirling around at anything up to three hundred kilometres an hour. Two lungfuls of that and they'd have been clogged up worse than a blocked lavatory.'

She really knew how to make history live. Penny coughed. 'Leaving a lot of expensive stuff around for the taking.'

'Exactly. The Toscanans did just what you or I would do in similar circumstances. Grabbed whatever they could—gold, jewels, money—and made for the harbour. Most of it's long since gone. Grave robbing's always been something of a cottage industry round any classical site. Still is. In spite of the guards, people break in all the time. That's why we keep the boat-chambers boarded up. We never even know if the thieves get away with anything. There are all sorts of outlets for archaeological artifacts.'

'Illegal ones?'

'Of course.'

Meg began walking back toward the place where Penny had found her. Her T-shirt clung to her back. Penny picked up her moccasins from a bit of wall and padded along behind. Trenches led off to either side, some of them almost resembling streets. Here, however, the buildings on either side were kept apart by heavy pipe scaffolding. The doorways had all been blocked with corrugated iron, to prevent entry. Or possibly exit.

'Are those houses shut off to prevent theft too?' Penny asked.

'Partly. Partly to stop anyone going down there. The last thing we can afford is to be sued by some widow or orphan for negligence, if one of our diggers should fall down a fissure or something. And believe me, in a place like this, anything could happen at any time.'

As if to prove the point, the ground suddenly trembled under Penny's feet. For a split second, the world seemed so silent she thought she'd gone deaf. Then far away, a car horn honked. 'Whew,' she said. 'For a minute there, thought I heard the Eternal Footman snicker.'

'Terrifying, isn't it?' Meg said. 'Makes you realise you can't rely on anything. This whole area is under constant deep-earth pressure. The ground literally goes up and down.' She jumped on it a couple of times, to demonstrate. The earth didn't move. 'It's always been like that here, though recently the activity's been on the increase. Since the last big earthquake in nineteen eighty, most of the poor devils who used to live round here have moved into *tendopoli*. Tent towns.'

'That can't be much fun.'

'It isn't. It's not just the cold in winter. There's rats. Disease. The constant risk of fire. It's better than living in a building that's liable to crumble round your ears at any moment. It's better than walking down streets that could open up and swallow you. But only just.'

'I can see why they might break in here at night hoping to find a bit of antiquity to sell. It must be their only chance to start a new life somewhere else.'

'Exactly,' said Meg. 'Even though it's strictly illegal, of course, either to buy or to sell. But there are always collectors and dealers hanging around, willing to look the other way when it comes to papers of authentication, ownership documents and so on.'

'I suppose you can't blame the diggers.'

'I suppose you can't. But of course we do. As archaeologists, our concern is for the past rather than for the present,' said Meg.

'Time present and time past are both perhaps present in time future.'

'And time future, my dear, contained in time past.' Meg looked up at the dishcloth sky hanging just above their heads and drew in a breath that lifted her shoulders. 'We keep hoping to uncover something that will give us the kind of archaeological respectability we need. The big finds, the spectacular ones, like Tutankhamun's tomb, or the Xian warriors, don't necessarily tell us much about the past, but they do increase public awareness. That always means more funding. The trouble is, because of its geographical position, Toscana was too accessible. We do occasionally turn up something valuable, but so far, they've got there ahead of us. We really need a big find. And last week . . .''

'What?'

Meg lifted her shoulders the way the British do to hide deep feeling. 'It could have been the end of all our troubles, if bloody stinking Bruno hadn't buggered it up for us.' The schoolgirl phraseology in no way disguised the real despair in her voice. 'The Government would have had to take us seriously at last. Underwrite us properly, instead of pouring everything into Pompeii and Herculaneum. I'd have been able to get on with my work, instead of spending hours and hours of my time trying to drum up financial support. We're working under licence, of course, otherwise we wouldn't be here in the first place, but without sponsorship, we might just as well not be. Especially with the other two just up the road. Even they're suffering from lack of funds for further excavation, and sources like the universities and the National Geographic Society are stretched very thin. And after Toscana, there are still six other buried towns to excavate.'

'What does this have to do with Bruno?'

Tarrance fists clenched against Tarrance thighs. 'What it's got to do with Bruno is this.' Meg threw back her head so the loose hair floated. 'He and that bloody Sandy— Cindy—have stolen the very thing we've been hoping to find ever since excavation started. The big find. The thing which we only uncovered a few days ago. Which *I* uncovered, to be perfectly precise. The major discovery.'

'Where did you find it?'

'In one of the boat-chambers, the last one we'd opened up. Come on. I'll show you,' Meg said.

She led the way to the top of a rampart of excavated dirt. She pointed. Between modern buildings painted ochre and yellow, the sea gleamed, pale blue, darkening to navy at the horizon's edge. Once, Meg explained, it had lapped at the quayside almost below their feet. Now it lay a quarter of a mile away, pushed back by the huge volcanic flow of nearly two thousand years ago.

'They came down to the harbour, hoping to get away by boat, but it was impossible,' she said. 'The sea kept being sucked away and then flung back on land in great tidal waves. As I'm sure you know, Pliny the Younger watched the whole thing from Misenum, at the far end of the bay, so we have an eyewitness account.'

'I've read it.'

They climbed down, using steps cut out of the earth. The entrances to the boat chambers were high and arched, like wine-vaults. The remains of the brick edgings were clearly visible. Most of them were boarded up.

'I just couldn't believe it when I found them,' Meg said. 'I'd been working on the Governor all afternoon, and there they suddenly were, lying under his rib-cage.'

'The Governor being a skeleton.'

'Yes.'

'Them being the statuettes.'

'Yes.'

'Which aren't bronze.'

'Which are by no means bronze.'

'What are they?'

'Gold, my dear,' said Meg. 'Solid gold.'

5

'A PAIR OF FIGURINES, TO BE EXACT,' MEG SAID. 'ONE male, one female. Egyptian, probably representing a member of the royal house and his consort. Not that I got much chance to examine them very thoroughly. I locked them up immediately they were found, and then bloody Bruno had swiped them before I could get back for a more detailed look.'

'Why?' asked Penny.

'Why?' Meg turned her upper lip outwards. 'Don't ask me. He wanted the bloody money, I suppose.'

'Why the rush to get them under lock and key? Did you suspect someone might try to nab them?'

'No,' Meg said. She looked flushed. 'I—uh—just didn't want to take any chances.'

They were sitting in a restaurant in the derelict town nearby. It wasn't one of your four-star eateries. It would never make the Michelin Guide. If pushed with an index finger, it probably wouldn't make the end of the week. It was almost the only sign of life left in the narrow street. Most of the other tradesmen had already skipped town, their shop-fronts boarded up or covered with sheets of corrugated iron. Political slogans were daubed everywhere, most of them calling for the resignation of a government that had left the town to rot since 1980. Complicated structures of scaffolding cat's-cradled the streets. They seemed to be the only thing keeping the buildings upright on either side of the roadway. Such citizens as hadn't already moved to the safer discomfort of the *tendopoli* were making good use of them. Jeans and shirts had been hung out to dry. Rag mats were being aired. Occasionally, cats stalked from one side of the street to the other, a hundred feet up.

'We think they were burial offerings originally,' said Drusilla. 'Funerary figures from the tomb of some high-ranking Egyptian official.'

Drusilla was the girl in the Indian cotton Penny had seen earlier. She had a long, thin body and long, thin hair which hung down into her wine-glass and her spaghetti. Her feet were also long and thin. She wore muddy flipflops like Meg's, and kept taking her granny glasses off and putting them beside her plate. If she had a mind of her own, she didn't let on, copying Meg's gestures like an understudy. When she talked, bits of her hair stuck to her mouth. They both worked in Cambridge, she in the Department of Modern Languages, Meg as the Wilfryd Professor of Archaeology.

'Royalty,' Meg said firmly. 'Only royalty would have been buried with such valuable gifts to take to the other side.'

'That's why we called them the Royal Pair,' said Drusilla.

'How come Egyptian,' Penny said, 'in a Roman seaside resort?'

'Looting is *not* a modern phenomenon,' Meg said fiercely, as though Penny had just roundly declared that it was. Drusilla looked fierce, too. 'Some provincial gover-

45

nor may have retired here, bringing his *lares et penates* with him. Things he'd collected while serving time in Egypt, perhaps. Or been given.'

'Or exacted as fines,' said Drusilla. She gawped at Meg through the lank strings of her hair as though she thought she was wonderful. She probably was. Just didn't want people to know.

'Perhaps,' Meg said. 'Who knows? Whatever they were, unless we get them back, we shan't bloody well find out, shall we?' She turned to Penny, the lines biting deep into her forehead. 'I could kill him. I could kill Bruno Ferlinghetti for what he's done.'

'Just a goddamned minute.' Penny leaned forwards. For a second, the ground trembled. Under her elbows, the surface of the plastic table was gritty with plaster-dust. 'Why're you so sure Bruno's taken them?'

On the other side of the room a man watched them. He wore a double-breasted pin-stripe suit and gold-rimmed glasses. He kept looking at a watch which he pulled from a waistcoat pocket. Every now and then he brushed at his jacket and wrinkled his nose at the dust that flew up. He could have been a top lawyer or a high-ranking member of the Mafia. Or both. There was a heavy gold ring on the fourth finger of his right hand. He picked up the bottle of wine in front of him and rapped it on the table twice. From a shadowy recess, the restaurant owner ran forward and listened while the man spoke from behind his hand, his eyes not leaving the women.

'Instinct,' said Meg. She hadn't noticed the man. Drusilla had. She wasn't thrilled about it.

'Come on, now,' Penny said. 'You surely don't expect me to buy that. Not from a scientist. Instinct.'

'Backed up, of course, by some fairly damning circumstantial evidence,' said Meg. She looked as though she had her foot firmly on the neck of a fallen adversary.

'Let's hear it.'

'Dru,' Meg said.

The ends of Drusilla's hair were dragging in her tomato sauce. She sucked them clean. Yecch. There was an easy-to-squeeze limpness about her that reminded Penny of a caterpillar. The sort you feel no qualms in murdering because it's walking all over your salad.

She gave a frail smile, the first independent action Penny had seen her make. Picking up a salt shaker the size and shape of a hand-grenade, she scratched at some dirt encrusted round the cap. 'It's not exactly proof,' she said, 'but I did overhear Bruno and Sandy talking about the statuettes after Meg had locked them up, the day they were found.'

'Do you remember when that was, exactly?' Penny asked.

Dru looked over at Meg. 'Was it Thursday or Friday? I know it was the day Riordan and Dunlap drove up to Rome.'

'Thursday,' Meg said.

'Anyway,' said Dru. 'They were talking about the security arrangements at the museum, how bad they were, how anyone could just walk in and help themselves to anything they wanted.'

'Museum,' Meg said with scorn.

'They were saying how easy it would be to dispose of them on the black market, and what a huge price they would fetch.'

Meg drank some wine impatiently from a thick tumbler of bluish glass. So did Drusilla. The pin-striped *mafioso* watched suspiciously. There was a goitrous growth behind his left ear. 'Go on, Dru,' she said, looking hard at Penny.

47

'Bruno even said how simple it would be to get them out of Italy. He said they were small enough to stick in a pocket, and anyway, because he had some kind of a title—'

'Visconte,' Penny said.

'—the Customs people never stopped him, just waved him through whenever he arrived at airports.'

'It sounds like the sort of conversation someone worried about security might have,' Penny said, although it didn't. Not quite. Not if Drusilla was telling the truth.

'That's what I thought,' said Drusilla, 'until we discovered that Bruno and Sandy had gone.'

'Added to which,' said Meg, 'the bloody woman was no more an archaeologist than I'm a disco-dancer. Less.'

'How can you tell?'

'If she was really an archaeologist, why didn't she ever speak to any of the rest of us? Ask questions and so on? We've all got areas of special interest, even the amateurs like Dru. But the only one she ever spoke to was Bruno. Frankly, I think he made up the first lie he could think of to make us accept his bloody girlfriend hanging round.'

If there were a tactful way to pass that bit of information on to Giulia, Penny couldn't think of it. Anyway, she'd as soon beat up a baby.

'Typical bloody male,' Meg said. 'If they've got to choose between work and sex, they'll choose sex every time. Did you know that before the age of forty the average man thinks of sex up to six times an hour?'

'I expect the average woman does, too,' said Penny.

'Well, I certainly don't,' Meg said.

Which didn't prove a thing. 'When did you start suspecting that this Sandy person wasn't what she was supposed to be?' Penny said.

'We didn't *know* what she was supposed to be,' Meg said.

'Arriving with Bruno,' said Drusilla, 'we just assumed she was another archaeologist. It certainly didn't occur to *me* that she wasn't.' In the dim light, her dreary hair seemed almost green.

'Quite,' Meg said. 'Obviously we didn't ask to see the woman's credentials.'

'Why would we?' asked Drusilla.

'Naturally, when our so-called supervisor brings along a body willing to help, we don't question his right to do so.'

'Nor the helper's fitness for the purpose,' said Drusilla. She gave the very dimmest of smiles.

'The trouble is,' said Meg, 'we're not only grossly underfunded, we're running out of time. Everything on the site has been preserved intact for nearly two thousand years. At Pompeii, it was the form of the objects that was preserved, when the pumice and lava hardened round them. Here, because of the prevailing physical conditions, it's the objects themselves. Furniture, foodstuffs, fishing-nets. They're all here, just as they were when the ash started raining down. But once we expose them to light and air, they start to disintegrate. We need hands, not just to dig but to preserve as well. So we're always grateful for an extra pair.'

'Especially when they don't need paying,' said Drusilla.

'Quite. Dunlap brought those two students down last year, for instance. One of his pupils and her brother.'

'Boy-friend,' Drusilla said. She looked strained. But anyone would, with a *mafioso* watching her round his glass.

'Who informed the press?' asked Penny.

'Not me,' said Meg. 'Christ. Certainly not.'

'Nor me,' Drusilla said.

'Publicity's the last thing we want,' said Meg.

'Why?'

'Isn't it obvious, my dear? As soon as the papers got hold of the story, every thief in the world who specializes in antiques was going to be after Bruno. If they ever find him, that's our figurines gone for a burton. And with them, any chance of increased funding from the Ministry of Works.'

'What did these statuettes look like?'

Meg settled on her elbows. 'Two seated figures,' she said. 'Very straightbacked. He had his hands fisted on his knees. She had a child on hers. Kind of growing out of them. He had the square beard and heavy wig that you associate with Middle Kingdom figures of this sort. She wore the vulture head-dress that showed she was a queen. The implication was that she was the ruler and he was her consort.'

'Why would Bruno want to steal them? He doesn't need the money. Hightailing it with stolen goods is hardly going to earn him a place in the archaeologists' Hall of Fame.'

'Nobody's so rich they don't need more,' said Drusilla.

'I wouldn't be surprised if Bruno's not much worse off than you seem to think,' said Meg. 'That bloody Institute must take every spare penny he's got.'

'He could have been kidnapped,' Penny said.

'What, him *and* Cindy? Don't be bloody stupid. They've gone off together. It's obvious.'

Drusilla nodded. So did the man in the pin-stripes.

'He's probably sitting on Copacabana beach right now, negotiating a price with some South American collector,' said Meg.

'There's an awful lot of collectors in Brazil,' Drusilla said, nodding some more.

'While one of the most valuable historical sites of modern times is allowed to disintegrate under our very eyes,' said Meg.

'The reports I read didn't mention the fact that the statuettes are gold. How come all these crooks know?'

Meg looked quizzical. Drusilla tried to. 'Half the locals who work with us are runners for the Mafia,' she said. At the word, the pin-striped gentleman looked up. He poked one side of his face forwards, as though trying to hear what she was saying. 'And the other half's probably in touch with every crooked dealer in antiquities this side of the Ural Mountains.'

'Or the other,' said Drusilla. She inspected the ends of her hair, sucked the tomato sauce off them again, pushed them back futilely behind her ears. 'They keep a close watch on us. They know there's always the possibility of a valuable find here.'

'I don't hack it,' said Penny. 'Not Bruno. He's just got no reason to steal the damn things.'

'If not for the money, how about for love,' Drusilla suggested. Dust fell quietly on to her hair. 'If he's in love with Sandy.'

'Impossible,' said Penny.

'Of course it's not bloody impossible,' said Meg.

But it was. Meg didn't know Bruno like Penny did. Bruno was already in love. With Giulia. Always had been. Always would be. He couldn't have fallen for anyone else. A person had to believe in something.

'Who else was around at the time?' she said. There were minute specks of plaster-dust on her wine. She moved her finger across the surface to attract it. Under her chair the ground rumbled again.

Meg and Drusilla looked at each other. 'Dunlap,' Meg said.

'And Riordan,' said Drusilla.

51

'You mentioned them before. Who are they?'

'Riordan's an amateur. From Virginia. Made a fortune in fertilisers or something similar,' Meg said. She locked her fingers round her wine-glass and stared down into it. 'He's put a lot of personal money into Toscana.'

'And Dunlap?'

'Another amateur. Also American. He teaches literature at the Hands Across the Sea. It's one of these American sixth form colleges, up in Rome,' said Meg. She took a cigarette holder out of her pocket and began stuffing an oval cigarette into it. If she was hoping to prevent nicotine staining, she was years too late.

'Do you trust both these guys?' asked Penny.

'I'd trust Riordan with my life,' Meg said. For a lady whose opinion of the male sex had up until now appeared to register Statistically Insignificant on any scale you cared to use, it was an emotional remark. It was an emotional remark, period.

'Mr Dunlap's all right,' said Drusilla.

A puff of Turkish-flavoured smoke swirled round Meg's head. She was watching Drusilla's legs. There was quite a bit to watch. The two halves of Drusilla's skirt had fallen apart, showing smooth brown thighs and a triangle of white cotton pantie. Drusilla didn't seem to notice.

'How come you're picking on Bruno as the fall guy? Why not one of these others?' said Penny.

'Because, my dear, although the figurines have gone, they're still around. Whereas Bruno most definitely isn't.'

'Not that we realised until later that they'd disappeared,' Drusilla said. 'I shared a hire-car up to Rome with Dunlap and Riordan, so we all left together.'

'Any one of you could have had figurines in your pocket,' Penny said.

'Right,' said Meg. 'Except that there was no sign of

forcing on the safe. And Bruno Ferlinghetti was the only one with the keys, having relieved me of them as soon as he decently could. After which, he just drove off. Him and that Cindy Wotsername.'

'What *is* her name?' Penny said.

'Sandy,' said Drusilla.

'I thought it was Cindy,' said Meg.

'Sandy,' said Drusilla. 'Sandy Leon.'

'His car's parked right outside his flat in Rome,' Meg said. 'I checked with his mother but she says she hasn't heard from him for weeks.'

'When do you two go back to England?'

'I don't,' said Drusilla. 'I'm taking a sabbatical term, spending it in Rome.'

'Full term starts next week,' Meg said. 'I'll have to be back in Cambridge by next Monday.'

'Look. Just in case I need to get in touch with you again, could you give me your Cambridge addresses?' Penny said.

Meg wrote them down on a piece of paper. She looked over at Drusilla and then at Penny. 'I really couldn't manage without Dru,' she said. 'Not having the language. She's marvellous at dealing with the jumped-up little bureaucrats who're always coming round asking damn-fool questions.'

'Good,' said Penny.

The pin-striped man got up. He had the tightly girdled look of a 1930s movie gangster. Drop his gun on the floor, he'd just have to leave it lying. No way he'd ever bend far enough to get it back. As he walked towards the street door, dust scuffed up around his feet. More sat on his shoulders like dandruff. He spoke briefly to Drusilla as he went by, his hand brushing her bare shoulder. He needed a shave.

Drusilla watched Meg through her hair. She looked as though she was waiting for something to happen.

Something did. 'You bloody like it, don't you?' Meg said violently. 'You like it when they say things to you. Sitting there with your legs wide apart. You were making eyes at that sod all through the meal. Don't think I didn't notice.'

Drusilla looked down. She pulled her skirt together.

'What the hell did he want?' Meg demanded. 'Bloody nerve. The attitude to women over here is absolutely unbelievable. Straight out of the Middle Ages.'

'Don't be silly,' Drusilla said. She was trembling. 'You know they'll try it on with anything in skirts. It's just a reflex action. They can't help it. You know it doesn't mean anything.' Her eyes flirted with Meg. Penny hadn't noticed before just how hungry they were.

'The trouble is, I don't speak Italian,' said Meg. 'Otherwise I'd give the bastards a word or two they wouldn't forget in a hurry. Dru speaks it perfectly, of course.'

So did Penny. And the *mafioso*'s words had not been a come-on.

Unless you were excited by threats.

'One week,' the man had said. 'You were given one week.'

H E LAY FACE-DOWN IN THE POOL, ROCKING VERY GENT-
ly in the motion from the underwater filters. He had to be
dead. Nobody could hold his breath that long and live. And
she could see the ragged exit wound in the back of his
head. He must have been standing on the edge of the pool
when the bullet caught him. Must have spun round, staggered, arms flailing in reflex, brain already nonexistent,
body about to be. Must finally have fallen, the water
splashing rainbows. Must have floated ever since, waiting.

There were flies at the wound. Big ones. Shadows
passed between them and the sun. She looked up. Buz-
zards. Two of them, almost motionless in the flat, blank
sky, wings hardly stirring.

Around the body, the water was flushed, the stain
spreading, growing fainter towards the edges, like a Chi-
nese water-colour of a peony, a lotus-blossom, incredibly
pale and delicate.

She looked up at the hills. The silver leaves whispered
quietly. The green pines were still. It was sentimental to
see anything more in their stillness. Higher, by the crumbling wall, there was no activity. There was nothing.

Why had he come down so close to the house? What had he seen? Or who?

At the bottom of the pool, under his shadow, was his gun. He must have realised at the last minute that there was danger. Or had it been in his hand all along, his nerve gone, eyes bunched against a threat he didn't see? She could see the tender red skin across his shoulders. Death was one sure way to cure sunburn.

She walked up through the trees. His bag was behind the wall. His book, his binoculars, his shirt, his tanning cream. She wondered how he got there each day, how he got away again, where he went. Was there a wife, a child? What would they ever understand of his violent death in a far-off country?

For a moment she glimpsed a future man, visiting the hot hills where the father he'd never known had died, and finding comfort in the patterns, the way life's paths turned back, arced upon themselves. In my end is my beginning.

Whoever had killed him must have been standing just about here. She brought the bag down with her and put it by the pool. The police would learn from the badge in his shirt pocket who he was. She'd call them on her way to Rome.

Anonymously.

7

THERE WAS A BAG OF PEACHES ON THE PASSENGER SEAT of the Lamborghini. Also some rolls, some olives and a bottle of wine. On the back seat was a bottle of San Pellegrino. In the glove compartment were two new paperbacks. No reason why a stake-out shouldn't be comfortable.

Penny was parked across the square from Lucia Formaggio's flat. It was a small square. There was just room for an equestrian statue in the centre and some cobbles round it. Beneath Lucia's windows, two young men with cameras round their necks were playing a version of *pétanque* with plastic balls. A third sat astride a motorscooter playing himself at draughts on a portable set. Three crash helmets sat on the pavement beside him. Under the horse statue, a long-legged hippie type lounged against his backpack and read *In Cold Blood*. The horse's head was much too small for its body.

Penny ate a peach. She didn't want to put the top down in case Lucia looked out of her window. She wouldn't have much trouble recognising Penny if she did. By their braids ye shall know them. It got hot. She drank some of her wine. She read her book. It got hotter. She leaned back and closed her eyes. The window was open. She'd hear anyone coming out of the iron-and-glass ornamental doors of Lucia's building. She wiped her forehead. The white beads on the ends of her braids pressed into her neck. She lifted them. For a couple of seconds her neck felt cooler. She pulled at the front of her shirt. She'd have been even hotter if she'd been wearing a bra.

Around four o'clock, a man selling ice-cream from a box in front of his bike pedalled into the square. He pedalled all round it. This was the third time he'd come by since lunchtime. He looked hopefully at the hippie. He looked even more hopefully at the boys with cameras. The one on the scooter bought a cornet from him. Penny put an arm out of the window and bought one too.

Around five o'clock, the boy on the scooter put one of the crash helmets on his head and trod heavily on the starter-handle of his machine. The noise bounded round the square. The hippie woke up. So did a couple of dogs. They barked. Some girls walked past in cotton dresses and white shoes, laughing. One of the boys with cameras snapped them. They shook their heads at him and laughed some more. Penny ate another peach. It was beginning to get cooler.

In Bruno's office at the site, she'd seen his logs for the last three years. The current one wasn't there. They were large books, and cumbersome. Not the sort of thing you'd take to Copacabana. Nor on a kidnap.

At six o'clock, the boy on the scooter said he'd have to go. The others said they would too. They packed up their game. They looked up at Lucia's windows and shouted something. They put on the black helmets and all three climbed on to the scooter. They roared insolently away. The hippie yawned and stretched. He took out a bottle of

Listerine and a hairbrush. Slowly he brushed his long blond ringlets. He put the Listerine bottle to his lips, rinsed out his mouth and spat into the gutter. A pigeon landed on the too-small horse's head. The hippie shouldered into his back-pack and went away.

At half past eight, lights appeared in Lucia's windows. A hand, reaching out between heavy lace drapes, adjusted the catch to allow more air in. A few people went into and out of buildings around the square.

At half past nine, a man in the apartment opposite Lucia's began to sing selections from *La Traviata*. He seemed to know it all. He sang it badly. Penny wished he would stop.

So did his wife. At ten o'clock, she told him he'd wake the little girl if he didn't stop. At ten thirty, she said the little girl was awake and what did he plan to do about it? He asked her what the hell she *wanted* him to do about it. He said she was the mother, wasn't she? He went on singing. At ten forty-five, the wife said she was going to see the priest first thing in the morning and she'd had about enough of his damn singing to last the rest of her life. At ten fifty, she hit him on the mouth. For a while, Penny listened to him hitting her back. To her screaming. To the neighbours screaming. To the husband saying he was sorry. To the wife saying, Oh yeah? Well, he could just show her how sorry.

At eleven ten, the lights went off in Lucia's apartment. By midnight the lights had gone off just about everywhere in the square. Penny ate her last peach and drove to her hotel.

She was back the next morning at six thirty-five. At seven fifteen, a man who looked like he'd always wanted to be an opera singer came out of the building opposite Lucia's and walked away. There was a deep cut on his upper lip. All round the square, other people emerged. Some carried handbags, some satchels, some neither. At seven thirty-seven, Lucia herself came out. She went down the street, swinging a slim-cut executive briefcase. Office hours are much earlier in Rome than in London.

Penny looked at the paper she'd bought from the old man who lived on the pavement outside her hotel. Lavette hadn't made the front page. The politicians contesting seats in the elections had. Penny couldn't tell them apart. American Drowned in Pool appeared at the bottom of page 6, just above a picture of some kneeling monks praying for the miracle that would restore their lost treasure to them. For some reason, no link was made between Lavette's death and Bruno Ferlinghetti's disappearance. Amazing how absolutely power can corrupt. Interesting to know who had the power to keep the press in check. And why they should want to.

She read an interesting article about the resignation of Craxi over the *Achille Lauro* affair. And another about the leaders of the various parties making up the new coalition Government.

At nine o'clock, the hippie or someone very like him appeared. He sat down under the equestrian statue and scratched himself comprehensively. Today he was reading *Die Welt*.

At ten o'clock, the *paparazzi* boys showed up on their scooter.

At eleven, Oscare Torella appeared.

She'd known he must be there. As she always did whenever she saw him, Penny told herself she'd have joined the Foreign Legion, gone on the game or down a mine, anything rather than marry him. A man who wore suits made out of butchers' aprons had to be wholly bad. But then she hadn't been brought up like Giulia, as a dutiful daughter both to the Church and to her parents. Oscare was handsome, if you appreciated full jowls and appraising eyes. He gave the impression of being forceful, both on the boards of his many companies and in bed. It wasn't just an impression. Some women liked that. Lots, in fact. Giulia didn't. Giulia sometimes cried when she told Penny how forceful Oscare was in bed.

Penny watched him walk across the square. He was wearing a suit that even Harry the Horse would have balked at. It only needed spats. She started her car. She knew he wouldn't be walking far. Oscare went in for too-tight shoes. Today they were made of black alligator. Some people had no ecological conscience.

Around the corner, he stopped beside a bright blue Fiat Strada. He looked up and down the street as he inserted the keys, furtive as a rat. Could be he'd seen a lot of gangster movies. Could be he had something to hide. Could be his normal paranoid reflexes. Penny hovered while he adjusted the wing mirror then pulled out into the road. She followed him slowly. They left the district behind and went through several others. By the Colosseum, a nun on a Yamaha overtook Penny. She was wearing sunglasses. It was good to see the Church was moving with the times.

The pavements were crowded with rubbernecking tourists. Long-skirted priests walked in pairs, their hands constantly being seized and kissed by passers-by. The guys not selling ice-cream were selling hotdogs. Scooters zipped through the traffic. There was a persistent, insistent noise of blaring horns. The place was full of dust and dogs and dangerous drivers. Tattered election posters were everywhere, wrapped round trees and news-stands and the backs of public benches. If you weren't careful, you could easily miss the grandeur that was Rome.

In a street just off the via Condotti, Oscare drew up in

front of No 171 and double-parked. A man in a baggy suit of azure blue came running out and opened the car door. Oscare went into the shop. Penny spent the next fifteen minutes finding a parking space.

No 171 was double-fronted and very chic. You could tell from the door, which was bronze. The numerals 171 in polished brass formed the door handle. Also from the windows on either side of it, circular and tinted to tone with the door. In one of them a stone mask of chilling beauty rested on a cube of grey slate. The eye sockets were almond-shaped and peaceful, the lips curved in an archaic smile. The other window contained a shallow-bowled goblet of green glass, the sort of thing Agrippina might have passed the poison in. The fascia was brown with elegant white lower-case lettering that spelled the words *galleria itaro*.

Penny pushed open the door. The shop stretched away from her, softly lit, tastefully quiet. Dove-grey walls exactly matched the expensive carpeting. Floor-to-ceiling display cases jutted out into the room like theatre wings. Some held urns. Some held pots. Others had swords or vases or oriental lacquer. Standing against the walls were some anthropoid funeral jars. Apart from the personnel, everything in there was at least a thousand years old.

What was probably Marcello Mastroianni's twin brother was examining a bronze relief of a well-hung charioteer kissing a better-hung horse. An Al Pacino look-alike with a vicuña coat hanging off his shoulders appraised an alabaster cosmetic spoon, pushing his lips in and out. A couple were looking at some pieces of jade spread on a black velvet cloth. The female was in a feathered hat. The male wore an almond-green wool suit with a navy-blue singlet underneath and navy canvas shoes. Pure *Miami Vice*.

Everyone looked as though their current accounts never got much below a quarter of a million, even at the end of the month.

Penny threw her shoulders back. She was wearing her Issey Miyake culotte suit in white and cream. Not exactly haute couture, but striking. Especially if you knew what Issey was charging these days. She couldn't see Oscare. For the moment, she was glad. Having had her hunch confirmed that he was around, and possibly involved in some way with Bruno's disappearance, she now had to work out what she was going to say to him. I suspect you are engaged in the illegal purchase of antiquities? I think you murdered your cousin? Oscare would love that. He'd probably get violent. Even if it was true, she'd never make it stick. At least, not yet.

She wondered if *galleria itaro* was one of his businesses. Giulia had never mentioned any connection with antiquities. But then she rarely spoke of her husband if there was any other possible topic of conversation. Import-export was a vague term. Penny had always supposed it covered a two-way traffic in things like cheap copies of the Rubik cube and spare parts for agricultural machinery. Floodlighting systems travelling out, pirate videos coming in.

A man approached. He was darkly attired. His eyes were full of money and she wasn't adding up to much. She wished she'd kept the price-tag for her outfit.

'I am the manager. Can I help you?' he said coldly, certain he couldn't.

Penny pointed to a tiny gold box hinged with a pin that was lying on some pink velvet. The lid was carved with the face of Hathor, Egyptian goddess of love and fertility. 'I'd like to look at that,' she said.

He raised thin eyebrows. Penny could read him like a book and the contents indicated that she could look at it perfectly well through the glass-topped counter without putting her hands all over it. But haunted, as all shop people are, by the tales of eccentric millionairesses who, if not treated right, buy up the whole shop and not only fire the rude sales assistant, but make sure he never works again, he took out a bunch of tiny keys attached to a chain round his waist and opened the case. The box was light as pumice in Penny's hand, and vibrant with the past. 'What's the date on that?' she said.

'Thirteenth century,' said the manager.

'Is that so?' said Penny. 'I'd have thought it was older.'

The man closed his eyes. 'BC,' he said.

'And how much would that set me back?'

He named a sum that would have purchased Harrods, Neiman-Marcus and Bloomingdale's, and still have left enough to put a deposit down on the Dorchester. 'However,' he added, 'we already have two potential buyers. I'm afraid it's not for sale.'

'Actually,' Penny said, lowering her voice, 'I'm interested in gold, but I had statuettes in mind, rather than this kind of thing.'

The manager's face glazed over. He took the gold box away from her and opened its lid a couple of times. Then he returned it to its rose-coloured nest and tucked the keys back into a waistcoat pocket. Easing himself out from behind the counter, he used a hip to edge Penny away from the other customers. 'Statuettes?' he said. He didn't look at her.

'Figurines,' Penny said. 'You know.'

'Gold ones?'

'Yeah.'

The man looked towards the back of the shop. He seemed nervous. 'You want to buy,' he said, 'or sell?'

'Well, now,' said Penny. 'Which would interest you most?'

'Naturally,' said the man, 'we are always interested in an opportunity to purchase first-class antiquities, provided their origins and documentation are satisfactory to us.'

'How interested would you be in a pair of them?'

The manager obviously longed to confer with someone. He stared at the curtain at the end of the room as though praying it would suddenly be rent in twain. Nothing happened.

'What you are describing would be virtually priceless,' he said, although she didn't remember describing anything. 'If, that is, you are talking about—'

'I'm talking about funerary figures,' interrupted Penny. 'The sort of thing a royal personage might want to take on her journey to the other side. So they didn't mistake her for some old bag lady.'

The manager fiddled with his keys. He cleared his throat. 'I think I could say we'd be interested,' he said softly.

'How interested?'

'Very,' the man said.

'Right.'

'Very interested indeed.' The manager glanced at Al Pacino and added quietly, 'With or without the necessary authentication.'

It was another triumph for man's inalienable right to turn a dishonest penny.

'Don't call me. I'll call you,' Penny said. She smiled.

She wondered who'd actually got the figurines.

Oscare suddenly appeared through the curtain. He came towards her. He stood on tiptoe and kissed the air to the left and right of her face. 'Penelope,' he said warmly. Which was some kind of a giveaway, if not a dead one. Warm was not how Oscare usually greeted her. 'What can we do for you?'

'You're supposed to be in Cairo,' she said.

'Cairo?' Oscare's eyes shifted about while he tried to remember what lie he'd told and who he'd told it to. 'Ah yes. Cairo. Luckily I was able to complete my business there sooner than I had expected. So I flew on here, to visit with my sister, Lucia.'

'And recover those vitally important papers from the Villa Ferlinghetti.'

'You have lost me, Penelope. Which papers? Why should papers of mine be at Bruno's house?'

'Exactly what I wanted to know. But Lucia was there yesterday, hunting for them.'

'You misunderstood her,' Oscare said. He was moving her towards the door like a bouncer.

'I don't think so.' Penny bent to admire a black-figure kylix showing Prometheus and Atlas being punished by Zeus. Either Oscare or Lucia was lying. Which one? She looked up at Oscare. 'Nice place you got here.'

'I? Oh no,' Oscare said. 'This is not my business. It belongs to Pietro Bernini. Do you know him?'

'No.'

'He has been involved in antiques for many years, although he has recently gone into politics.'

'How long have you been interested in them yourself, Osc? I thought you were strictly a late-twentieth-century man.'

'Since I married my wife,' Oscare said. He pulled open the door of the shop.

Penny found herself out on the pavement.

She found herself wondering if there was a link somewhere between Oscare and the figurines. And if so, what?

And where was Bruno?

8

THE HANDS ACROSS THE SEA SCHOOL WAS UP IN THE hills outside Rome. Lots of American money had gone into fronting it with a perfect replica of a classical Roman villa. The effect was spoiled by the modern blocks which rose behind it. Difficult to kid yourself Cicero and Livy might once have walked here debating abstruse legal and philosophical points when faced with prestressed concrete and aluminum window-frames.

The school's cafeteria looked on to a stretch of scrubgrass. There was a small fountain in the middle of it, featuring a statue of Neptune poking his trident up a dolphin's nose. Vines hung from trellises, many of them heavy with grapes. The spire of a cypress poked above the red pantiles. The sky was absolutely blue.

Antony Dunlap looked like an advance man for the seven years of plenty. It was obvious that in his forty years or so he'd never bothered leaving anything on the side of his plate for Mr Manners. He was extremely pink. The suede patches on the elbows of his English-type tweed jacket were fake. So were large areas of his hair. He smiled a lot behind octagonal rimless glasses.

He was smiling now, across a jumbo pizza with all the trimmings. 'You say you've been asked by the Instituto Ferlinghetti to enquire into the disappearance of Dr Ferlinghetti,' he said.

Penny nodded. It was only a little more than the truth. Or less.

'I see.' The canteen noises were muted by air-conditioner hum. 'I'm truly sorry I can't be more helpful to you, but I was devastated by a series of stomach upsets for most of the time I was able to spend at Toscana this vacation.' Despite his Virginian drawl, he spoke with the grave orotundity of an Oxbridge regius professor.

'How inconvenient,' Penny said.

'How aggravating,' Dunlap said. He stuffed a wedge of pizza into his mouth and chewed energetically. Each time he did so, his jaw clicked.

'So you saw nothing? Heard nothing?'

'Nothing whatsoever.'

'Pity.'

'It most certainly was.' Dunlap scanned his pizza like a demolition expert wondering which way to direct the wrecker-ball. 'Personally, I blame the *fritto misto* I had the first night I got down there. As soon as I saw the mussels in it, I should have known. I mean, one bad mussel and your gut turns to slop, don't you agree?'

'What I meant was—'

'And after that, I couldn't seem to shake the bug or whatever before I was down with something else '

'—that it was a pity you'd heard nothing—'

'So I virtually spent five weeks with my head inside a toilet bowl. Which, as you'll be aware if you know anything at all about Italian plumbing, is not a particularly pleasurable way of passing the time.'

'—which could give me a lead to Dr Ferlinghetti,' Penny said loudly.

A girl in Tretorns and a preppy-type denim skirt lined with madras tried to pass behind Dunlap's seat. She rolled her eyes as she squeezed between the wall and the extra flesh which strained over the sides of his moulded plastic chair and was extruded through the oval space at the back. Coloured plastic bulldog clips clung to either side of her head like butterflies.

'Dr Ferlinghetti,' said Dunlap. He licked one finger and used it to lift a bacon morsel from his salad. He put it on his tongue as though it were a Communion wafer. 'Such a nice man. I must say I was surprised to discover he'd done the dirty on his own institute. I mean, after all the work he's put into it. When he took over the place, it was very run down. It's taken him years of effort to restore its reputation as a serious academic establishment.'

Penny frowned. 'Bruno's never ripped anybody off in his entire life.'

'He's been having a hard time adding to the collection at the institute,' Dunlap said. 'And, of course, you need new attractions if you're to keep attendances up. For a while there he was doing brilliantly. Lots of press coverage of those wild journeys of his into the unknown, and all the goodies he brought back with him. There's not been much of that recently. Yet it's the paying public that funds the research going on behind the scenes. And some of Ferlinghetti's was very good. Which, as I say, is why I was so surprised that he should take off like that.'

'But these missing statuettes weren't anything to do with the Instituto.'

Dunlap looked over the tops of his glasses. 'Surely Meg explained.'

'About pyroclastic flows, she explained. And someone called Sandy.'

'Ah.' Dunlap moved into professorial mode. 'Ferlinghetti had agreed a deal with the Italian Government—the Belle Arti Commission, to be exact—that anything of real interest would be displayed at the Instituto—provided, of course, that the security arrangements met with official approval. There was to be a press conference, and a considerable amount of fanfare. The idea was to boost both the prestige of the dig at Toscana, and the receipts of the Instituto.'

'All the more reason why he wouldn't steal them.'

'Maybe.'

Penny cut a tiny portion of her own pizza and chewed it daintily. Teaching by example. It was lost on Dunlap. He doubled over another slice of his own and rammed it into his mouth, trailing strings of melted cheese.

'Have you any other theories about why Bruno might have taken the statuettes?'

Dunlap waved smooth white fingers about. They hovered in the air beside his face like the tentacles of a *calamare*. His fingernails were covered in clear varnish. Jeez. 'I did rather wonder if possibly it was some kind of publicity gimmick. The idea being to stir up public interest and then reappear at the appropriate moment, saying the whole thing was an error.'

'Bruno doesn't work like that.'

'Or possibly he'd finally decided to do a Gauguin.'

'You don't know him very well.'

'He's never married,' Dunlap said. 'Yet he's clearly not a homosexualist. Perhaps he felt it was time to chuck up his responsibilities and light out for the wilderness. Taking with him some security for his old age.'

'That's ridiculous. He doesn't need that kind of hassle

71

to get his hands on some cash. Anyway, he wouldn't have the first idea how to find a fence.'

'Under that sophisticated veneer, you're obviously still an innocent,' Dunlap remarked. He reached across and rubbed the material of Penny's top between finger and thumb. 'Tell me, do I detect a hint of the mysterious East about your garments? A touch of the wily oriental?'

Penny jerked herself away. Condescending prick. Condescending *racist* prick. 'Can you describe the statuettes to me?' she said.

Dunlap lifted his fingers again. 'I'm afraid not. I've never actually seen them. Reilly Riordan and I drove over to consult the people at Paestum about something the morning that Meg Tarrance uncovered them. I gather she whipped them into the museum safe so fast you'd have thought they were red hot, being extremely jittery about losing them. I suppose you can't blame her, but no one was allowed to look at them until the Government official had been down from Rome. Except by then, Bruno had done his vanishing act.'

'Tell me about Sandy Leon.'

'The gorgeous Sandy,' said Dunlap. 'She was making a big play for Ferlinghetti, that much I do know.'

'How?'

'My dear, I saw them.'

'I thought you had your head down the john.'

'Not the entire five weeks,' said Dunlap. 'I may have exaggerated my condition a little. I did manage to stagger round the site a few times and while I did so, I could hardly fail to note the attraction that seemed to exist between Miss Leon and Ferlinghetti.'

'Did you speak to her?'

'I might have done, had I been able to prise her away from the good *dottore*.'

'What was she like?'

'Blonde hair, dark eyes, very attractive. A bit of a feminist, I imagine, since she always wore those one-piece things that remind one of Amelia Earhart. Or dungarees and shirts with slogans all over them. And wore them very well, I might add.'

'Had you ever seen her before? In Rome, perhaps?'

'No.' Dunlap gripped his salad bowl with one hand and pushed most of the contents into his mouth. Blue cheese dressing glistened on his chin. 'What makes you think I might have?' he asked sharply. Hard to be sharp with a mouthful of iceberg lettuce, but Dunlap made it. She could imagine him in a leather skirt, whipping galley-slaves into hamburger.

'I wondered if you knew her professionally, is all. None of you experts seem to have questioned her credentials.'

'She arrived under Bruno's aegis,' Dunlap said. 'Why would we? Besides, she kept her credentials in her sweat-shirt, where we could all see them.' His eyelids squeezed together. Some chins shook. Penny couldn't see the joke.

'Very droll,' she said.

'Experts is perhaps a misnomer,' said Dunlap. 'Whatever claim to expertise we may have in our own fields, archaeologically speaking we are ignorami—'

'Ignorami,' said Penny. 'Hey, that is class.'

'—and likely to remain so. These days, the chances of an amateur making any kind of a mark are slim indeed. I, for instance, have contributed numerous papers to the journals, but it's one of these Catch-22 situations. If you haven't got a name, they won't publish, unless the paper is world-shaking. And if you haven't published, you can't make a name.'

'What's in a name?'

Dunlap looked at her over his glasses. 'You'd be surprised,' he said. 'When I say ignorami, I naturally except Meg and Bruno. The rest of us, however, are merely enthusiastic amateurs. Riordan, myself, Meg's dreary little sidekick.'

'Drusilla.'

'I, for example, am on secondment from a seminary for young ladies in Charlottesville, employed to teach English literature, though my specialist field is the Russian novel. Not that there's much enthusiasm for Russian literature among the young these days. Particularly not in an establishment of this sort, which is little more than a poor man's finishing-school for the brainless daughters of *nouveaux-riches* insurance salesmen in the more southerly of the United States.'

'I bet they didn't ask you to write the prospectus.'

The fat man sighed. A fragment of Roquefort flew on to the side of his wine-glass. Gaahd. At least it hadn't been hers. 'Teaching them is a soul-destroying job, believe me. For the most part they simply can't be bothered to plough through the wordage. They're too used to having it all spelled out for them. 'Oh, Mr Dunlap, I can never remember who's who in those dreary old Russian novels.' He spoke this in a high falsetto, and sighed again. 'Attention spans of grasshoppers, most of them.'

Two girls in Oxford cloth button-up shirts and madras bermudas went by. They were holding loose-leaf binders to their chests. Neither of them looked as if they'd know the brothers Karamazov from the Hardy boys.

'And they're not just stupid. One girl was sent here to get away from some lowlife boy-friend she'd picked up. As a matter of fact, I took her with me to Toscana last summer. Her father asked me to keep an eye on her.' Parts of his face went red. Penny guessed the father had paid heftily for the privilege. 'Her boy-friend came along too, a couple of times.'

'The lowlifer?'

'Jesus, I hope not.' Dunlap thought about it. 'No. It can't have been. He took rather a liking to Godzilla.'

'That's Drusilla,' Penny said.

Over by the coffee-machines, someone dropped a tin tray. It clattered on the tiles. There were screams and giggles of the coed kind. She felt odd.

'To get back to this Sandy Leon,' she said. 'Did you ever have any reason to suspect that she might not be what Bruno implied she was?'

'None.'

'She fitted in on-site all right, did she? Looked as if she could handle a pick and shovel?'

'Frankly, she looked as if she could handle an army.'

Darn it. There had to be a reason for Sandy Leon. Other than the one Meg and Drusilla had suggested, which Dunlap had reinforced. He was eating chocolate cream pie. A double portion. She watched him remove the swirls of cream which decorated it and lick them one by one off his spoon.

'Do you have an address for Mr Riordan?' she asked.

'Only in the States. He left Rome last Friday.'

'Expecting him over again?'

'No. But come back to my office after lunch and I'll find his address,' Dunlap said. 'I ought to carry it in my head, considering how long I've known him. In fact it was through him that I got on to the Toscana dig in the first place.'

A lot of purposeful streaming had begun. Girls shifted back and forth, book-bags slung over their shoulders, straw hold-alls in their hands. Every one of them had a perfect tan. Most had perfect teeth. Those who didn't were busy putting it right with steel constructions that made their mouths look like the insides of computers.

After another piece of pie—pecan, this time—and three cups of coffee, Dunlap was ready to leave. Penny followed his large buttocks out of the cafeteria. He must have weighed three hundred pounds at least. His thighs swished together when he walked. As they moved into the sunlight, the discrepancy between the real hair and the fake was more noticeable. Much more. Funny how keeping the years at bay was expected of a woman but sad in a man.

They walked across a garden of sculpted box and gravel. The sun was very hot, bringing out the thick, aggressive scent of the little hedges. The gravel was noisy. Dunlap's office was in one of the modern blocks, surrounded by balding lawns. No one grew grass the way the English did. At least there was something left to be nationalistic about.

Dunlap took her up to the second floor. His office looked out on to tennis courts and a swimming pool. There were chaises set around the pool, and tables with striped umbrellas. It looked more like a resort than a school. Nearly all the chaises were empty. Of the two which weren't, one contained a girl in half a bikini, the other a man in a flashy red maillot. He was reading a book and squeezing suntan cream on to his arms.

'That, believe it or not, is the chaplain,' Dunlap said.

'What is he, hearing confession? Or working on a sermon.'

'Working on a tan,' Dunlap said.

'Guy ought to be rooting out evil,' Penny said.

Dunlap didn't give a damn about evil. 'And then he has the nerve to lecture me about *my* gross habits,' he said.

'Grossness is in the eye of the beholder,' said Penny.

With Dunlap around, the beholder didn't have that much choice about what was in his eye.

It was the standard academic's office. Desk, shelving, filing cabinets. A pole with hooks on it. A sleazy raincoat on the hooks. On a sidetable, piles of term-papers. The window-sill was dusty. It held a small clay jar, a shard of iridescent Roman glass, and four flies, three of which were dead. The room smelled of wood-glue.

Dunlap sat down at the desk. He began poking through papers. 'Riordan, Riordan,' he said. 'He gave me his card just last week. He lives quite near my home—my former home. What on earth did I do with it?'

'In your address book?'

'Could be. It's around here some place. Black leather. Can you see it?'

Penny couldn't. She tried. There were so many papers everywhere it was difficult. She put her hands on either side of the nearest pile to lift it and look underneath. Term-papers. The top one was entitled *Jane Austen and the Politics of Fear: an interpretation of Mansfield Park by Anne-Marie Huizinger. Her Own Original Work*. It certainly sounded original. There were hand-drawn daisies in each corner of the title page.

Dunlap's hands came down over hers. Amazing. It wasn't so much that he moved with deceptive speed. More that because he was so huge, you were surprised he could move at all. His hands clamped Penny's to the pile. He gripped them and pulled them away. 'I'll take those,' he said, smooth as butter. With just about the same percentage of saturated fat.

He picked up the essays and put them on the shelf behind him. But not before Penny had seen several sheets of squared paper, one edge raggedly torn. They were written in brown ink.

'Okay, Jack,' she said. 'You've stalled long enough. Where is he?'

'Where is who?'

'Who the heck've we been talking about? Bruno Ferlinghetti is who.'

'Why on earth should I know? I already explained that I find his disappearance inexplicable.'

'You've got his notes. I just saw them.'

'My dear Miss Wanawake. Those are some rough notes of my own.'

'Don't bullshit me, Dunlap. I know my friend's handwriting when I see it.'

Dunlap produced some nicely judged impatience. Added a touch of irritation. Glanced at his watch.

'I fail to see why I should have to justify myself to you,' he said. 'But if it will put your mind at rest...' He pulled at a lower drawer in his desk and took out a large book. It was hard-spined, with a navy-blue cover and red corners. He opened it.

Squared paper, all right. Like Bruno's. And the first few pages had been torn out.

'Ah,' Penny said. She couldn't think of much else to say. Except to accuse him outright of being a liar. She wasn't sure that was wise. He might be a murderer as well.

'I always use a book like this for writing up my notes,' Dunlap said. 'A lot of archaeologists do—it's easier for charting measurements and diagrams.'

'Do a lot of archaeologists use brown ink?'

'I can't speak for all of them.' Dunlap reached into the spaces of his jacket and brought out a gold Schaeffer. He jiggled it across the open page and turned the book towards her. He'd written 'Never send to know for whom the bell tolls.' In ink that was indisputably brown. In a hand very similar to Bruno's.

Why didn't she believe him? Was it the gleam she caught, behind the octagonal glasses, of something that could have been complacency? The triumphant gleam of a man well-armed against possible questions?

'Why don't I believe you?' she said.

'Some people have trouble relating to the truth.' Leaning back in his chair, Dunlap capped his pen. He smiled. A tiger's smile. With the young lady not only inside but well and truly digested. She stepped back. It was easy for a fat man to be taken for a clown. Easy, and dangerous. No one had taken fat men seriously since Charles Laughton died. Ask for an associative adjective to go with fat, and most people would hand you jolly. But look at Hitchcock. Look at Orson Welles.

She folded her arms across her chest. Scrunched up her eyes. Lifted her lip from her teeth. Body language designed to intimidate. It might have worked if she'd been a dog. Or if Dunlap had.

'I ought to warn you that I can beat the shit out of you if I have to,' she said.

Dunlap gazed back at her. Very bland. Very unintimidated. 'Oh, my God,' he said. He slowly bunched a fist. The fat on him suddenly had purpose. It didn't look like fat any more. It looked like a lot of muscle.

Penny swallowed. 'I don't give up easy,' she said.

'Would you like to leave, Miss Wanawake? Or would you like to duke it out right now?' asked Dunlap. He grinned. The gentlemanly air of scholarship had vanished.

She didn't want to, but he definitely had the weight. She left.

9

THE INSTITUTO FERLINGHETTI WAS IN ONE OF ROME'S northern suburbs. Statuary littered the grounds, some of it marble and pensive, some bronze and immodest. The place had originally been built for a cardinal's mistress. Later she'd married a member of the rising merchant class who had cornered the market in Bohemian silver. Palladio's influence was strong.

There'd been some changes since then, unless the cardinal's mistress also kept a skeleton of *Diplodocus* in the hall. This one had several vertebrae missing and a neat cylindrical litter-bin beside its right foot. Someone had scrawled Gianni è Carla on the rear kneebone. Penny had noticed before that Italians had no respect for history. Probably because there was so much of it about.

The Instituto had been founded by Bruno's great-grandfather, an amateur anthropologist and keen collector of practically anything. His enthusiasm had begun when a sailor uncle left him several shrunken heads and a grass skirt. A large legacy from a maiden aunt had enabled him to purchase the building from an early-nineteenth-century property speculator and found the Instituto to which he continued to add eclectically for the rest of his life. Bruno's father, an amateur anthropologist, had built the laboratories behind the building. Bruno himself had given the Instituto an international reputation with some solid, occasionally even exciting, anthropological research.

As a child, Penny had been fascinated by the totem poles and beaded head-dresses, the kayaks swinging up among the cobwebs, the collections of semi-precious gems. Now, however, she'd have been the first to admit she wasn't wild about sharks' teeth. As for totem-poles, she'd have taken a new Emma Lathen any day.

In one corner of the hall was a desk skirted by posters advertising exhibitions of Esquimaux art and Maori weapons. Someone you would unerringly have picked out of any crowd as a professional hit-man sat behind it. When she asked to speak to Dr Cesare Lunghi, he scowled. He pressed a button somewhere behind him and spoke into it. A voice squawked back at him. He watched Penny as if wondering whether garrotting was too good for her. When Dr Cesare Lunghi, Bruno's second-in-command, showed up, the desk man made a few hostile sounds in his throat and shifted postcards of the Pietà about.

Dr Lunghi was in his fifties. He wore his hair high and was obviously dedicated. As they passed between formal-dehyded pythons and shields of rhinoceros hide towards the offices at the back of the building, he couldn't resist showing Penny some of the treasures the Instituto contained. Ammonites. A stuffed cockatoo. A Tiahuanaco beaker. Penny was grateful. They weren't things she'd ordinarily have spent much time looking at. Lunghi didn't ask for comment, nor did he make any. As they paused beside a sod hut once occupied by Chipaya llama herders and transported bodily from Bolivia, she thought he might, but after twitching a loose bit of straw from the thatch which crowned it, he moved on without speaking.

One case particularly caught her attention. It was smaller than the others in the room. There was a red light set into the front of it, like an electronic eternal flame. Inside it, small objects stood on beige platforms of different heights. There was plenty of room for more.

'What are those?' she asked.

'Funeral offerings,' said Lunghi. 'As you see, we have categorised them generically rather than by period.'

Penny pointed to a small gold box carved with the face of the hawk-headed god, Horus. 'I saw a box very similar to that this morning,' she said.

'Ah yes.' Lunghi smiled mournfully. 'That would have been at the *galleria itaro*, I have no doubt.'

'Spot on.'

'We're very hopeful of negotiating a price with them for their box. Very hopeful. The two obviously belong together. And as a pair, they would be worth far more than they are singly.'

'The man at the shop told me there were two potential buyers.'

Lunghi seemed distressed. 'Oh dear,' he said.

'What's wrong?'

'That means we shall almost certainly lose it.'

'Why?'

'We shall be outbid, whatever price we offer. It happens a lot. Only last week we were after a very rare Numerian cooking pot that would have completed our collection . . .' He shook his head.

'Are you short of funds?'

'No. It just seems that whatever we want, someone else wants it worse. But a place like this does depend to an extent on a turnstile revenue, and without new attractions we aren't going to get the visitors. They've been falling off at an alarming rate in the past months.'

He pushed open a door with his name on it. It appeared his office was also his laboratory. He offered Penny a tall stool beside a work bench. The room smelled, as such places always do, of acid and slowly seeping gas. What looked like a dodo stared out at Penny from behind smeared glass doors. There were microscope boxes on the window-sill. Along one work-top were some teeth laid out on a strip of paper towel. A roll-down display board had things written on it in blue Magic Marker.

Lunghi picked up a tooth and scratched at it with his fingernail. 'What exactly did you wish to speak to me about?' he said.

'Sandy Leon.'

'Oh, yes,' Lunghi said.

'Obviously I'm hoping to find a motive for Dr Ferlinghetti's disappearance. But anything you tell me will be strictly confidential and non-attributable.'

'I am most relieved,' said Lunghi. 'Or would be, certainly, if I had anything to tell. But I don't know this person. Who is he?'

'She.'

'I am sorry,' Lunghi said. He looked sad but sexy. Penny had long ago decided that Italians couldn't help it.

'She's a colleague of Dr Ferlinghetti's. I understood they were working together on some project right here at the institute. He took her down to Toscana three weeks ago to assist on the dig there.'

'She is not from here.' Lunghi put down the tooth and picked up another. He held it very close to his eye and turned it round. It wasn't a tooth that had ever made much contact with a Water-Pik.

'But I was told—'

83

'Whatever you were told was wrong,' said Lunghi, tightening the belt on his lab coat. As high fashion went, lab coats didn't rate much as far as Penny was concerned. Especially the short ones.

'Do you have any idea at all where Bruno might have gone?' she said.

'None.'

'Do you think he could have stolen the statuettes?'

'What else can I think?' Lunghi said. 'Dr Ferlinghetti was the only one with keys to the safe at Toscana. There is a spare set in a safe-deposit box at the Banco Roma. I checked with them the day after the disappearance of the statuettes and no one had asked for them. And the safe itself had not been forced, according to Professor Tarrance. I can only conclude that Dr Ferlinghetti himself removed them. For some good reason.'

'Such as?'

'To clean them, perhaps.'

'You don't believe that any more than I do.'

'I would rather believe that than believe the *dottore* was a thief.'

'Me too, boy.'

'Dr Ferlinghetti has been under much stress recently,' Lunghi said slowly.

'Why?'

'The Government has asked him to head a commission of enquiry into ways of safeguarding Italy's art treasures. As you will know, there is a considerable traffic in stolen and smuggled goods. I know he has been very distressed by the statistics. And all too often the major foreign auction houses contribute to them by accepting goods without proper authentication. Perhaps you read of the recent case where one of your own auction houses refused to halt the sale of some black glazed vases that had been looted from an Italian site. And that was despite the fact that *they* had no authentication and *we* had proof that they were stolen. On top of that, Dr Ferlinghetti has recently received a number of phone calls of an unpleasant kind.'

'Not heavy breathers, I presume.'

'People offering him bribes. As you can imagine, certain interests make a lot of money from smuggling antiquities and art treasures out of Italy. They naturally are not very happy at the thought of losing a source of considerable income.'

'Trying to spook him?'

'Exactly.'

'Bruno's not easy to scare,' said Penny. 'Under that Byronic exterior, he's as tough as old boots.'

Lunghi looked down at his own, a suede pair with a patch of something old and glutinous on the instep of the left one. 'Any man has his price,' he said. He cleared his throat softly. 'Or there is another possibility. Suppose he was told that something would happen to him if he didn't co-operate with certain parties. Suppose someone close to him was threatened.'

Giulia. Sickeningly, Penny wondered if someone had threatened to carve up Giulia. Throw acid into her face, stroke a razor over that thick white skin, kidnap or torture her. Bruno could never stand out against such threats. But how many people knew of his attachment to Giulia? Not more than half a dozen, all of them either family or very close friends.

'All this is so bad for the reputation of the Instituto,' Lunghi went on. 'And now the newspapers have got hold of the story. I have wondered if Bruno removed the figurines himself to prevent them from falling into the wrong hands. But in that case, he could be in the gravest possible danger. You must realise, Miss Wanawake, that on the whole, archaeologists prefer *not* to come across buried treasure. It gets in the way of their legitimate business of advancing man's knowledge of the past. Gold brings all sorts of complications, in particular, the attention of the criminal element. And today's hoodlums are so ruthless.' He looked at Penny from under his eyebrows. 'In South America, archaeologists finding gold hoards have actually been shot dead by professional bounty hunters.'

'Do you think he might already be dead?'

'It is possible.' Nervously, Lunghi put down the tooth, picked up another, put that down too. 'Of course, I have considered that.' He jammed his hands into the pockets of his lab coat so that the knuckles bunched out under the fabric, as miserable as a basset-hound with piles. 'Because, you see, if he *had* been blackmailed into stealing the figurines and handing them over, the people concerned might have killed him to prevent him identifying them later.'

Penny touched his arm. 'No one's found a body,' she said.

'Not yet.' Lunghi bowed his head for a moment. 'Not yet.'

'May I look round Bruno's office?' Penny said.

'He hasn't been in it for three weeks,' Lunghi said. He led her down a hall floored in polished herringbone parquet. 'I doubt if you will find anything significant.'

'To the trained eye, anything can be of significance.'

She said it to reassure him. But would she recognise anything that could be of help in finding Bruno? Probably not.

As far as dust and gas leaks went, Bruno's lab was the twin of Lunghi's, though there were attempts at interior decoration. A woollen tapestry woven on some primitive loom by a long-dead female Inca. A photograph of Giulia.

86

Some large pottery jars of coruscating dullness. A small prayer mat.

'I shall leave you,' Lunghi said, looking at his watch. 'If there is anything further you wish to know, please ask.'

Penny went through the place. The files. The desk drawers. The cabinets. She looked behind the wall hanging. She stared into the jars. Mostly, there were papers. Every now and then she came across a glassine envelope containing bits of dead human. Hair. A sliver of bone. Fragments of scorched skin. But no clues to the whereabouts of Bruno or the figurines.

After quite a long time, during which a pretty girl in a pink smock brought her some coffee and a wrapped *biscotte*, at the back of a drawer she found something that was definitely of interest. An envelope of cuttings. She had no means of telling how significant it was.

Slowly she ate the *biscotte*. One cutting went back more than eighteen months, the most recent only a couple of weeks. Bruno had clipped a report of looting from a site near Alexandria; an account of the acquisition of two pre-Columbian mummies by a museum in New Zealand; an article on the theft from a Tuscan monastery of part of the treasure donated by an uxoricidal knight back in the fourteenth century. Under a picture of a boring pot that had gone for an astronomical figure in an auction just the week before, a word caught Penny's eye.

She went next door and found Lunghi. 'Is this the cooking pot you wanted?' She showed him the photograph.

'Isn't it superb?' he said.

'Glorious.'

'Does it say who the buyer was?'

It did, in very small print, among a lot of other names. Oscare Torella.

Back in Bruno's office, she examined the cuttings more

carefully. The only unifying factor she could find was that on three occasions Oscare Torella had been involved. Once as seller, twice as buyer.

How long had Oscare been dealing in antiquities? Why had Bruno marked those particular items? And what was niggling her about them?

She hadn't answered herself by the time she left.

10

FOR ONCE THERE WAS AN EMPTY PARKING SPACE OUT-
side the building where Bruno's mother lived. It had been a
palazzo. Now it contained high-rent flats. Penny backed
into the space, beating out a Fiat with eight big women in
it. Somebody obviously knew the secret of getting ele-
phants into VWs. The women all shook their fists.

If the press was hanging around, hoping for a break in
the Ferlinghetti case, it was keeping a very low profile.
The only people to be seen were a man sadistically whipping an off-white horse between the shafts of a cart, and a
back-packed US tourist in earth shoes and a Pendleton
shirt. Three cars down from hers was a black Citroën with
a star in the corner of its windscreen.

A maid showed Penny into the large salon on the second
floor. There was a man standing by the window, staring
down into the street. The Vicontessa Ferlinghetti was sitting on an ottoman looking cute and thumbing through carpet samples. Her arm lay across a sphinx-head. Winged
lions supported a glass table-top beside her. A mummy
case stood behind the ottoman. It was enough to make your
nose bleed.

Palma Ferlinghetti had bones like a bird and liked you to think her brain matched. Long ago, she'd gone to Hollywood from her native Pittsburgh and starred in a film about a girl who saw something nasty in a Transylvanian graveyard. The film had bombed, but not before Palma had allowed Bruno's father to sweep her off her feet. In a moment of passion, he had told her she reminded him of Bardot and she'd been trying to jog people's memories ever since. Nowadays, all she reminded anyone of was the passage of time.

She looked up when Penny was announced.

'Honey,' she cried. *'Benvenuto.'* She wore a simple garment that allowed glimpses of her thighs when she moved. Very classical. Very sexy. This year her hair was dark and tied up in a topknot. When in Rome, Penny always tried to think as the Romans did.

'Ave, Miz Ferlinghetti,' she said.

Palma pouted in the sultry way Bardot had made her own some thirty years earlier. 'Palma, please,' she said.

'Or should I call you Cleopatra?' The mummy case seemed to be ajar.

'Do you like it?' Palma said.

'I am trying, Egypt, trying.' Difficult, with an outsize golden foot, toenails and all, monopolising one wall. Very difficult, with black marble pillars guarding each door, and a twenty-foot-high statue of some dog-headed dude in a tennis skirt staring from the other end of the room. Where furnishings were concerned, Palma rang more changes than a team of sponsored bell-ringers. Only two months earlier, it had been country house chic, with chintzes and labradors and decoy ducks, and Palma herself in tweeds fingering copies of *The Field*.

'Ah tell yew, ah'm about to dah of nervous prostration,' Palma said. She made a big production about having been born in New Orleans. She made less of the fact that her parents had returned to Pittsburgh the minute the gynaecologist gave them permission to travel. Palma was closer to death than she'd ever been to a Swannee-Ribber accent but she gave it a darn good try. When she remembered.

'Why's that?' Penny said.

'Tryin' to get this place ready.'

'Oh.'

'Why do you say it like that, honey?'

'Thought you might be worried about Bruno.'

'What are you sayin', chile?' Palma produced a first-aid-box laugh. Trouble hadn't arrived but she'd be prepared when it came. 'There's nothing wrong with Bruno. Now. You simply have to meet Alex.'

Alex was the man at the window. Alex was a really sensational *numéro*. His sweater had been knitted with yellow string. He wore baggy cotton trousers, also yellow. He was religious. You could tell by the crucifix hanging from his ear. Perhaps he was moonlighting from the College of Cardinals.

'Alex, sweetie,' Palma said. She uttered small cries of a bird-brained nature. 'This dahlin' gull is an old friend of the family.'

Penny held out her hand. 'Hi,' she said. 'I'm Penny Wanawake.'

Sweetie bowed over her hand. Someone had spent a great deal of time on his hair. Not just on the highlights, but on backbrushing as well. His chin was as smooth as a blackjack. He murmured something in the light androgynous voice of a hairdresser.

'Alex knows just about ever'thing there is to know about the third dynasty,' chirped Palma.

'Swell.'

'Or is it the fourth?'

91

Alex looked at Penny, then down at a clipboard he was carrying. 'The carrrrpets, Vicontessa,' he said. 'You 'ave choose?'

Palma smiled. It was the only thing to do with such an accent. Penny held back. When he moved long blond eyelashes up and down at her, she was sure of one thing. Alex was as precious as grandma's Spode, but he was nowhere near as fragile. The guy might be fooling some of the people all of the time, but he sure wasn't fooling Penny Wanawake. Not with a handshake like that. Not with the callouses on the knuckles and the bend in the nose.

'Such a talented decorator,' Palma said. 'He's done all this for me.' She waved at the Egyptian splendour. 'Ah just love talented people.'

'Bruno,' Penny said.

Alex looked at her again. He took in a good deal. She wondered whether they did his sweater in white.

'Wine!' Palma called. There was a wary expression on her face. 'Let's have some wine.' She tinkled a little bell with a pharaonic motif round it.

'Where is he?' Penny said.

'Now you know that boy nevah did pay me no nevah mahnd.' Vivien Leigh's southern belle had been a lot more convincing than Palma's.

'You're his mother.'

'That doesn't mean a thing these days.'

'Knock it off, Palma.'

'I tell you I really don't have the least idea,' Palma said. She rang the bell again, sharply.

'Sure you don't.'

Palma glanced at Alex. He'd gone back to the window and was staring down into the street. 'Alex,' she said.

'The rugs,' Alex said. 'The carrrrpetti.' He waved the clipboard about. Even with the calloused knuckles he might have got away with it if the religious medal round his neck hadn't nestled between pectorals Sly Stallone would have given blood for. Also, he walked on the balls of his feet. Only two breeds of men did that. Boxers and bodyguards. Three, if you counted ballet dancers.

The maid came in. She carried a tray containing some small bronze bowls and an amphora of wine. Beside it rested a bronze strainer. Nobody had ever accused Palma Ferlinghetti of restraint. If she was going to play a part, she did it up to and beyond the limit. An amphora, for God's sake. Thing was, why was she so deep into Egyptology? Could it possibly have anything to do with two missing Egyptian statues? Statuettes. And if so, what?

Somewhere, a phone rang. Alex was sitting on the windowseat, looking up the street now, instead of down it. He was on his feet before the first ring died away. He moved quickly towards the door. He stood just outside it, keeping it open with his foot. Penny couldn't hear what he said except 'Yes, sir.' He said that three times in the kind of voice that hopes it isn't being overheard but if it is, doesn't want to give anything away. He came back into the room and walked back to the window, keeping to one side of it.

'When did you last see Bruno?' Penny said. Worrying it like a bone.

'What was it?' Palma said vaguely. 'About three weeks ago?'

Alex nodded. Something was bugging him.

'What did he think of the décor?' asked Penny.

'Dahlin', he *loved* it. Well, I should just hope so. It was his idea, for heaven's sake. Isn't that right, Alex?'

Alex indicated that it was. His head was cocked to one side. Real cute. Also real easy to listen with. He held his hands loosely at his sides. Ready for anything. The decorator, right? Who did Palma think she was kidding? There was plenty of room in his baggy trousers to hide a gun.

Palma poured wine through the bronze strainer into the shallow bowls. It was a process that probably had some point when Nefertiti was dishing out the purple plonk to Akhenaten. They weren't too adept at clarifying the stuff back then. With last month's Lambrusco, it was ridiculous. It was camouflage.

'Did he tell you he was going away?' Penny asked, cautiously drinking from her bowl. Last month's? It tasted more like last week's.

'No, honey, he did not. He's a big boy now. He doesn't discuss everything with his mamma. Besides, you know how vague he is. Maybe he decided to take a little vacation. He certainly needs one.'

'Maybe he's taking one he didn't decide on,' said Penny. 'Did you think of that?'

Palma put a hand to her chest. On Bardot, there'd have been curves. Palma had dieted all hers away. 'Oh, my heavens,' she said.

'Not only that, I found a man floating in Bruno's pool yesterday,' said Penny. 'A dead man. He came from some kind of Pinkerton agency in the States. He'd been watching Bruno's place.'

'Dead?' Alex said. 'How dead?'

'Very.'

'But how?' Alex drew a finger across his throat, made a gun with his hand, jabbed an imaginary knife into his heart.

'Shot,' Penny said.

'That's just terrible,' Palma said. She was looking kind of sick.

'Especially for him,' said Penny.

'Shot,' Alex said. He touched the crucifix in his ear and looked down at his clipboard. He went back to his station by the window.

'You can see where this laid-back attitude of yours might get a person thinking,' Penny said. 'Thinking that maybe you know where Bruno is, so you don't have to worry about him.'

'I've taught myself never to worry about anything,' said Palma. 'It only causes facial wrinkles.'

She must have done a lot of worrying before she finally caught on. 'So you don't know where he might be?'

'No.' Palma sipped from her bowl. A woman entirely free from care. A woman who'd have had no problem failing a lie-detector test.

'Is that Bruno's car out front? The black Citroën?'

'Yes.'

'How long's it been parked there?'

'Weeks,' Palma said. She looked over at Alex and patted her topknot.

'Do you know anything about the things he's supposed to have stolen?'

'Things?'

'Statues. Statuettes. Whatever.'

'He hasn't stolen anything,' Palma said. 'A man in his position.'

'He rang Giulia last Friday and told her he was in danger,' Penny said.

'Giulia!' cried Palma. 'How is that dahlin' child? Is she expectin' yet?'

'Only the worst,' Penny said. 'That's why I'm here.'

'That gull should be worryin' about havin' babies, not about my son.'

'Have a heart, Palma. Who'd want to make babies with Oscare?'

'Well . . .'

'Tell me about Alex,' said Penny. 'Who hired him?'

'I did, honey. I told you. He's my decorator.'

'And I'm Ashley Wilkes,' Penny said. 'What is he? A minder? A gumshoe?'

'The idea,' said Palma. She pushed her lower lip out. You had to admire her. The way she'd been juggling Bardot, magnolia blossom and the Nile was little short of miraculous.

'Decorators look at interiors,' Penny said. 'He's concentrated on the exterior ever since I got here. And for a guy who speaks such crappy English, he doesn't have any problem following it.'

'Isn't that always the way? I'm just the same in Spanish. Hardly speak a word but—'

'What's shaking, Palma? I'll find out one way or another.'

'Now, Penny. Don't tell me you're doin' some more of that detectin',' Palma said.

The maid appeared and said there were some men at the door. Alex sprang forwards, blocking the way so nothing could get past him. Not without a struggle. Horatius couldn't have kept the bridge any better.

The maid stared at the golden foot. She breathed in through her nose, at the same time shaking her head. There was some Italian conversation going on outside in the foyer. From the little Penny could hear, Alex wasn't a native speaker. But she'd already sussed that one. She stood aside as some men in grey overalls appeared with a terrific third-dynasty commode decorated with hieroglyphs. Another carried in a life-sized wooden ibis on a stand. Things were getting more Nilotic by the minute.

If Palma wanted to act like a clam when her own son was in danger, she could do so. Penny certainly wasn't there for the chowder. When a curly-headed boy came in, carrying two hand-painted papyrii, she left. As far as she was concerned, it was the last straw.

11

BRRR. BRRR.

'Savoy Hotel. Reception.'

'I'd like to speak to Barnaby Midas,' Penny said.

They said they'd see if he was in his room. He was.

'Hi,' said Penny. 'I've been out of town.'

'I know.'

'Thought I'd see how you're doing.'

'Lousy without you.'

'Me too. Wish you'd come home.'

'Have you considered my proposal?' said Barnaby.

'Yeah.'

'And?'

'And what?'

'What conclusion did you come to?'

'Said I'd considered it, man. Didn't say I'd concluded anything.'

'I see.'

'My views haven't changed,' Penny said gently.

'You do realise, don't you, that a lot of girls would give their eye-teeth to be married to me?'

'I've seen just the box you could keep them in, too.'

'Keep what?'

'All those teeth. A little gold thing with a fertility goddess on top. Beautiful. Thirteenth century BC.'

Barnaby couldn't resist the bait. 'Where did you see it?'

'A shop in Rome,' Penny said. 'From which city I've just returned.'

'*Galleria itaro*, I bet,' said Barnaby.

'Right. What do you know about them?'

'It's a chain. There's one in most major capitals,' said Barnaby. 'The one in New York's called *galleria itany*.'

'Let me guess,' Penny said. 'In London, it's *italo*.'

'*Itato* in Tokyo.' Barnaby said. 'And you don't get past the door without a credit rating of six figures. Per week.'

'They didn't check *my* bank account.'

'They're trained to recognise class when they see it.'

'How come they let Oscare Torella in?'

'He's class, baby. Even sleaze gets graded.'

'Do all these places specialise in antiquities?'

'Yeah.'

'How do you tell whether the stuff they've got is really antique and not just fakes run up in some backstreet sweatshop?'

'On the whole, you don't.'

'Pity.'

'But *I* might. You're not an expert and I am. Mind you, there are techniques for ageing things like bronze or ivory that would pass all but the most stringent tests.'

'And what about authentication and provenance?'

'They're easy to fake.'

'The folks at *galleria itaro* didn't bat an eyelid when I hinted that I might pass something their way that was not only highly valuable but known to have dropped off the back of a chariot.'

'Sounds like what I've heard of them.'

'Any connection between them and Oscare?'

'Not that I know of.'

'Listen,' said Penny.

'Don't I always?'

'Gold figurines. Egyptian. Gone missing from Toscana.'

'From where?'

'Toscana. In southern Italy.'

'Oh.' Barnaby sounded surprised.

'The poor man's Pompeii.'

There was a pause. 'About nine inches high. He's wearing a size X hairpiece. She's got a bird on her head,' Barnaby said slowly. 'A falcon.'

'You're a real smart kid, you know that?' Penny said. 'Where'd you *hear* that stuff?'

'They were stolen recently.'

'Yeah.'

'Must have read it in the papers.'

'The bit about the falcon wasn't in them,' Penny said. As always with Barnaby, unease nibbled. 'Hey. Weren't you in Italy recently?'

'*Moi?*' Barnaby moved away from the receiver. He spoke to someone nearby.

'Who the hell was that?' said Penny. She swung her braids about so he could hear.

'Room service.'

'What kind of service they provide?'

'Just about anything you ask for,' said Barnaby.

'What did *you* ask for?'

'Champagne.'

'Celebrating?'

'No. Just thirsty.'

Outside Penny's windows, a man from a messenger service roared past on a powerful motorbike. He was sashed in yellow Dayglo. His helmet informed her that if she were in a hurry, Kwikrun gave the best service. It sounded like a prescription for dysentery. Or maybe a constipation cure.

'Come home,' she said.

'Not unless you've changed your mind. I'd rather languish here.'

'Languishing there must cost a bomb.'

'It does.'

'So come home.'

Have you changed your mind?'

'No.'

Silence.

'Let's talk about something else,' Penny said.

More silence. 'I heard a rumour there's a contract out on those figurines,' Barnaby said finally.

'Where'd you hear it?'

'Around.'

'Who put it out?'

'There was mention of the Mob. There was also mention of individuals. The gold freaks always get restive when there's a theft like this. If they themselves weren't responsible for it.'

'Gold freaks?'

'Collectors. People like Fazal, the man from Cairo. Cheng Su Lei, from Peking. Reilly Riordan, in Virginia. There are others.'

'I've heard of Riordan. He was on the Toscana dig. But if he was going to steal them, why not do it right there and then, on the site?'

'Perhaps he meant to, and Bruno got in first.'

'Why? I can't figure it out.'

'If you catch up with him, you'd better tell him to offload the loot pretty damn quick. People like Fazal and Riordan don't horse around.'

'Barnaby.'

'I hear you.'

'You don't think he's dead, do you?'

'I'd have thought they'd have found him by now, if he was.'

'Only I couldn't break it to Giulia, if he was.'

'Marry me,' Barnaby said.

'No.'

'Are you going after these figurines?'

'I'm going after Bruno.'

Barnaby sighed. 'I can't stop you, I know. But take some protection. A gun.'

'You know how I feel about guns, sugar-baby.'

'Want to hear how I feel about dead black girls?'

'About the same as I feel about marriage. For instance, if we were, you and me, I couldn't go after Bruno. As you say, you couldn't stop me. Not physically. But deep down, you would. I wouldn't be free. If anything happened to me, I'd have left you on your own. I couldn't take the responsibility. It's bad enough,' said Penny, 'the way we already are.'

'Don't think there's no responsibility, just because we aren't married,' Barnaby said.

'I don't.'

'Don't think you wouldn't be leaving me alone. If anything happened. Just don't ever think that.'

'I know.'

'And if there *are* people after these gold things, they won't be kidding. The prize is too big. They won't waste time. They'll shoot first and not bother with the questions.'

'I know that too,' said Penny. 'But I got a pretty big prize of my own. Giulia. She's already lost Bruno once. If anything happened to him, if he—uh—died, she would too.'

'And she's not even married to him.'

Very gently, Penny put the phone down.

Upstairs, she could hear Peter Corax singing. More accurately, she could hear Fischer-Diskau singing and Peter helping him out. Rats. Whenever the Literary Gent played Schubert, it meant he was about to fall in love again. Again.

'*Knabe sprach ich breche dich*," howled Peter. Gutturals don't lend themselves to howls. Penny knew this could go on all day. She went visiting.

'If he was alive and free, he would have called me on the phone,' Giulia said. 'He'd know how much I'd be worrying.'

She breathed in sharply, trying to startle the tears into not falling. It didn't work. She gasped a couple of times. She banged her fist against Penny's knee. Penny held her. What was there to say when your friend cried for the man she loved, who might be dead?

Through the long Knightsbridge windows, the wet sun caught the auburn lights in Giulia's long, thick hair. She kept it off her face with a rich-lady Alice-band. The band looked as if it were made of mottled brown plastic. On anyone else, it might have been. With Giulia, you knew that somewhere some tortoise was going round mothernaked. Her skin was very white. In places, the veins showed through. Penny remembered what Lunghi had said. It was all too easy to imagine the ugly razor lines across it, like ski-tracks on virgin snow.

They were sitting on a long sofa, one of four which surrounded a shallow pit in the middle of the long drawing room. The pit was floored with squares of alabaster, tinted alternately red and cream. Lit from below, the white ones had a faint cheesy glow.

'You told me Oscare was going to Cairo,' said Penny.

'That's what he said.'

'I saw him in Rome.'

Giulia raked her long fingernails through her hair in a gesture worthy of Antigone. 'Was he with a woman?'

'He was coming out of a woman's apartment.'

'Of course.'

'His sister's, as it happens.'

'That didn't stop the Egyptians.'

'Oscare's not Egyptian.'

'You don't know him as I do.'

'Even Oscare would draw the line at incest.'

'Oscare can't draw,' Giulia said.

Beside her there was an electronic keyboard sunk into a cube covered with the same material as the sofa. She flicked tears away from the outer corners of her eyes and pressed one of the keys. Some foot-high chessmen began moving erratically about on the floor of the pit. Oscare liked gadgets.

'So will you go to the States and see this Riordan?' Giulia said.

'I'm not sure it will be of much help.'

'But you *said*.'

'If he's after the missing statuettes himself, he's not likely to help me.'

'If he's not, he could have seen something at Toscana. Bruno might have spoken to him.'

'He might not.'

'You have talked with all the others who were there.'

'And gotten precisely nowhere.'

'With him, you might get somewhere.'

'The guy lives in Virginia, for chrissake.'

'I am paying your expenses.'

'It's not the money,' Penny said. 'You know that.'

'I know.'

104

They were silent for a while, each thinking about Bruno. Then Giulia, gazing round, said, 'God, I hate this apartment.'

'Mmm,' said Penny.

The room reflected nothing of Giulia's taste. Before her marriage, she had been studying for a diploma in fine arts. The only object in the room belonging to her, a Venetian looking-glass with a flower-garlanded rosewood frame, hung in an alcove by the fireplace. The seventeenth-century master craftsman who had designed it would have torn out his hair if he'd seen the place. It was as if, by marrying Oscare, she had abdicated her own personality. She loathed ultra-modern furniture. But since Oscare loved it, that's what there was. Not too much. A couple of Rossellini chairs, shaped like giant hands. A smoked-glass table with a moving sculpture on it. Light bulbs on the end of chrome worms. That was more or less it. One wall was painted in shocking zigzags of clashing colour.

'Hideous,' said Giulia. 'Absolutely hideous.'

'Always reminds me of a pedigree warthog,' Penny said. 'Ugly, but expensive.'

'And look at that,' Giulia said. 'He brought that home with him last week. What on earth is it?'

There was a clay pot standing on the low slate hearth. 'Bet you anything you like it's a Numerian cooking vessel,' Penny said.

'Oh?'

'Just a guess.'

'I don't know why Oscare should buy such a thing,' Giulia said.

Neither did Penny. Not yet.

She stood up. 'Don't get neurotic. But it could be Bruno did a vanishing trick to protect you.'

'Me? What do I have to do with it?'

Penny explained about the Commission of Enquiry. 'Maybe he protects you better by not being around. It's hard to make threats if there's no one around to listen. Have you seen anything odd? Heard anything?'

'A couple of weird phone calls,' Giulia said.

'What sort of weird?'

'Putting the phone down when you pick it up. Or breathing at you. But nothing special. You get those in any big city these days.'

'What about people following you? Someone watching the house?'

'Not that I've noticed.' Giulia stared down at the chessmen. She pressed the back of her hand to her mouth and bit the knuckle of her middle finger. For the first time, Penny saw lines in her friend's face, feather-thin strokes etched on the white skin. Were those what you called marriage lines? As a good Catholic, Giulia was tied forever to her Oscare. Time present and time past had no meaning when time future had none either.

The rims of Giulia's eyes were very pink. But Penny wasn't going to think about Barnaby. He'd said he was languishing. It took real dedication to languish at the Savoy.

Giulia was wearing very tight black trousers with a shimmer in them, and heels so high they'd have qualified for a caber-tossing contest. She touched the electronic keyboard again, pressing down several keys at once. The Red Queen staggered aimlessly across the giant chessboard.

'I am so afraid for Bruno,' she said. 'Afraid that maybe he has been—murdered.'

An ugly word, murder. One you didn't want rattling around in your drawing room if you could help it. Penny was afraid of the same thing, although she wasn't going to admit it. Like Giulia, she believed that if Bruno had taken off from Toscana under his own steam, however low he might be lying he would never have left Giulia to worry like this. *Ergo*, he had not left under his own steam. So where was he? And in what condition?

'I'll find him,' she said. Dead or alive.

'You will be careful, Penny?'

'You betcha.'

'I shall go to Rome,' Giulia said. 'To my parents' house. You can call me there.'

She fidgeted with the keys again. Pieces slid about the floor like dodgem cars, bumping into each other. A shard of alabaster flaked off the Red Bishop.

'Oscare will be furious.' Giulia sounded as if she couldn't care less. She felt under the cushions of the sofa and brought out a tiny gun with a silver handle. You might have brought down an escaping balloon with it, but not much else. 'Penny. Do you want to take this with you?'

'No, ma'am,' said Penny. 'Me and guns don't mix.'

'It may be small, but it's quite effective,' Giulia said. She aimed at the Red Knight. She pulled the trigger. The top of its head flew off. The body fell slowly on to its side and cracked into two pieces. Giulia put the gun back under the cushions.

'Hey, now. That was a bit over the top, wasn't it?' Penny said.

'I wish it had been Oscare.'

'Perhaps next time.' Penny was joking. Trying, anyway. It was probably best to believe that Giulia had been too.

12

S HE CABBED IT TO KING'S CROSS AND TOOK THE NEXT
train to Cambridge. The town was all sunshine and tourists. They were selling geraniums in the market, and new
potatoes. Windcheatered men offered handfuls of bright-
coloured nylon bikinis out of cardboard cylinders. Huge
women belligerently handled bananas. The Senate House
looked as if it had just been scrubbed down with a wire
brush. Pale, bearded people cycled slowly about with bas-
ketfuls of books.

Penny went into the Body Shop. Japanese ladies in
black raincoats sniffed testers of raspberry bath oil and car-
rot face cream. Penny bought some bright green soap in the
shape of a heart. Maybe she'd give it to Barnaby. Maybe
she wouldn't. In St Mary's, bellringers were practising
changes.

She walked on towards the bus station. It was full of
spotty youths eating chips and nasty meat pies out of paper.
Drusilla's address was a small brick house behind it. She
rang the bell.

A kid in flannelette opened the door. His outfit was
dotted with Star Wars figures. He carried a gun.

'I just took Marty's comic-book,' he said.

'Didn't anyone ever tell you that crime doesn't pay?' said Penny.

'I'm going to go and hit him on the head in a minute,' the kid said. A kid with a plastic pistol in his hand can get pretty mean.

'You just wait until he's big enough to hit you back.'

'He already is,' said the kid. 'But he never does.'

'Is your mom in?' Penny asked.

A very thin young woman appeared with *Language, Truth and Logic* in her hand. She wore a blue cardigan over a cream-coloured blouse. Both had been unkindly treated by the washing machine. Both needed pressing. Behind her, a grubby kid was screaming about a book someone had stolen from him. She put a hand to her forehead. 'Marty,' she said. She looked at Penny. 'Yes?'

'Hi there. I'm a friend of Drusilla's,' Penny said.

'Are you?' The woman sounded surprised that anyone would admit to it.

Penny eased on into the hall. 'The thing is, I'm flying back to Italy soon and Drusilla asked me to pop in and see if there's any urgent mail waiting for her.'

The woman nodded. 'Urgent,' she said.

'That's right.'

'I don't know how you'd tell if it were urgent or not,' said the woman. 'Not unless you opened it.'

'Perhaps I'd better take the whole lot, unless it's obviously junk mail.'

'You can't always tell,' said the woman, in a logically positive way.

The pyjamaed kid edged round behind his mother. There was the sound of a blow. The other kid screamed in an unrestrained manner. 'Oh, Mickey,' said the woman. 'Why are you so violent? And where did you get that gun?

We belong to CND, you know that. Your father will have a fit.'

'I stole it from the shop on the corner,' said Mickey.

'Oh God,' the woman said.

'Shall I just look very quickly?' said Penny.

The woman lifted one bony shoulder in a shrug. 'I suppose it's all right. It's upstairs. Third door on the left.'

The stairs and passage were covered in thinning linoleum. The woodwork needed painting. People like Mickey were hard on a house. Drusilla's room was small and pitiful, with windows looking out on interlocking backyards of concrete and coalbunkers. A bird bath sprouted from bare earth in the garden next door.

The bed was covered in a candlewick spread of faded green. A black-and-white television stood on a small table. Its screen was fingerprint-foggy, its white plastic shell yellowed. Shoes with run-down heels poked out from under the bed. On a hook behind the door were some dresses and skirts. They lacked any kind of hanger-appeal. They didn't look as if they'd have much wearer-appeal, either.

The place smelled. Of unwashed tights. Of showers not taken. Of poverty. Of lack of love. In one corner was a small handbasin that needed cleaning. The cold tap dripped, leaving a brown bib of scale. On the floor beneath was a grey bathtowel that might once have been pink. Penny tried not to think about Drusilla standing on it, washing her narrow feet.

She opened the bedside drawer. Nivea creme in a flat greasy tin. An unsigned Valentine card in an envelope with a Rome postmark and an extra heart drawn on the flap. Contact lens liquid. A photograph of a handsome man in a dinner jacket with his arms round a young girl in a chiffon evening dress. The girl wasn't Drusilla.

Under a formica-topped table long ago thrown out of

someone's kitchen, were two wire supermarket baskets. Drusilla's filing system. One held some lecture notes, two unused Christmas cards from a pack of five, and a child's drawing of a house, signed Marty. The other contained three dictionaries and a couple of folders. One of the folders was empty. In the other was a picture cut from a newspaper. It showed a man standing in front of a portrait of President Craxi. It was the same man as in the photograph in Drusilla's bedside drawer. He wore a decoration of some kind round his neck. Newsprint made him appear less jowled, better looking. Penny had seen the face before. Many times. All over Rome, in fact. Smiling from hoardings, from the back windows of cars, from the pages of newspapers. Whoever he was, he was running for public office in the forthcoming elections.

She tugged open an awkward little drawer in the table. It held a plastic file of bank statements, and a building society passbook. At last accounting, Miss D.A. Ross had nine thousand pounds in the bank, plus some loose change. She also had twelve thousand pounds in the building society.

Well, now. What to make of that?

Twenty-one thousand pounds wasn't a fortune. On the other hand, it certainly wasn't peanuts. It was a sum more than adequate to pay the rent on a decent flat and buy clothes that didn't look like jumble sale rejects. It showed that, whichever way you looked at it, something about Drusilla Ross was as phoney as a drag-queen's tits.

Penny looked again at the bank statements. At the end of each month, a regular sum was paid in and immediately withdrawn. From the code letters accompanying it in the credit column, it was almost certainly Drusilla's salary cheque. In addition, there were other payments. Three thousand one week, two thousand another, nothing for a couple of months and then a further payment. The largest sum of all, nearly five thousand pounds, had been paid in September of the previous year. The building society account showed a regular monthly payment of two hundred pounds. A regular and quite large sum was withdrawn monthly.

If you asked Penny, something stank. And not just the room.

She looked round it once more. It didn't improve. It would never improve. It indicated an impoverishment of the spirit in anyone who could tolerate living there for long. Or else a preoccupation so fierce that surroundings became unimportant. Penny remembered Drusilla's craving eyes. With that kind of cash behind her, Drusilla Ross had to be going after something. It might be interesting to find out what. Or whom.

As she was leaving, Penny saw a bag hanging limp as a pelican's beak beneath the clothes on the door. Inside was a card, the sort that eating places hope you'll hand out to your friends. Or enemies, depending on how you rated the cuisine. This one plugged someting called the Caffè La Strada. Under the name was an address and phone number. Under those, a line drawing of a clown face beneath a hard round hat with a bite out of the brim. Four big eye-lashes above sorrowful eyes. A big blob on the end of the nose. Unmistakably Gelsomina.

Downstairs, Marty was watching Mickey smash Action Man's head into the wall. Bits of plaster had fallen on to the lino.

'Hey, you guys,' said Penny. 'What're you trying to do here?'

'I hate Action Man,' said Mickey.

'Even the one with the beard?'

'Him most of all,' Mickey said. He definitely had aggression problems.

'Where's your mother?' asked Penny.

'Inna kitchen.'

Marty began to scream very loudly. It was probably his Action Man.

His mother came out into the hall. She was holding *The Concept of Mind*, a finger keeping the place. She looked cold. She put a hand to her head and pulled her cardigan closer round her. Penny wondered when she'd last eaten meat.

'Uh—Drusilla asked me to give you this for the kids,' she said. She gave the woman two tenners. Wanawake as God. 'She—uh—she said she thought it was one of their birthdays or something.'

'She did?' The woman looked astonished. 'But she's never—'

'How long is it now she's lived here?'

'Oh, must be, um, nearly two years,' said the woman.

'That's right,' said Penny. 'Amazing how time goes.'

'Is it?' The woman spoke tiredly. You could see she wished it would go faster, to a time when Mickey and Marty were older and didn't scream so much and she could find time to press her sweaters and read her books. 'She came here straight from university. Leeds, I think it was.'

Penny nodded.

'And she did some kind of post-graduate work in Italy, too, didn't she?'

'Right,' Penny said. She nodded again, as if the woman was merely confirming stuff everyone knew.

'We've been glad to have her, actually,' the woman said. She was folding the ten-pound notes into spills. 'My husband and I are both doing post-graduate work, and with four of us it's not always very easy.' She looked down at the children. 'Of course, we never intended to start a family quite so soon.'

'I expect Drusilla helps with baby-sitting, doesn't she?' Penny said, hating herself.

'Well, she's out quite a bit. Goes over to Italy a couple of times a month, on some kind of exchange programme, she told me. And then she spends a lot of her evenings with Professor Tarrance.'

'She's the one there was all the scandal about, isn't she?' said Penny. Big wide eyes. Enquiring eyebrows. Naive smile. You'd have trusted her with your innermost secrets and your wallet as well.

'Scandal? Oh, you mean the business last year where someone accused her of trying to sell things to the black market?'

'Yes,' said Penny.

'I remember my husband talking about it. It wasn't a very big scandal. Not picked up by the papers or anything. In fact, Drusilla said it was all complete nonsense.'

'I'm sure it was. By the way, I've left her letters upstairs. She said not to bother if it was only bills.'

'What about her chance to win the two-hundred-and-fifty-pound jackpot plus free notebook bound in simulated leather?'

'Guess she'll have to miss out on that one,' said Penny.

She wondered about Drusilla all the way home. A visit to Meg's address, a small Barratt house on an estate surrounded by lawnfuls of interested neighbours and barking dogs, had proved useless. At her college, the porter had told her Professor Tarrance was away until the beginning of term and her rooms were locked. He had then come out of the lodge and watched her go back out of the gates. He made it fairly plain that any attempt on her part to re-enter the college in the next thirty years would be foiled.

Was there some connection between the so-called scandal and the payment every month into Drusilla's building society account? Was Drusilla putting the squeeze on Meg Tarrance? If so, why should Meg be the only victim? What about that Italian politician whose picture was in her room? Try as she might, Penny couldn't dislodge the word blackmail from her mind. She also wondered where Drusilla's contact lenses were.

When she got back to the Chelsea house, the eggs looked as if they'd been buffed up with floor wax. So did the carrots in the vegetable rack. Lucas had been in again. He'd left a gay magazine on the kitchen table, open at the centrefold. She recognised the naked figure at once. What was this? Some kind of subtle wage demand? See what I'm reduced to because you're too tight to pay me the going rate for the neat way I sterilise the rubber gloves and vacuum the place-mats? Maybe she should try a spot of blackmail herself. Let the magazine's publishers know that Lucas was in fact married to an ex-Hot Gossip dancer and was the father of two kids.

As well as the magazine, he'd left her some messages.

Miss Ivory says she's put £15,000 to win on Isaak D (by Blixen out of Africa). Says you must watch race at 2:45 on TV.

Signora Torella has booked you a flight on PanAm, eight p.m. today. You must telephone to confirm booking.

Mr Midas telephoned. Says stop nonsense, must get married immediately. Said wouldn't be answerable for the consequences otherwise. Said you must face facts.

Must watch, must book, must marry. Sometimes she wondered whose life it was.

There was a tap on the kitchen door. A whiff of Eau Sauvage Extrême. A bigger one of Gordon's. Peter Corax came in, stately in checks.

'My dear,' he said. 'I simply had to see you. Look.'

He showed her a picture of a punk in a collarless shirt. There was a week's stubble on the handsome sullen features. A rich person had autographed his skintight jeans. He wasn't someone Penny was ever going to give a blank cheque to. She knew some day he'd break Peter's heart for at least a week.

'Isn't he heaven?' said Peter.

'Triff.'

'I've fallen in love,' said Peter.

'Even educated fleas do it,' said Penny.

Peter looked at her with concern. 'Do I detect a touch of citrus about you, dear girl?' he asked.

'Perhaps I envy you.'

'Me, my dear? *Me?* A poor writer, barely able to keep body and soul together.'

'It's common knowledge that you sold your last novel for an undisclosed six-figure sum.'

'That has to be salted away for my old age,' Peter said. He rolled his greenish eyes at her. 'My lonely, sad, disillusioned old age. It is the curse of my condition that while people like you will be wallowing in the sunset with your chosen partner, I and my kind will inevitably be alone at the end.' He picked up an egg and looked at it closely. 'Tell me. Is there such a thing as a spot of gin about the place?'

Penny poured one and added several spots of tonic. Watched him drink it. Watched him stare at the photograph of the young punk.

Two, four, six, eight, gay is just as good as straight. Better, she thought, in some ways. For one thing, if you weren't a het, people didn't keep trying to marry you.

13

SHE'D ASKED FOR SOMETHING ZIPPY AND THE RENTAL company hadn't fooled around. The tomato-red sports car cut along Route I-95 between Washington and Richmond like a ladybird whose house was on fire. She loved the sense of space in the States. Everything was so big and new. America the beautiful. As long as you kept well away from downtown. Floating along the freeways, you could make-believe it was all still there, the way the White House wanted you to, the clambakes and quilting bees, the pioneer spirit, the simple honest faith in a new found land.

In Richmond, she found a hotel near the Museum of Fine Arts. Its architectural style tried to give the impression that Mr Jefferson had just stepped out to sign the Declaration of Independence. Standing on the steps was someone got up like a banana-republic dictator, in epaulettes and frogging. He wanted to take her car away from her. After an argument, she let him.

Outside, a marquee announced the arrival of the Sweetwater Cultural Club. It added it was glad to know them. Inside, a sign on the reception counter spoke of Virginia's twin traditions of gracious hospitality and historical continuity. The overnight charges were neither gracious nor hospitable but Penny paid up without a murmur. Murmur in a place like this and, with skin her colour, she'd be out on her ear before she could say John Brown.

In her room, she flicked on the television. It was still early enough for David Hartman to be wishing America good morning. She hung up her clothes. A nice man with a blue tie told her the winds were light to moderate that morning, and the temperature in downtown Richmond was in the low seventies. She was glad to hear it. She took a shower, washing away the miles between her and London. A person could get pretty tired of jetting across the Atlantic if a person allowed herself to. From the wardrobe in the bedroom, she took out a managerial-type two-piece. Slim white skirt with open vent at the back. Mannish sort of jacket, designed to get answers. Under it, a cotton top designed to get questions.

She went down to the lobby to ask for directions out to Riordan's place. Having left without the address, she'd been forced to ring Dunlap and eat dirt in order to get it. She'd hated it. He hadn't. One day she'd get even with him. The guy behind the desk told her the route. He was black. He wore a jacket in banjo-player red, and a bootlace tie held in place by a piece of pressed tin.

Riordan lived on the far edge of the ritziest part of town. The homes were big, the landscaping expensive. Sun glazed the leaves of magnolias and dogwoods. Some of the homes had little black kids standing on plinths at the drive entrance, holding out lanterns. None of them had been vandalised, which said a lot about local feeling for Virginia's historical continuity. Or about guard dogs.

Riordan's place was surrounded by a tall hemlock hedge. On the inside of it was a twelve-foot cyclone fence with a reverse-curve top. The fence was electrified. Inside a pair of barred iron gates stood a man in a tailored semi-military uniform. He was holding a Doberman on a short thick leash. Behind him was a gold-coloured Firebird with a sticker that said GOD, GUNS AND GUTS MADE AMERICA GREAT: LET'S KEEP IT THAT WAY. In a kind of armoured toll-booth, another guy was doing his best. He looked like he had shares in the National Rifle Association. He watched Penny with a rifle held loosely over one arm. He was pretty serious about it. Penny tried to be too.

'Professor Meg Tarrance,' she said when the first guy asked her name.

The guy in the toll-booth leaned over a console and spoke. The rifle was still pointed at her. Riordan obviously kept a tight hold on security. Which indicated that he had a lot to secure. The guy straightened up. He stroked the shield-shaped badge on his khaki-coloured sleeve and pressed something. The gates swung open, and Penny drove in. The guy with the dog pointed up the drive which curved around some leafy growth that hid the house from the road. The Doberman yawned.

The house looked as if it had been transported stone by stone from Stratford-on-Avon. Shortly after she'd stepped inside the front door she discovered that it had. Lying on an antique table was a reprint from some architectural journal that explained it all. She read it, while a Jeevesian person went to find out if Riordan was decent.

Fertilisers weren't a career option she'd been offered at school, but Riordan had obviously done pretty well out of them. She sat down in a carved oak chair and watched a piece of the panelling in the hall slide open just wide enough for some kook to stare at her. What was it with these people? Did they think she'd given a false name, or something?

The manservant came back. He too looked as if he'd been imported from England stone by stone. She resisted the temptation to goose him as he led her into an Elizabethan chamber full of diamonded windows with bits of stained glass let into them. Portraits of Renaissance scholars in slouchy black caps looked down their noses from the linenfold. The ceilings were so ornately plastered you wondered how they defied gravity. Logs burned in a fireplace big enough to hold a dance in. The room was full of soft yellow light. Definitely historical, and exceedingly gracious to boot.

Riordan was sitting in a swivel chair with his back to the door, playing chess with an IBM. From behind, it was hard to miss the fact that he was going bald on top.

'Professor Tarrance,' announced the manservant.

'You didn't say you were coming, Meg,' Riordan said. 'Have you found them?' He pressed a key. The VDU flashed up THAT WAS DUMB. He swung round, holding out arms covered in a yellow velvet jacket that was a size too small for the bulk of his chest.

'Hi,' Penny said. 'I'm Penny Wanawake.'

'You're who?' Riordan's arms dropped. His small round eyes tightened so she couldn't see what colour they were. He was going bald in front too.

'Penelope Wanawake.'

Riordan was having trouble figuring it out. 'But Jarvis said Meg Tarrance was here,' he said. 'Professor Tarrance.' He peered behind Penny.

'It's an easy mistake to make,' Penny said.

'An easy mis—'

'Mr Jarvis was acting on information received. Just happened the info was dud.'

'Are you saying that you wormed your way into my house by lying about who you were?' said Riordan. He had one of those southern accents that sound like a sponge dipped in cement. Behind him, the screen kept flashing THAT WAS DUMB.

'Yes.'

'You better have a very good reason,' he said.

'Oh, I have.'

Getting up, Riordan came towards her. 'What exactly do you want?' he asked.

Quite a lot of what you've got, Penny thought. Barnaby had called him a gold freak. She could see why. For instance, the dissolute cavalier housed in a small picture-frame covered in gold and precious stones. For instance, the stuff the crystal drops of the chandelier were hanging from. For instance, the small gold chest with a domed lid inset with baroque pearls.

There were a couple of glass-topped tables against a wall. One contained a chessboard, its squares made of ebony alternating with gold. The chessmen were made of the stuff too. It looked like a lot more fun to play chess with than a computer. On the wall were some glazed cases containing a considerable number of gold burial masks, softly lit from below. She wondered if Riordan had read *Goldfinger*. He probably had. He probably had it bound in gold somewhere, in a gold bookcase.

'I asked what you wanted,' Riordan said. He touched the IBM. The screen displayed THAT WAS DUMB one last time and expired.

'I want Bruno Ferlinghetti,' Penny said.

'I don't have him,' Riordan said.

He walked over to a Tudor table in dark oak and picked up a magazine. He thumbed through it, looking as nonchalant as anyone in a too-tight jacket can. The cover showed a marble lady scratching the back of her ankle while a naked *putto* held her foot up, to make things easier. Penny

121

recognised it at once. A back copy of *Hermes*. Barnaby had the same issue at home in Chelsea. So did Bruno, in his office in Rome.

'I understand you were on site at Toscana al Vesuvio when he disappeared,' Penny said. She undid the buttons of her jacket.

'When I left, he hadn't disappeared,' Riordan said.

'He had. You just didn't realise it. I wondered if, looking back, you could remember anything that might be helpful in tracing him.'

'Looking back, I can't remember anything. Where're you from, the sheriff's office?'

'No. From the Ferlinghetti Institute. They've asked me to see if I can find out where Dr Ferlinghetti went.'

'And who gave you the idea that I'd know?'

'Not just where he's gone,' Penny said. 'But who took him there.'

'Are you nuts?'

'Not yet.'

'Just because he visited my place a couple of times last year doesn't mean I've eloped with the guy,' Riordan said roughly. His face was suddenly very red. So was his short thick neck. 'What is this? Some kind of shake-down?'

'Do you know why he might have taken the Royal Pair?'

A lifetime in fertiliser probably isn't the best training ground for pretending you don't give a damn. Riordan had a shot at it and failed. Penny would have bet he gave a lot more than one damn. He was definitely not happy about her questions. He took a sudden fierce step towards her, then stopped. He went over and pressed a brass-surrounded bell attached to the woodwork.

'Of course I don't,' he said.

'I heard that you might've put a contract out for them,' Penny said.

That pulled some kind of string. Riordan started laughing. He wasn't what you'd call a neat laugher. Spit globuled the lapels of his velvet jacket. 'A contract for them,' he said. Amusement pushed his head back so Penny could see up his nose.

The door of the room opened fast. A big black man in a double-breasted suit came in. He was slim but hefty. His shoulders moved like they knew where they were at. He wore a pure cotton shirt and a red silk tie. As far as men went, he was definitely in the top percentile.

When he saw Penny, he stopped. He widened his eyes at her. She widened hers right back. Slowly he ran his thumbnail across his upper lip. She watched him do a visual check for concealed weapons and find some under her open-knit top. Watched him register that some bits of it were a lot more open than others.

'Everything okay, Mr Riordan?' he said, looking at Penny.

'Sure as hell is not,' said Riordan. 'Perhaps you'd escort this crazy lady to the gates, double quick.'

'Escort,' said the black guy. 'Did you say escort, Mr Riordan?'

'Sure did.'

'Did you say crazy, Mr Riordan?'

'You deaf or something, Kimbell?' Riordan said.

'It's just she don't look crazy to me,' said Kimbell.

'Well, I'm telling you she is. Seems to think I'm some kind of a goddamned crook.'

'You, Mr Riordan?' said the black guy. He straightened his tie. It didn't need it.

'Yeah, me.'

'Oh, my.'

123

'See what I mean, crazy,' Riordan said.

'Okay, lady,' Kimbell said. 'Better come along with me.'

'Better get help,' Penny said.

'Now, Miss Wanawake,' said Kimbell. 'It'd be easier for everyone if you come quietly.'

'That's not my way,' Penny said.

'As I recall,' said the black guy. 'Vividly.'

'You still scream in your sleep?' Penny said.

'Got nobody to tell me.'

'You lost weight,' said Penny.

'I got this anxiety disorder,' said Kimbell. 'Keep sweating at night, dreaming I'm in bed with a tall black lady and then finding I'm not.'

'Hey,' Riordan said. 'What do you think this is? Dr Kildare or something? Just get her the hell out, Kimbell, would you mind? Busting in here, calling herself Meg Tarrance, accusing me of kidnapping Ferlinghetti.'

The black guy came over and stood behind Penny. He took hold of her arms and pulled her up hard against him. 'Come on, lady,' he said. 'Move it.'

Penny did. Just enough to give him a thrill. Then she looked at Riordan. 'Okay,' she said. 'That's fine. I'll go. Just don't dump on me when the boys in blue come round, hassling your wife and kids. Just don't blame me, is all.'

Riordan smiled. 'Don't you worry none about them,' he said, gently as a lion with a tamer's head in its jaws. 'The kids are away in college and Marshy's visiting her folks in Atlanta. Nice of you to care, though.'

'I'll have to report your unco-operative attitude,' Penny said.

'You do that,' said Riordan.

'You bet your sweet life I will. People gonna find it

pretty damn significant I come by here to ask a few simple questions and you try to throw me out on my ear.'

'After giving a false name,' said Riordan. 'Be sure to mention that, won't you?'

'Sounds like some serious stuff been goin' on here,' said the black man. 'Usin' a false identity to effect an entrance into a citizen's private residence.'

'Look. All I am is making enquiries on behalf of a friend,' Penny said.

Riordan seemed to decide something. He blew out a big breath, as though he'd been keeping his lungs full in case of emergency. 'Okay,' he said. There was a pause. Then he said, 'If you really want to know what I think, I'd say Ferlinghetti was trying to dodge that Leon woman.'

'So you did know he'd disappeared?'

'Heard something about it from Meg,' Riordan said. 'She was shitting bricks in case the cops got in on it.'

'Why?'

'The thing you got to realise about Meg is, she's a fanatic. The site at Toscana means to her what a kid would mean to a normal woman. More, probably. She doesn't give a shit that the place has been so thoroughly vandalised over the years there's nothing worth having left. Just a few skeletons and bits of marble too heavy to drag away.'

'And the Royal Pair,' said Penny.

'Okay. Also, there's the time element. Everything's going to disintegrate before we get to it if there's any delays. And once the cops get involved, you got all the delays you could ever need.'

'Why would Bruno want to avoid Miss Leon? Way I heard it, he couldn't get enough of her.'

'Any more than she could get enough of him.'

'She wasn't there on purely archaeological grounds, then?'

'Archaeological? Listen, honey, her interest in Toscana was purely Ferlinghetti. Simple as that. Don't ask me why. Guy's handsome enough, if you go for those Latin looks, which personally I don't. I like him, don't get me wrong. We've worked together many times. He's taken me around a bit, shown me things I'd never have seen without him. But that Sandy Leon really had a case. Last time anyone stuck that close to *me*, I ended up marrying her.'

'What did you think of Miss Leon?' Penny asked coldly.

'Didn't exchange that much conversation, to be honest with you. Anyway, I don't like women you can see the line of their panties under their clothes. If you want my opinion, Ferlinghetti quit while he was still ahead.'

'Where is she, in that case?'

'Probably chasing him up and down Italy,' Riordan said. 'I mean, she didn't have any time for the rest of us. Just stuck to Ferlinghetti closer'n a snail to its shell.'

'So you don't think she was after anything specific?'

'Sure she was. Like a justice of the peace pronouncing them man and wife. Like a little band of gold.'

'How about a little figurine of gold?'

'Hoo, boy,' said Riordan. He stared over at the burial masks, their gold faces as thin as onion skin and just about as expressive. His own held a mixture of anger and longing, of thoughts many times mulled over, now being re-examined. 'Hadn't thought of that, I have to tell you. I can't say I saw her as some kind of international art thief.'

'But she could have been?'

'I guess she could. But Meg had those figurines locked up so tight, the Pope himself would've needed a pass to see them. She wasn't taking any chances this time.'

'I heard there was some kind of scandal—'

'Scandal,' said Riordan. 'Yeah, I guess. Someone accused Meg of stealing some things that had gone missing, but in the end, far as I remember, turned out they hadn't. I don't think anyone got to the bottom of it. But there's always stuff disappearing on digs. The temptations are enormous and it's a seller's market. Too many people chasing too few items.'

'Surely someone like Meg Tarrance wouldn't be tempted.'

He indicated doubt. 'All I know is, she's one determined lady. She'd do almost anything to keep that crummy dig of hers going. Hell, she even persuaded me into putting some money up-front to finance the place.'

'What were these statuettes like?' Penny said.

'The Royal Family?' Riordan leaned forward in his chair and stared out through the diamond-paned windows. Penny did too. Two red cardinals, brilliant as Christmas decorations, were fluttering about on some topiaried yew. Clipped hedges bounded the edge of the lawn and marked the beginning of a formal sunken garden laid with bricks. A man was riding a mower up and down, striping the grass alternately dark and light. Spreading oaks stood about here and there, looking majestic. 'Pure gold. Beautiful. Did you know the ancient Egyptians called gold the flesh of the gods?'

'No, I didn't know that.'

'They connected it with the sun, the life-giver. That's why yellow was a special colour to them. It was its beauty they loved originally, not its value. They believed you'd survive in the after-life if you were buried with it.'

'The statuettes were Egyptian, weren't they?'

'. . . uh,' Riordan said. He dragged himself back from some Ozymandian dream. 'I didn't ever see them. I had some trouble with my teeth that day. By the time I got back from Rome, they were locked up. Meg'd whipped them into the safe the minute she found them. She was terrified of losing them. The first bit of real treasure we'd found in years. She was going crazy at the thought of the Government funding we'd get, the sponsorships. No more guys coming round waving building permits for cardboard apartment houses. Oh no. This was it. Fame at last.'

'Does the name Oscare Torella ring any bells, Mr Riordan?'

'Ferlinghetti's cousin, isn't he? My Italian subordinates've done deals with the guy. A slippery bozo if I ever saw one. Wouldn't trust him with my toothbrush,' said Riordan. He laughed. 'Hell. I wouldn't trust him with my wife.' He laughed some more, looking at Penny as though she ought to join in. She wasn't amused by that sort of sexist crap.

'I happen to know for a fact that he's been involved in some mighty shady deals,' Riordan went on. 'Smuggling. Authentications. I even heard a whisper that he was involved in faking. There's a lot of cash money to be made out of faked antiquities.'

'So I'm beginning to discover.'

Riordan raised his hands and let them fall hard on the chair arms. 'I told Meg,' he said. 'I told her the security was the worst I ever saw. Christ knows who tramping all over the site. Half the bad-asses in Italy standing out like extras on a coffee break. Anyone could have just walked out the gate with something under his coat.'

'Do you believe Bruno—Dr Ferlinghetti—did?'

Riordan shrugged. 'Maybe.'

'Look,' Penny said. 'If you think of anything further that might help, please let me know. It's Bruno I'm interested in, not the statuettes. I'm at the Pleasant Oaks Hotel, near the Museum of Fine Arts, until tomorrow.'

'Come on, lady,' said the man called Kimbell. He

moved her towards the door. Outside, in the hall, he took her by the arms. 'And just you watch your step,' he said.

'I always do,' Penny said. 'Saves me tripping over my feet.'

'Nice feet,' Kimbell said.

'How long you reckon from here to the Museum of Fine Arts?'

'Twenty minutes,' Kimbell said. 'Max.' He laid his thumbnail against his upper lip and stared at her.

Penny smiled.

14

THE BANANA-REPUBLIC DICTATOR WAS BEING SPELLED
by a girl with frazzled yellow hair tied up in a rag. Her
black tube skirt had a trashy see-through blouse tucked into
it. Mostly what Penny could see through it were hi-there
nipples and a yellowing love-bite. The girl had drawn in a
big black mole above her mouth. Desperately seeking
something. An identity? It might have been hospitable. It
certainly wasn't gracious. So much for hotel brochures.
The girl blew a huge pink bubble of gum and got into the
front seat of Penny's hire-car. She drove it round the back.

In the reception area were women in hats and shirt-
waists. Hundreds of them. Maybe thousands. Many of
them had flowers sprouting from their lapels. They wore
badges identifying them as the Sweetwater Cultural Club.
When they saw Penny, the plantation accents died away.
There was a broadminded hush. Penny tried to live up to
their expectations. She thought *Gone With the Wind* and
Harriet Beecher Stowe. She made a real effort to look like
she'd been raised on black-eyed peas and chitterlings. It
was hard looking deprived in a wild-silk suit.

At the desk, she asked the only other black person

around for her key. He gave it to her, along with an expression that implied she'd set back the cause of racial harmony by at least half a century. Behind her, a woman with a high voice and matching heels said, My, they'd certainly been having their problems, hadn't they, and she had to apologise for the bus being late. She mentioned Edgar Allan Poe. She quoted something inapposite from *Annabel Lee* and told them she just knew how fascinated they'd be when they finally got to the Poe Museum. The women looked as if they'd sooner believe Nixon. Several of them sat down on seating units set round a square black planter filled with leaves. They fanned themselves with copies of a guide to Virginia's historic homes.

Heat from the concrete walkway flared round Penny's feet as she walked towards her room. There was a faint smell of disinfectant. A maid pushed a cart piled with clean sheets. Behind one of the doors, someone was watching *I Love Lucy*.

She took another shower. Under the needle spray, she thought of Barnaby. They weren't communicating. It was the only time since they'd first met in Paris, however many years back it had been. She turned the water to hot. The steam smelled of chlorine, of Miss Dior. The scent of independence. The scent of sadness. The scent of someone who didn't need the cling-wrap of marriage. Why did he have to bring up all that stuff? They were just fine as they were. Correction. They'd *been* just fine as they were. You go your way, I'll go mine, they'd said, and been lucky that their ways conjoined, paralleled.

Paris. There'd been chestnut trees and street-vendors and praline smells along the quays. There'd been Pernod cloudy round ice-cubes and Algerians selling wallets on the boulevards and little *boîtes* where men with hollow eyes sang of love and faithlessness. I'm the gasman, Barnaby had said, when she'd caught him rifling through her jewel case, and she'd laughed, told him if he'd checked first he'd have discovered that her Left Bank apartment was all-electric.

She wanted Barnaby. She didn't want to get married.

The phone beeped beside the bed. She walked over to it. Above the headboard was a picture of Thomas Jefferson inside a stockade, handing a scroll to some people in tall hats while naked savages in breech-clouts peered in through gaps in the fence. Outsiders, looking in, watching uncomprehending while someone gave away their birth-right. Their freedom. She knew how they felt.

She picked up.

'Miss Wanawake?'

'Yo.'

'My name's Aaron Kimbell and I'd like to have a word or two with you about burial masks.'

'Uh-oh,' Penny said. 'The old burial mask ploy, eh?'

'Thought we could maybe toss around a few ideas.'

'What kind of ideas?'

'If you'd let me put them to you, I think you'll agree they're pretty forward-looking. Pretty thrusting.'

'Sounds good to me. Who did you say this was?'

'Just call me the Ace of Spades.'

Penny laughed. 'How'm I gonna recognise you?' she said softly.

'I'll be wearing a double-breasted suit in charcoal grey with a faint blue stripe. Black wing-tip cordovans. A one hundred per cent pure Sea Island cotton shirt. How about you?'

'I'll be wearing lip-gloss,' Penny said.

'Just couldn't believe my eyes at Riordan's place when you walked in,' she said, sometime later.

132

'Couldn't believe my *luck* when I walked in,' said Kimbell. 'Do you know how often I thought about you?'

Penny turned over on to her stomach. She poked a finger into Kimbell's dimple. She touched his ribs under their thin layer of muscle. His chest was smooth. She brushed her hand over it several times.

'How often?' she said.

'All the time,' he said hoarsely. 'All the friggin' time.'

'What're you doing out there?'

Squeezing her fingers against his mouth, Kimbell said, 'Security check.'

'He's already got all the security any mortal man could need.'

'Right. And I'm checking it.'

'Why you?'

'He let his fingers do the walking down Security Agents in the Washington yellow pages. They stopped at my name. He told me he wanted an expert from the big city to look over his arrangements. An independent, he said.'

'You didn't let on you're a private-eye-type security agent rather than a surveillance technologist.'

'Bet I didn't.' Kimbell pulled Penny closer. 'Jesus,' he said. 'Have I ever missed you.'

'How long's it been?'

'Fifteen months, one week and four days. I can give you the minutes if you hold on.'

'Didn't work out with Grace, huh?'

'Grace found herself a singer with some funky band and went off to Atlantic City with him. Or maybe it was Mexico City. I don't rightly recall.'

'What do you think of Riordan?'

'What do you?'

'I don't have him tabbed as a scholarly aesthete,' Penny said.

'A self-made millionaire doesn't get to be that way without cutting a few corners.'

'Usually off the people that got in his way.'

'So why you messing with him? Guy like that could eat you for breakfast.'

'Don't count on it. I got a few tricks up my skirt.'

'I'll say.' With one finger Kimbell stroked the long line of Penny's back, touched the curve of hip, the circle of breast. It tickled. The air-conditioning coughed. 'So what's *your* business with him?' he said.

'A friend of mine's gone missing,' Penny said. 'Another friend wants to know where he went. Riordan's name came up.'

'This Ferlinghetti character you mentioned?'

'Right.'

'You thinking Riordan's maybe got the figurines?'

'Who can say? I hoped he might give me a lead. So far, he hasn't. Just confirmed everything I already learned.' She put her face close to Kimbell's ear and blew softly into it. 'How long you been at Riordan's?'

'Four days.'

'Did he make any long-distance phone calls? Or receive any?'

'What you think I am, lady? Some kind of hired hand? I'm the surveillance specialist. Don't go round lifting no phones. Not when there's some kind of Uncle Tom butler to do it for me.'

'Find out, will you?'

'How? Phone-tapping's still illegal.'

'Ask Riordan. Say it's to do with security. You could make it sound good.'

'Think he'd tell me?'

'With a smile like yours, how could anyone refuse?'

'Ask myself that all the time.' Kimbell grinned, his teeth

white as sugar-cubes. He moved the muscles of his shoulders up and down a couple of times. 'They still saying no.' He looked at Penny seriously, then took her hand. 'You think this Bruno dude is still alive?'

'He has to be. No way I could face Giulia if he's not.'

'When're you going back to Europe?'

'As soon as possible.'

'Well, hey, hey, hey.' Kimbell sat up cross-legged in bed. His kneecaps were pale where the skin stretched from molasses to cream over the bone beneath. 'Have I got some news for you.'

'Let's have it.'

'Riordan wants me to go to Rome with him when he flies back there, a couple days from now. Act as his bodyguard-cum-safe-deposit-box.'

'What's that mean?'

'Don't know exactly.'

'I hope you're not going to disappoint him.'

'Not me. I did some heavy rescheduling,' Kimbell said. 'Put off turning out my closets for another week or two. Told the ladies they'd have to chase up their own missing kitties for a while.' He laughed, throwing back his head. 'You and me, babe. In Rome together. Think of it. Isn't that great? Isn't that the best thing you heard in years? Plus I got this real good friend over there, a cop I met last year. Enrico Manzi. You'll like him.'

'Sounds great, Kimbell. I've got one more thing to do here though.'

'What's that?'

'Ever heard of Steve Littel?'

'Who hasn't?'

'Me, for one.'

'He runs an investigation business out of Roanoke. One of the biggest in the south. Why you asking?'

135

'I thought I'd just run on over and visit with him for a while.'

'Wish I could come,' said Kimbell.

He smiled at her. She smiled right back. 'Don't let me stop you,' she said.

So he didn't.

15

Wherever the low-rent district of Roanoke was, the Crumhorn Building wasn't in it. Twenty-two floors of tinted glass don't come cheap. Nor does a security guard at the entrance. Even potted plants cost these days, and there were plenty of those about. The ground-floor décor was tasteful. The security guard was tasteful. Even the car park out front was tasteful.

Penny took the lift to the ninth floor. She passed an open door leading to a room where a man in a five-hundred-dollar suit was holding the hand of a sobbing woman and surreptitiously inspecting his watch. He could have been a funeral parlour director or an abortionist. The sign on the door said he was an accountant. Looked like Sir Jasper had foreclosed on the mortgage. Or the accountant had just presented his bill. Either way, he probably charged double for crying time.

Safe & Sound occupied a four-room suite further down the hall. It was plush. Glass frosted in a maple-leaf pattern. Polished hardwood doors. Brass accoutrements. In a place that classy, you couldn't call them knobs. Penny turned an accoutrement and went into a reception area of glass and

137

chrome. In a big aquarium were tropical fish, mouthing at multi-coloured gravel. A flat snail slid infinitesimally across the glass.

Over the sound system, the William Tell overture was just working up to a climax. The man at the desk didn't look like it was an experience he'd shared. His bowtie, black with little white handcuffs scattered over it, was definitely frivolous. The rest of him definitely wasn't. His white hair was parted in the middle. His suit was the kind undertakers die in. He wore small-lensed gold-rimmed glasses. Penny had seen him in a hundred westerns, playing the bimbo in the green eyeshade and armbands who dispatches urgent telegrams to Dodge City or hands over the payroll to the guys in black hats.

'Hi,' she said. 'I'm Penny Wanawake.'

'Is that right?' He sounded like she'd have to convince him. There was a warm smell of alcohol in the air.

'Sure is.'

'How can I help you?' the man said. 'Husband having an affair, is he? Or he's got hold of some incriminating personal correspondence? Business partner bilking you?'

'Not exactly.' Proposing marriage all the time, but not bilking. Far as she knew.

'Your mother's left the whole shooting-match to the local branch of Right to Life and you figure there has to be another will. Or the guy next door's murdered his wife but you need proof before you go to the cops.'

What a huckster. Any minute now he'd be handing out free cotton candy and a chance to buy a set of cheap saucepans. 'None of the above,' Penny said. 'I want to see Mr Littel."

The man touched his bowtie. He moved a cube of brown plastic about. It had F.A.O. Schwarz incised on its side in letters so small Penny had to lean forwards to read them. Sometimes she wondered if she needed glasses. 'Mr Littel is unavailable at the present time,' he said.

'When will he stop being?' said Penny.

'He didn't confide in me.' The little man cleared his throat. His larynx jerked, the strings of his neck standing out like wings. There was no flesh there, none on his face, either. Penny had seen men like him before, drunks dying slowly of starvation and vitamin deficiency, the compulsion to drink as raw as liver however well they hid it. He launched into what sounded like an advertising spiel. 'But I am authorised to help you in any way I can. Whatever the problem, Safe and Sound can solve it. Perhaps one of your sales staff is putting his or her hand in the till: S and S will find out. You want to throw a party: S and S will be on hand to provide your guests with that extra assurance. Your pedigree Blue Point has gone missing: S and S will get her back.'

'Not for me,' said Penny. 'I don't like cats.'

'Anonymous letters,' said the man. 'You've been the recipient of anonymous letters and you want to know who's sending them. S and S offers not only the most discreet—'

'Mr Schwartz,' Penny said. She spoke firmly. Behind the gold rims, the eyes were glazing, remembering the last drink he'd had and thinking it was too long ago.

'No job too small, we solve them all,' he said. He reached out and gave the cube a 90 degree turn. Now it read Mr Laverne Forrester, in much larger letters. 'I'm always doing that,' he said. 'F.A.O. Schwarz is the establishment in New York where I—'

'Mr Forrester,' said Penny.

Forrester smiled vaguely. His hands inched towards the drawer of his desk, then inched away again. He licked his lips.

139

'You want to find out who your real parents are,' he said. It was almost a whisper.

'I want to find out where Littel is.'

'I'm not authorised to divulge such information,' Forrester said. He stared at the gold ring on Penny's finger. At the chain round her throat. At her shoes. 'However, it is quite possible that my tongue could be loosened.'

'Not with a Twinkie bar, I'll bet.'

'Candy is dandy,' said Forrester, 'but liquor is quicker.'

'Does Ogden know you're using his best lines?'

'Ogden?' Forrester licked his lips again. They were very dry. Just like him.

'I don't normally pay calls with a bottle of hooch in my pocket,' Penny said. 'Marlowe's the guy you want.'

'Money,' said Forrester, 'isn't everything. On the other hand, it's still quite a lot.'

'What does Littel think about you putting the bite on the clientéle?'

'He hates it,' Forrester said. He held out his hand.

'You dirty rat,' said Penny.

'Not that he'd do anything about it.'

'He should.'

'I'm one of his best operatives.'

'I'd hate to see one of the mediocre ones.'

'Also,' Forrester gave Penny a hard stare, 'I know too much about the business.'

Penny gave him ten bucks.

When she upped it to twenty, he gave her Littel's address.

'The agency's working on a case overseas right now,' Penny said. 'Who hired you?'

She took another bill from her bag. Laid it on the desk. Looked at Forrester. He looked at her. He looked at the bill. Slowly he shook his head.

'That's a fifty,' Penny said.

Forrester shook his head again. The shake was slower this time.

'Not that far gone, huh?' Penny said.

'Not yet.' The lines on Forrester's face took a downward turn. 'Next week, maybe. Or tomorrow. But not today.'

Penny put the money back into her purse. There was a sad smile on his face. A man whose yesterdays had caught up with him. At the door, she looked back. He was already unscrewing the top from a green leather hip-flask.

Littel lived some ten miles out of town, in the middle of pasturage enclosed in white-painted snake fencing. A grove of live oaks shaded an imitation ante-bellum mansion with green shutters at the windows. Out front was a flagpole flying the Confederate flag. A long line of misty blue hills stretched across the background.

A neat woman in a pink coverup sporraned by an apron answered the door. She smiled. She said Mr Littel was right out in back. Penny followed her across a hall and out on to a patio. A swimming pool was contained inside the two Ls of the house. In the pool, a lady in a yellow bikini splashed around with a little kid. Watching them from the shade of an umbrella was a man. He sat at a table covered by a red cloth edged with white ball fringing. On the cloth were papers. On the floor beside him was a box file. He was obviously supposed to be working. Instead, he was watching the woman and the child, and smiling. Doting would be nearer the word. He was a good twenty years older than she. Penny guessed a second marriage.

'Someone to see you, Mr Littel,' said the woman in pink.

The man stood up.

'Hi, I'm Penny Wanawake.' Penny gave him time to digest the syllables.

'Hello there,' he said.

No one was ever going to cast Steve Littel in bronze and put him on public display. Homely was probably the kindest way to describe him. His glasses were framed in a material resembling barley sugar. He wore a maroon Lacoste shirt and maroon wasn't his colour. But he had a lovely smile. For a plumpish forty-five-year-old, his knees weren't bad, either, considering the rest of him. They were freckled and prominently on display beneath the sateen running shorts Penny very much wished he wasn't wearing.

'Have we met?' he said. He put out his hand. A silver fish hung from a chain round his neck.

'Not yet.'

'So what are you . . . ? How did you . . . ?' Littel made a gesture that combined puzzled but courteous enquiry with a desire not to imply that he rather wished he hadn't been interrupted in the middle of something important like watching his wife and child in the pool.

'Mr Forrester told me your address,' Penny said.

'Oh dear,' said Littel. Behind him, a paper wafted off the table and sideswiped its way to the floor. 'How much did you give him?'

'Twenty bucks,' said Penny.

'Here.' Littel picked up a wallet from the table and thumbed out a couple of ten-dollar bills.

'No, no,' said Penny. 'It was pleasure doing business with him.'

Littel sighed. 'He used to be one of my best operatives.'

'He says he still is.'

'Not since he took to the bottle, he's not. I only keep

142

him on because the poor old guy would never get a job anywhere else. As anything else.'

The child in the pool called. Littel went to the edge. He reached down and pulled the kid out. He brushed the wet hair off her forehead. 'Isn't she just the cutest little lady?' he said. The child gurgled happily. She was wearing the tiniest swim suit Penny had ever seen.

'Sure is.' Penny touched the child's cheek with her finger.

'What exactly can I do for you?' Littel said over the top of his daughter's head. 'Since you've taken the trouble to drive out here . . .'

'Wanted to say I'm sorry about Lavette.'

'Oh,' said Littel. Noncommittal as a butcher's block. He was good at noncommittal, no question. But the way his shoulder hunched was a dead giveaway.

'You do remember Jack Lavette, don't you?' Penny said. 'Guy in the Calvin Kleins and the Ray-Bans?'

'Do I?'

'He was spying on a house belongs to a friend of mine,' said Penny. 'He let drop he was one of your men, but wouldn't say who the client was.'

'Good.'

The child in his arms stroked his ear and made happy noises. At the far end of the pool were big green trees weighted by heat. Leaves hung weakly down like panting green tongues. The air beneath them was dark blue. A ginger ant walked across the flags by Penny's foot. It was followed by a line of others. They all seemed to be heading for a terracotta jar with a camellia growing out of it.

'Guess that means you won't tell me either,' she said.

'An agency like mine has to guarantee absolute discretion at all times.'

'Nothing going to change your mind?'

143

'Nothing.' To show it wasn't personal, Littel smiled again.

'Not even the fact that Lavette was found face down in my friend's swimming pool? By me.'

Littel didn't answer.

A thin, pale lady with a great many scarves came floating through the glass doors behind him. She carried a metal tray. On it was a hand-embroidered cloth, a pitcher of lemonade and some glasses. She put it down on the table and gave Penny an anxious glance.

'Where have all the flowers gone?' she said.

'Thank you, Leonie,' said Littel.

'I'll go and pack my bags,' said the lady. 'They're firing on the house now. It'll be the Russians next, if we're not very careful.'

'Don't worry,' Littel said. 'Everything's under control.'

'Under control,' said the lady. 'It most certainly is not under control. There are soldiers all over the roof at this very minute. It'll be rationing and petrol bombs next, you mark my words.'

'I'll see to it,' Littel said. 'Why don't you go look at the backyard for a bit? See if the flowers are growing.'

'Flowers,' the lady said. 'Yes. They stuck them in their bayonets, you know.' She wandered away through a gap in the screen of flowering shrubs around the pool.

'My sister,' Littel said.

Penny admired him for not adding anything else.

'You better watch out, Mr. Littel,' she said.

'Oh?' said Littel. He poured two glasses of lemonade and gave Penny one. There were pieces of fresh lemon cartwheeling around the top. 'Why's that, Miss Wana-wake?'

'Because any minute now I'm going to show you my dimples. And when I do that, I'm irresistible.'

'Try me.'

Penny brought her dimples into play. Littel looked at them. Then he shook his head.

'No go, huh?' Penny said.

'Sorry,' said Littel. 'You want to brush up on your thermodynamics.'

'You're an immovable object, right?'

'Right.'

'Rats,' said Penny. The lemonade was cool and almost not quite sweet enough. It roughened the inside of her mouth. It was good. She'd have been enjoying herself if she'd known where Bruno was. And if Lavette was still alive.

'I do have principles,' Littel said, 'as well as a sense of business ethics.'

'Absolute discretion at all times.'

'Precisely. I don't know who you are or what exactly you want, but it was naive of you to think I'd answer the questions of a complete stranger. Especially where it affects my work.'

'It was,' agreed Penny. She gave him a smile that would have melted a glacier. 'But I had to give it my best shot. I promised, see. I got this real close friend, back home in England, she's worried to death about *another* real close friend who's gone missing. She's terrified he might have been kidnapped. Even murdered. She asked if I could help out and I said I'd do what I could. Trouble is, I can't find out a single thing. The trail, such as it is, pointed this way, and I kinda hoped maybe you and I could put our heads together and come up with something.' She lifted one side of her mouth ruefully. 'Should have known a man like you couldn't be persuaded to break his professional code.'

'I see,' Littel said. He bunched his lips together.

'It's a real sad story,' Penny said.

145

'Tell me.'

Penny did. She pulled out all the stops. She made it sound like one Shakespeare'd been keeping in the in-tray. If there'd been any strong men around, they'd have wept. By the time she'd finished, she felt a little snuffly herself.

Littel looked across the pool to where the woman in the bikini was trying to duck-dive. He swung the child high into the air until she shrieked with laughter. Then he set her down on her feet and patted her little behind.

'Off you go, pumpkin,' he said. 'Go find Mommy.' He drank some lemonade. Stared at the trees. Spat out a piece of lemon pith.

'So?' said Penny.

'Just wondering how come Erich Segal passed that one up,' Littel said.

'You gotta have heart.'

'Where my business is concerned, Miss Wanawake, I keep my heart locked up with my personal jewelry at the back of my drawer.'

'My friend's not eating,' Penny said. 'Unless you count Valium. I just hope Bruno turns up before she gets benzo-hooked.' Giulia never took anything stronger than an anti-histamine when the grass-cutting season started. 'As for the booze . . .'

'Women shouldn't drink,' Littel said. 'Their systems aren't geared to cope with alcohol.'

''S what I keep telling her. But it's the only way she can get through the waiting.'

Littel finished off his lemonade and set the glass down on the red tablecloth. 'Miss Wanawake,' he said. 'You tell a good story. But however much this bitches you up, I'm not going to tell you who hired Jack Lavette. What I *would* have done, if Lavette was still around, was tell him he could start walking the minute this case is closed. I'm running a business here. A business that relies on the confidentiality with which I conduct it. And that includes my personnel.'

Leonie reappeared. Some kind of blossom trailed from the back of her hair. Her arms were full of flowers. She laid them down on a towel lying by the pool and wrapped them up in it very carefully. Then she threw the parcel into the pool.

'Gone to soldiers everyone,' she said.

'Aw, Leonie,' said Littel. 'You know what a mess that makes.'

'Suppose I'd come from the local paper to write an article on the gumshoe in today's society,' Penny said. 'Or a promotional piece on local security firms. Would you loosen up a little?'

'That would depend on the questions you asked.'

'Suppose I asked where your operatives come from? Do they sit about your office reading magazines and waiting for a client?'

There was a smile on Littel's face. 'Sounds more like a cat house,' he said.

'So how does it work?'

'I have a stable of people, part-timers, mostly. Students. Actors. Musicians. Athletes. People whose employment doesn't fully occupy them or is in some way seasonal or occasional. I pay them a small retainer and when I want them on a job, I expect them to drop everything else and get out there and do it. If they possibly can.'

'How often do you get jobs abroad?'

'Sometimes.'

'And when you do, how does it work?'

'We use what contacts we have locally. Obviously we prefer to use someone already in place if we can. Unless it's a situation where an American is going to fit in easily.

147

It's amazing how big a network you can come up with if you really try.'

'How about when—'

'Miss Wanawake, way I understand it, you're *not* from the local paper, right?'

'Right.'

'So I don't guess we need go on talking about this.'

'One last question,' said Penny. 'Your client—whoever he or she was—contacted you for someone to watch the Ferlinghetti place. And you sent Lavette over there. Was the other guy—the one spelling Lavette—was he local?'

Littel thought about it. His head turned this way and that, like a rat wondering whether to risk it and go for the Warfarin. Then he said, 'No.'

'You've lost an operative on this job, Mr Littel. I'm looking for the guy whose house he was watching. Wouldn't it be better if we co-operated? Pooled our information?'

'From what you say, you don't have any to pool.'

She couldn't argue with that one. 'Was the person who hired you from around here?' she said quickly. She could tell he was getting impatient by the way the freckles on his kneecaps moved about.

'Around here?'

'Like, say, from Richmond. Or maybe from a classy girls' school in Charlottesville.'

'Miss Wanawake,' Littel said, 'I am not, now or ever, going to tell you who approached me. I'm not going to tell you anything further about my operatives, local or non-local, rich or poor, male or female.'

'Ever heard of Riordan? Or Dunlap?'

Under the maroon shirt, his shoulder hunched. He shook himself vigorously. 'Must have got water in my ears,' he said. 'I don't hear a word you say.'

148

The little girl tottered towards her father and held up her arms. He hoisted her on to his hip and blew against her stomach.

'Do you know where Bruno Ferlinghetti is?' Penny said.

'I can tell you nothing else at all,' said Littel.

'Please.'

'Nothing,' said Littel. 'At all.'

He looked apologetic. But not terribly. There is nothing so intractable as a man with principles. Or a man with a business to run. Which meant Penny would have to decide for herself which of the names she'd mentioned had made his shoulder jerk hardest. Riordan, or Dunlap. And when she'd decided that, whether it meant anything. Maybe he just had a wasp under his shirt. Or a nervous tic.

In the pool, the towel had opened. It hung just beneath the top of the water. Flowers were drifting across the surface. The lady in the bikini swam about trying to round them up. The lady in the scarves was holding her nose.

'No, Leonie,' shouted Littel.

'A life on the ocean wave,' Leonie said. She jumped, fully clothed, into the deep end. Littel closed his eyes and shook his head.

Driving away from the house between the white fencing, Penny clashed her braids together. The beads on the ends clicked. She was frustrated. From what Littel hadn't said, it was clear that someone had hired him to put a tail on Bruno. But who? Dunlap? Riordan? Or someone trying to make it look like Dunlap or Riordan? Because if it wasn't one of them, why else use a private investigator from this neck of the woods? And what was the purpose?

She was beginning to feel she'd just about run out of places to look for Bruno. Or questions to ask. Maybe she should follow Leonie's example and throw in the towel.

Not just the towel but the towel rail as well. Except she couldn't. Not yet. Not when she thought about Giulia.

Would there be any percentage in showing up at the Crumhorn Building again, filling Forrester up with Old Grandad, squeezing another sliver of info out of the guy? She thought not. Littel was much too smart to let a long-time boozer like Forrester in on anything worth knowing.

And how about that Littel, anyway? He acted like his heart was as big as the Grand Canyon. Crazy sisters, cute kids, drunks on the payroll. A fish round his neck, for chrissake. In actual fact, he was about as soft as a taffy-puller's slab. What had she got out of him?

Absolute zero was what.

16

KIMBELL HAD QUICK REFLEXES. HE PICKED UP BEFORE the first ring was over.

'—uh—*Pronto*,' he said. He sounded as though he was either suffering from sinusitis or had been woken from a deep sleep.

'Only been in the country five minutes and already you sound like a native,' said Penny.

'*Ché?*'

'The sort with a bone through the nose.'

'Who are you?' The voice was guarded, the mouth held close to the receiver.

'You asking in the metaphysical sense?'

'Asking in the need-to-know sense,' said the voice. It was happy now. It had tabbed her.

'If you need a bit more than that, Kimbell—'

'Do I ever.'

'—meet me at a place called the Caffè La Strada in about an hour.'

'Is this one of your toney places?'

'Could be.'

'Because I didn't pack my tux. Also, Mr. Riordan didn't pay me yet.'

'Relax, kid. Dinner's on me.'

'You are one sweet momma, you know that?'

'Yeah.' Penny gave Kimbell directions.

Sixty minutes later, she was walking down a grey high-sided street of wall-to-wall cobbles. A ginger cat with one ear watched her from a peeling window-sill. Behind the romanesque outlines of Santa Maria in Trastevere, the evening sky was purple, as ripe and smooth as a grape. Motor-scooters belched in nearby alleyways. The air was dark and hot and full of gasoline fumes.

Kimbell was waiting for her. He leaned against a wall, hunky under a cream-coloured jacket. There was an airline bag slung over one shoulder. When he saw her, he stroked the left half of his upper lip with his thumbnail.

'Hi,' she said.

'Didn't we meet last year in Marienbad?' he said. He had a rose in his buttonhole.

'You thinking of Delphine Seyrig,' Penny said. She bumped him with her hip.

'Never thought about the lady in my entire life.'

'Lookin' good, Aaron.'

'You too, Miz Penny.'

They smiled at each other. Two of a kind. All round them, life was being lived. Balconies hung like warts from the front of shabby blocks of flats. Shadows twisted, sleek as otters. In a room open to the street, a woman was on her knees in front of a plaster Virgin Mary. Two kids passed by, laughing, zonked on something. Blue-white light flickered on the ceilings of silent rooms. The opiates of the people. Television. God. Ammies or 'ludes or acid. What the hell. In that quarter of town, the people needed a fix of something—anything—to get them through.

The windows of the Caffè La Strada had been painted matt black. A stylised face was stencilled on to the glass, crowned by a hat with a bite out of it. In the dark little lobby, Kimbell pulled her towards him. He kissed her, his mouth as sweet as flowers. There was a gun on his hip.

In front of them the darkness lessened. A curtained door opened. They were led into a room painted entirely in black and lit by wandering spotlights. Without background depth, the objects touched by the beams lost meaning. A woman's arm. A white dish. A crudely painted banana. Faces, outlined in silver. Meaningless. Smoke hung like an eiderdown below the ceiling.

Small women in wigs of straight hair moved about. Giulietta Massina clones, mournful-mouthed, big-eyed, sad enough to lump your throat. On each table was a hooded candle encased in plastic netting. Every now and then, one of the restless beams stood still over a table, a modern star of Bethlehem, giving the patrons a chance to order. Against a wall, a group of young men in black jeans and sweaters were making a rhythmic sound on black-sprayed instruments. Their hands had been painted luminous green.

The restaurant was crowded. Easy to see why. It was so dark in there, you could bring who you liked and no one would recognise you. You could bring your wife and no one would recognise you. Not even her.

One of the clones appeared at their table. Penny wondered how many of the people drinking Campari sodas at the bar had actually seen *La Strada*. They didn't look like an arts-theatre crowd. Two many cufflinks. Too many bare backs. She watched luminous fingers rippling up and down an invisible clarinet. Piano chords drifted through the smoke.

They ordered. The glancing beams picked up flat

washes of colour from women's dresses, highlighted the deeper glow of wine in glasses. People laughed, teeth suddenly brilliant in the spots. Diamonds flashed as a woman turned her head.

The seediness of the place was spurious. Perhaps it made the rich folks' food taste extra spicy if they came down this end of town to eat it. Perhaps it gave them a feeling of stepping warily into the jungle, an extra frisson when they made it in one piece back to their ritzy flats on the Janiculum.

'Why we here, exactly?' Kimbell said.

'I don't know exactly,' said Penny. 'It's a lead I'm following up.'

'Not a hunch, I hope.'

'No.'

''Cause there's nothing worse, in my book, than a woman with a hunch. Jeez. Once a woman's off on that intuition kick, she's—'

'I said no, Kimbell. No. Okay?'

'Okay.'

'Where I come from, there's a difference between a lead, which is what I said, and a hunch, which is what I didn't say.'

'*Okay.*'

'And don't you forget it.'

'No, ma'am.'

'Intuition, for chrissakes.' At this stage, if she had any about almost anything, she would use it. She still didn't have the faintest idea where Bruno could be.

'Hey,' Kimbell said. 'Almost forgot.' He reached into his jacket. 'Something for you to work on. Look what I found in Riordan's trash-can.'

He held out two pieces of paper. Across a Parmesan cheese shaker shaped like the leaning tower of Pisa, Penny took them from him. Both were smeared with something red.

She examined them closely. 'Definitely not Heinz,' she said. 'You want an opinion off the top of my head, I'd say Van Camp's.'

Kimbell grinned. 'Sorry about that. Riordan eats a lot of pork and beans.'

'I can tell.' Penny smoothed the papers out. They were drawings of a stylised couple. The woman had a child on her knee. There was a circlet round her head from the centre of which reared a bird of prey. Riordan had taken a lot of trouble over the beak. He'd drawn the man with a square beard hanging from his chin and a pageboy haircut. There were hedgehog lines radiating out from both the figures to show that they shone. Like gold.

'Tell you anything?' Kimbell said.

'Sure does.'

'What?'

'That no one's ever going to ask Riordan to redecorate the Sistine Chapel.'

'Thought you'd be interested,' said Kimbell. 'I don't sift through garbage for just anyone, you know.'

'I *am* interested.'

'These the figurines you're after?'

'They might be.'

'You mean you don't know?'

'So far I haven't been issued with an Identikit,' said Penny.

'How come?'

'Because so far, apart from Meg Tarrance, none of the people I've spoken to has seen them. Including Riordan. Or so he said. Which makes it real interesting that he's drawn them in such detail.'

'I knew he was a crook,' Kimbell said.

'I didn't. But I'm beginning to wonder.'

'Tell you something else he is. And that's violent. Heard him bawling out that butler of his the other day. Thought he was going to explode. And all because the guy was late picking up the mail.'

The Gelsomina clone reappeared. Or a different one. She had two serving dishes in her hand. One held something flat in a reddish sauce scattered with pulverised parsley. There were buttered snap beans lying on one side of it, and aubergine fritters on the other. She put it down in front of Penny. The other dish she placed in front of Kimbell. Except that it was bumpy, instead of flat, it was identical to Penny's.

'What's this?' Kimbell said.

'Issa brains of little cows.'

'Issa what?'

'Calves' brains,' Penny said.

'Brains? I didn't order no brains,' said Kimbell. 'Leastways, if I did, I sure didn't mean to.' He pushed the dish away. 'Sorry, lady. You'll have to bring me something else.' He pointed at Penny's food. 'Like the signorina's. *Como la signorina.*' The clone went away.

Now that her eyes were used to the gloom, Penny was able to see the other diners. Particularly one of them. Four tables away, someone was staring at her and pretending not to. She could see he had silver hair.

'Don't look now, but the dude over there wants to get acquainted,' Kimbell said, jerking his head towards the man. He drooped his eyes.

'I know,' Penny said.

'Can't blame the guy.'

'Probably the local rep for the NAACP, wants me to picket a MacDonald's or something.'

'Just what I was thinking.'

The clone waitress returned. She put another dish down in front of Kimbell.

'What is it this time?' he said.

'Same as signorina,' said the waitress.

'Yeah, but what *is* it?'

'Issa very nice. You will like.'

'Looks the same as what you brought me before.'

'Plus ça change, plus c'est la même brain,' Penny said.

'Issa sweetbreads,' the clone said. 'Very nice.'

'Issa lovely,' Penny said.

Kimbell poked suspiciously at his plate. 'Sweetbreads,' he said.

'Pancreas, if you prefer,' said Penny. She poked her fork into his food and tasted it. 'Issa *gorgeous*.'

The man who had been watching her still was. When he saw her looking, he spoke, barely moving his lips, to the man who sat opposite him. Immediately his companion dropped something on to the floor and bent to pick it up. Very smooth. Also, a good way to check someone out. One of the beams hovered over Silverhair's table and she saw him clearly for the first time. Big head, light eyes, a smoothly handsome face of the kind that keeps second-rate actors in work portraying crooked congressmen and financiers on the fiddle.

She showed him her teeth. He spoke again, and the man in the dark suit got up and headed over to where a green-lit sign indicated the whereabouts of the EXIT and the GABINETTI. Two rolls of rubbery fat hung over his collar, front and back. Pure muscle, with no ambition to be anything else. She wondered why Mr Smooth was sitting at a table with him, what they talked about.

She wondered who Mr Smooth was. Other than the man in the photographs in Drusilla's room in Cambridge. The guy she'd come here hoping to see.

He was staring at her again, eyes quizzical, on the make. He was obviously a politician because he moved his head once, gently enough to be no more than an involuntary movement, forcibly enough to be an invitation. Bet-hedging, in case she refused it.

She didn't. She got up.

'What'd I say?' asked Kimbell.

'I gotta see a man,' Penny said. 'If I'm not back in ten minutes, call out the SWAT team.'

She hipped it like a *Dynasty* starlet over to his table. Her beads banged along her forehead. Her drop-dead de la Renta was slit just about every place it could be without causing a riot.

She leaned over the man's table. Even in the gloom he could see as much as he wanted. He wanted quite a bit.

'Hi,' she said. 'I'm Penny Wanawake.'

He stood up. Placed a chair. Held out a hand. 'Pietro Bernini,' he said.

Gracefully, she sat down and crossed her legs. The silk of her dress fell away from them. Bernini enjoyed the show. He snapped his fingers at one of the clones and creased his face into a Paul Newman smile.

He brought her fingers to his mouth. Oh wow. It wasn't the same as having her palm kissed. Definitely not. A man who kissed her palm could more or less name his terms. Palm kissing made her feel fragile, which, at six foot and counting, wasn't something she got a lot of chance to feel. Finger kissers just had to try a little harder, was all. One of these days, her weakness for men was going to prove fatal, she knew it.

'I wanted to ask you something,' she said.

'Of course.'

'Where does a girl get a bodyguard like him?' She gestured towards the EXIT sign.

For a moment Bernini was nonplussed. Perhaps she wasn't supposed to have sussed the other man's function. Then he smiled. He could handle this sort of thing. 'First a girl has to have a body worth guarding,' he said. He'd taken the bait. He was still holding her hand, running his thumb over the fingernails.

Big-eyed and dimpled, she said, 'Really?'

'And I imagine you'd qualify,' said Bernini. Bet that wasn't all he was imagining, the creep. Any man who was sucker enough to go for that sexist shit deserved everything he got. Men like Bernini were two a penny up in the top echelons of whatever field they'd chosen to excel in. Ruthless, hard-headed, expecting no pity and giving none. Pushing, publishing, prostitutes, pols or profs, they all looked the same. The thirty-dollar blow-dry lifting the thinning hair off the scalp. The capped teeth. The smooth skin creamed every night. The carefully cut clothes. Image was all. Reality was nowhere.

The thing about appearances is, if you present the right one, people don't always check to see if it's deceptive. Men like Bernini didn't rate women much outside the bedroom, so it didn't occur to them that the women they met might really be quite different from what they seemed. Men like Bernini were pushovers when it came to women. It was just as well she wasn't unscrupulous.

Another clone arrived. Bernini ordered champagne. She knew he would. He looked at her to see if she was impressed and she played along. She knew when an ego needed massaging, even if she hadn't been parlour-trained.

'Champagne,' she said huskily. It nearly killed her. 'For me?'

'What else?' he said.

Jesus.

He picked a breadstick from a glass in the centre of the

table. He peeled off the cellophane wrapping, nice and slow. Lips slightly parted, tongue just showing. Even without a two-way mirror, you knew he looked the same way when he undressed a woman.

There was no denying he had an aura. Big bucks sat back of his eyes. Power quirked the corner of his mouth. Penny liked power. Even when allied with obduracy, as it was in Bernini. When his silvery eyes started doing a tarantella over her body, she had to remind herself she was there on business. Took a minute or two to remember *what* business, but she managed it.

'Perhaps I should mention that I'm a friend of Bruno Ferlinghetti's,' she said.

'Ah,' said Bernini. He leaned back in his chair. 'The *professore* who is also a thief.'

'You want to rephrase that?' Penny said.

'Isn't it the truth?'

'Bruno is straight arrow.'

'He may well be,' said Bernini, 'but right at the moment, not too many newspaper-reading Italians would agree with you.'

The champagne came. After pouring it, Bernini lifted both glasses. He touched the rim of one with his lips and offered it to Penny. Gaahd. He was hamming it up even worse than she was. Difference was, he expected to be taken seriously. She only hoped to be.

He leaned towards her. 'Do you, then, know something about these missing statuettes that Ferlinghetti has stolen?'

'Something.'

'Indeed.'

'Do you know something about Drusilla Ross?' Penny said.

For a moment she thought she'd blown it. His expression didn't change but all of a sudden the charm was gone.

A layer of angry muscle bulged under his ears for a second, making his shirt look too small.

'Drusilla Ross,' he repeated. Neither question nor statement. Two words laid out in the open. Something to think about while he decided what to do.

'Know her?'

'No.'

'Does the name mean anything to you?' It quite obviously did, but she wasn't going to push it. Not right then.

'Nothing,' Bernini said. 'Is she a friend of yours? Or of Dr Ferlinghetti's?'

'No.'

'Why, then, do you mention her?'

'Because she was working down at Toscana when Bruno disappeared.'

'So, undoubtedly, were others.'

Yes, but the betting is they don't keep photographs of you beside their beds. 'Yes, but . . .' began Penny.

Bernini made a fist and pushed it gently against the table-top. 'I am extremely concerned about those missing figurines,' he said.

'Why?' Penny wondered whether he would mention the *galleria itaro*.

He didn't. 'Although I was trained as a lawyer, my business is now primarily antiques and fine art. I am a connoisseur,' he said, giving it a smidgin of *double entendre*. His fingers moved very lightly up and down her thigh. They were cold.

'I can tell,' she said.

'Moreover, I am a patriot. For too long Italy's artistic heritage has been at the mercy of unscrupulous men. Smuggled out of the country, melted down, sold to private collections and thus lost to the citizens whose birthright it is. Objects such as the golden figurines from Toscana must

161

be preserved. They are part of our historical legacy.' It was beginning to sound like a campaign speech.

'Even though they're Egyptian?' Penny said.

'That is beside the point. At all costs we must see that they are not lost to us forever. This illegal traffic must be stopped. This plundering of our nation's history must be halted. It is up to those of us who have influence to pull what strings we can to preserve these and similar artefacts for Italy's future. I shall leave no stone unturned in my efforts to recover them before it is too late.'

By golly, it *was* a campaign speech.

'Gee, Mr Bernini,' Penny said. 'You must be the noblest Roman of them all.'

'Perhaps you understand how I feel,' he said. He smiled into her eyes. She reminded herself he went round with an ape. You only did that if the stuff you were into was strictly non-legit.

At the back of the room, the door under the EXIT sign opened and Bernini's gorilla peered cautiously out. He stared at them. He looked like he had trouble breathing through both nostrils at once.

The door of the restaurant opened and the candle on the table guttered, giving off a smell of hot plastic. Bernini looked up. His mouth tightened. 'We must talk further,' he said quickly. 'But here is not the place.'

'Why not?'

'There are too many ears.'

There were a lot, agreed, but none of them seemed to be turned in their direction. 'When, then?' Penny said.

'Tomorrow.'

'What time?'

'Twelve thirty.'

'Your place or mine?'

'Mine,' said Bernini. He smiled, giving it a lot of the

162

Newmanesque crinkle. He told her the address. 'Already I am impatient to see you again,' he said.

'Oh, me too,' said Penny.

The gorilla came and stood at the table. He rested his knuckles on the cloth. Didn't say anything, just acted kind of heavy. He flexed the top part of his arms.

'Could I ask you something?' Penny said.

'Anything at all,' said Bernini, smiling.

'Does he often stuff water-melons down his sleeves?'

'No,' said Bernini.

'Didn't think so,' Penny said.

Kimbell came over. He had the shaker of Parmesan cheese in his hand and a napkin over his arm. 'The SWAT team *con formaggio* you ordered, ma'am,' he said.

Bernini half stood. 'I am detaining you,' he said. 'My apologies.'

'Not at all,' said Penny. She pulled her mouth ripely forwards, raised her eyebrows. 'A *domani*,' she said.

She followed Kimbell back to their table.

'Jesus,' he said. He pushed his mouth into a sultry pout. 'A *domani*.' He spoke in a high voice.

'Jealous, Aaron?'

'Where'd you learn crap like that?'

'Went to night school.'

'Who is that guy, anyway?'

'Someone to watch, if I'm any judge.'

Bernini saw her looking at him. He crinkled again.

'If we're into judging,' Kimbell said, 'far's I'm concerned, you get first prize. Every time.'

'Aw*right*.' Penny drew it out. What else do you do when people tell you nice stuff like that?

Kimbell coughed. 'Remember that business associate of yours? Midas?'

'Perfectly.'

'How's he doin'?'

'We're still in business together, if that's what you mean.'

Kimbell gave a big sigh.

'At least,' Penny said, 'I think we are.'

Their dessert came. They drank some more of the wine. It was probably the anti-freeze which gave it that rich pastoral flavour.

'Ever thought of getting married, Kimbell?' Penny said.

'Frequently,' said Kimbell. 'And always to you.' He picked up her hand and kissed the palm. Oh wow. How'd he *know*?

'You don't see marriage as an outdated bourgeois convention, imposing pressures and restrictions on a relationship that should essentially be free?'

'No, ma'am.'

'You don't feel that bits of paper are quite irrelevant between two mature people who know how they feel about each other and don't need the law to tell them?'

'Nothin' like that.'

'Particularly when there are no children to be taken into consideration.'

'Midas hasslin' you?'

'Yeah.'

'Only natural,' Kimbell said. 'When a guy hits a class-act like you, he wants to make sure it's his and no one else's.'

'That's exactly what I mean,' Penny said. 'Pressures. Restrictions. Who needs them? I'm *mine* and no one else's.'

'I'd do the same as him, you were my chick.'

'Bet you would.'

'Let me know, things break down between the two of

164

you,' Kimbell said. 'I got no objection to standin' in line for my chance.'

'I'll keep you in mind.'

While they were drinking coffee, Bernini passed their way, the gorilla shuffling along behind. Bernini touched Penny's back with a cold forefinger. He opened his mouth.

'A domani,' Kimbell said. 'Now beat it.'

The way back to the hotel took them past the Casa Ferlinghetti. The lights were on behind the curtained first-floor windows. Penny wondered if Alex was still there. If he was, he wouldn't be measuring up for any of that Egyptian-type carpeting. Interior designer, my ass. He couldn't have designed his way out of a condom. In the car mirror, she saw movement in the dark street. She caught a glimpse of curls, a neutral jacket, an impression of stealth. A shadowed man, walking in shadow. Sometimes the world seemed full of them.

There was another couple waiting to go up when they stepped into the lift at Penny's hotel. Kimbell drooped his eyes at her. He was good at it. He held her hand very tightly. She stood up close, feeling his heat. The other couple smelled of brandy. Without encouragement, they introduced themselves. Nancy and Arnold. Very polyester. Very J.C. Penney. Here on a second honeymoon and having a whale of a time.

'Swell,' said Kimbell.

Arnold looked at Nancy and scratched the underside of his chin. He intimated that the whale could turn into a ball without any problem at all, if Penny and Kimbell were agreeable.

'Wife-swopping,' Nancy said clearly. 'That's what Arnie means.'

'We aren't married,' said Penny.

''Sides, we got our own balls going, thanks,' said Kimbell.

'I can see that,' said Nancy. She laughed, showing the back of her tongue. 'And most of them is yours, right, big boy?'

'Don't get fancy, Nancy,' said Penny. Jesus. Where were people like that coming from?

'We were on the verge of breaking up a couple years back,' Nancy said. 'Isn't that right, Arnie?'

Arnie said it was. He looked as though he rather wished he'd gone right over the edge.

'Then we decided to swing,' Nancy said. 'It really saved our marriage.' She blew VSOP into the air.

What kind of marriage had you saved, if you saved it like that? Penny thought of her and Barnaby. If they got married, might they some day need to swing? God help them if they did. 'Keep it for *True Confessions*,' she said.

Nancy laughed again. 'Don't knock it till you've tried it.'

Arnold said they were in Room 156. He said if they changed their minds, why just to come on down. He and Nancy would be as happy as hogs at a hoedown if they did.

'I can see what you've got to gain,' Kimbell said. 'How about me?'

'You haven't tried it yet, big boy.' Nancy winked.

The lift stopped. Arnold and Nancy got out. 'Remember now,' said Nancy. 'Room 156.'

'Don't hang by your thumbs,' Kimbell said.

The lift doors closed.

Kimbell shifted the thick leather strap of his airline bag. The brass edgings shone. 'Do I look like an idiot?' he said.

'What kind of question is that?'

'I'm serious. I mean what in hell makes those turkeys

think I'd be fool enough to swop something like you for a moose like her?' He shook his head. 'Shee-it.'

'Don't knock it till you've tried it,' Penny said.

At three o'clock in the morning, the phone rang. A voice like a broken hangnail ripping down nylon satin said, 'Keep away from Toscana.'

'The hell I will,' Penny said.

'You'll be sorry,' said the voice.

The line went dead.

17

PENNY SPOKE BRIEFLY TO KIMBELL ON THE PHONE.

'Hi,' he said. 'How're ya doin'?'

'Just off to lunch with Mr. Hotshot Bernini,' said Penny.

'And you want my off-the-cuff reaction, right?'

'Wrong.'

'A guy goes round like he does with his back covered, you gotta wonder why. Place like this, the answer's not too hard to figure.'

'Maff?'

'That's my guess.' She heard the phone shift in his hand. Then he said, 'Listen, hon. Want me to come along?'

'Might cramp my style. I'll tell you what would be a much better idea.'

She did.

From the hotel wardrobe she picked out a white linen suit. The skirt was very short and very slim. The jacket was big and loose and tied with a sash. It didn't have any buttons. Unstructured was the word for it. The only thing she wore underneath was Miss Dior. Miss Dior was demure. Miss Dior provided a contrast with the big square diamond on a heavy gold chain that she slung round her neck. Barnaby had given it to her a couple of months earlier.

That wasn't the only reason she wore it. She figured Bernini was turned on by money. Especially other people's. Also by women. And a turned-on man is not in one-hundred-per-cent control. She believed in using sex where she could. However bright a woman might be, and whatever the feminists liked to pretend, in a patriarchal society it was still the best weapon. Born to be exposed on hillsides, clitorectomised, burned alive for not bringing enough dowry to a marriage, women often hadn't got a lot else going for them.

A white-gloved houseboy with a hyacinthine face let her into Bernini's flat and showed her to a room made entirely of glass. Plants flowed over the outside of it. Beyond them a distant prospect of Rome acted as wallpaper. White-painted iron pillars like the ones in the Palm House at Kew held the structure up.

On either side of a white flokati rug spread over sanded floorboards were chesterfields covered in maroon velvet. There was a Steinway in one corner. Half the florists in Rome must have delivered that morning. It was cool and classy.

On the piano, there was a photograph of the girl Penny had seen in the picture in Drusilla's bedside table. She wore a riding jacket that flared out over cream-coloured jodphurs. Penny was looking at it when Bernini came in.

'My daughter.' He smiled sadly. 'Poor child.' He took the frame from her.

'Why?'

'Her mother died eighteen months ago. They were very close. My daughter has not yet recovered from the loss.'

'Have you?'

'We were not so close, I am afraid. Perhaps that is why my daughter and I are not...' He broke off. He put the photograph back carefully on the piano, beside a pale green porcelain vase. Its celadon glaze had probably crackled ten centuries earlier, in a country far to the east of Rome. He sighed melodramatically. 'But this is not interesting.'

Since there were probably fifty Roman matrons happy to call him a liar, Penny didn't sweat it. She had other things to do.

She went for the kill. 'How well do you really know Drusilla Ross?' she said.

Bernini moved away from the piano to a small gilt table holding drinks. He poured her one of the bitter jewel-coloured apéritifs the Italians are so big on. Penny never liked them.

'You are something of a detective, I believe,' he said. From his tone, detectives weren't a class of person he'd normally want to share a desert island with.

'Been checking me out, Mr. Bernini?'

'I am a careful man, signorina. When a beautiful woman approaches me in a restaurant, I am naturally flattered. I also wonder what she wants?'

That wasn't exactly how Penny would have described the way they'd got together at the La Strada. She let it pass. 'Perhaps you underestimate your personal magnetism,' she said.

'Perhaps.'

Bernini took Penny's arm and led her out to the roof garden. In spite of the sun, it was damp and green out there, with leaves trained over trellises and little trees standing in wooden planters. A lead *putto* dribbled water like a geriatric with a prostate problem.

'Wanawake,' he said. 'I recognised the name last night

170

but could not remember in what connection. This morning, it came to me.'

Penny wondered what would happen if she dumped her drink in one of the planters.

'Monsignor Capet was a popular man here in Rome,' Bernini continued. 'It was a relief to his colleagues to know that he was murdered.'

How many years was it now since she'd found the plump Monsignor swinging in the sunshine at Hurley Court, his feet bare, the amethyst rich on his fat little hand, blood beading the sacreligious wreath of holly pressed into his hair round the silk skull cap?

'Murdered,' she said. His had been the first one. A long time and a lot of grief ago.

'I mean, of course, rather than being a suicide.' Bernini touched her hand. His fingers were still cold. His silvery eyes stared into hers, full of unspoken questions. She gave him a few unspoken answers.

'Has anyone ever told you how beautiful you are?' he said.

Of all the dumb questions. Of course they had. As if she'd admit it if they hadn't. She stepped over to the waist-high balustrade round the edge of the terrace. Below them, the Roman hills simmered under a brilliant sky. Around their edges the light was the colour of cream.

'Why would Drusilla Ross have a picture of you in her bedroom in Cambridge?' she said. It might make her un-popular, but once she had the scent in her nostrils, she kept right on sniffing.

Frowning, Bernini put down his glass. 'Yesterday I told you that the name meant nothing to me. Perhaps that was not strictly accurate. In the past, I have received letters from someone signing herself in this way.'

'I knew there was something.'

'There is no mystery here, Miss Wanawake, whatever you may think. No detecting to be done. It is very simple. When a man achieves a certain status, as I have done, he immediately becomes a target for unfortunates like this woman. I do not know her. I do not know where she found a photograph of me, though it would not be difficult. A man in the public eye is often photographed.'

'What did she write to you about?'

'She had some absurd bee in her bonnet,' Bernini said. 'You get used to such letters after a while.' He heaved a politician's sigh. 'There are many confused people around.'

'What sort of bee?'

'I do not wish to discuss it.'

'But it was definitely a crank letter?'

'Yes.'

'How many times did she write to you?'

'Half a dozen, perhaps,' said Bernini. 'But this is not extraordinary. I get such letters all the time. So do other prominent people. It is one of the prices you pay.'

Drusilla as crank correspondent? Penny could all too easily imagine her in that bitter Cambridge bedroom, sending off poison-pen letters to the famous. Wasn't it supposed to be something that unmarried women went in for? Perhaps she'd made unspeakable suggestions to Bernini, accused him of bizarre sexual perversions. It made sense of a kind. But did it have anything to do with Bruno?

Bernini brought a slim case of green leather out of some inner pocket. Using a jade lighter, he lit a long grey cigarette that had his initials on it, then blew out aromatic smoke. 'It is a long time since she last sent one of her letters,' he said. 'I had forgotten all about her.'

'She has a photograph of you and she's at Toscana when Bruno Ferlinghetti vanishes,' Penny said. 'There has to be

172

a tie-up somewhere. One thing I really despise is a coincidence. It's like making *gazpacho* in the Cuisinart.' She gave Bernini the sort of stare that needs a snap-brim pulled down over the eyes. 'Know what I'm saying here, Bernini?'

'No.'

Penny didn't either. She was trying for hard-boiled and coming out half-baked. Yet there *was* a connection. There had to be.

'I mean, you get your oil and your tomatoes and your garlic and your cukes and whatever. You stick them in the bowl and give the thing a whirl and what happens?'

'Cukes?' said Bernini.

'Instead of recognisable and separate ingredients, you end up with an homogenised gloop. I'm saying I got the soup,' Penny said. 'I need to know exactly what's in it.'

The cute houseboy came out. His white jacket was almost as baggy as Penny's though she was prepared to swear the topography underneath was different. He stood expectantly by the open door on to the terrace.

'Lunch appears to be ready,' said Bernini. As they went back into the big glass room, he put a hand on Penny's shoulder and squeezed. If she'd been a peach, he'd have left a bruise. They went into a dining area walled off from the big room by a lot of greenery. The air-conditioning made quiet noises. They sat at a glass-topped table bound with ebony and polished steel.

The boy brought in a porcelain tureen and served a soup that was pale green and chilled. He poured a cold white wine from Alsace. Bernini's patriotism didn't seem to go as far as drinking Asti Spumante.

Ever the graceful conversationalist, Penny leaned across her soup-spoon. The diamond swung between her breasts. Bernini watched it.

'I understand you're up for re-election any day now,' she said.

Bernini inclined his head in a way that suggested he practised it a hundred times every night. All of his moves came straight off the silver screen.

He smiled vote-catchingly. 'Where did you hear that?'

'A little turd told me.'

'A little what?'

'Oscare Torella.'

'Ferlinghetti's cousin,' said Bernini.

'Yeah.'

'I don't know him.' Bernini didn't sound as if he planned on changing that. He patted his mouth with a napkin of linen that was the same colour as the soup. It had an elaborate B embroidered in one corner. 'All right, Miss Wanawake. You have asked me a lot of questions. Now I should like to ask one.'

'Go ahead,' said Penny. She loosened her jacket very slightly.

'What do you know about the missing statues?'

'Zilch.'

'Which means?'

'Nothing.'

Bernini raised his eyebrows. 'That is extremely disappointing,' he said. 'I had certainly hoped for more than that from this meeting. In fact, I must tell you I had hoped for very much more.'

'Well, excuse me.' Penny moved her fork around in the pasta that the houseboy had just slid on to a plate and put in front of her. It had shrimps in it and some kind of nut.

Bernini tilted back his head, the napkin held to one corner of his mouth, and manoeuvred himself carefully about in his chair. The chair was made of black leather and rubbed steel and went with the table. He gabled his fingers.

174

It was another of those gestures, the only people who made them were assistant district attorneys in late night re-runs, trying to pin a rap on the wrong guy.

'Because it has been brought to my attention that a pair of gold figurines has recently been offered for sale, right here in the centre of Rome.'

'Hey, man,' said Penny.

'By a young woman not unlike yourself. Tall and—uh . . .'

'Black?'

'In point of fact, yes.'

'I suppose there's no mistake?'

'None.'

'People would remember,' agreed Penny. 'Not too many of us souls around in Rome. Matter of fact, I've been feeling like a token ever since I got here.'

Bernini didn't seem to care too much about immigration quotas. He brought out another of his monogrammed grey cigarettes. He tapped down the tobacco on the corner of his cigarette case which also had his initials stamped on it. Gaahd, how gross could you get, lighting up in the middle of eating and not bothering to ask a person if they minded. Which this person most certainly did.

'I doubt if I would be too far wrong in thinking that that was the first approach,' Bernini said, blowing smoke. 'And that the statuettes mentioned were the Royal Pair.'

'It's a fascinating theory.'

'The timing of this offer, so soon after Ferlinghetti's disappearance, would suggest I am right.'

'If that was the first, what about the second?'

'What better place for it than the Caffè La Strada?'

'I see,' said Penny. 'So we're expecting the third approach any time now.'

'Precisely.' Bernini smiled up at the ceiling.

'And how do you see the third approach shaping up?'

'I imagine that the girl—the go-between—would get down to basics.'

'Basics,' Penny said. 'We're not talking strip-tease here, are we?'

'We're talking price,' Bernini said. Soft as chrome-plated marbles, his eyes honed in on the place where the two edges of Penny's jacket met. 'In so far as the Royal Pair have a price. Their value is historic as much as intrinsic. And history cannot be assessed in *lire*. But I imagine that any moment now, some kind of outrageous demand will be made and negotiations will begin.'

'Well, if you want to play it by the book . . .'

'Unfortunately, negotiations have a way of dragging on. And I have a particular interest in bringing this matter to a speedy conclusion. I therefore hope to eliminate any further steps.'

The boy removed Penny's plate and replaced it with another. He put small fresh vegetables on it, and a couple of pieces of meat. Veal. Thin as birchbark, tender as snow.

'I suppose there'd be no point in saying that I haven't the faintest idea where the statuettes are,' Penny said.

Even with a mouthful of veal, Bernini managed a hateful laugh. 'Like you,' he said, when he swallowed, 'I prefer to leave coincidences to the fiction writers. How many tall black girls do you think are at present in Rome who have approached my shop with offers to see a pair of gold figurines?'

'Would you go for one?

'That is what I suspected.'

Bunches of tiny grapes clustered round an embossed B on the handle of Penny's fork. Either Bernini had a poor memory or a low self-image, the way he needed reminding all the time who he was.

'Obviously Ferlinghetti himself cannot risk being seen on the streets,' he said. 'He therefore sends you—his accomplice—to the natural outlet for his merchandise.'

'The *galleria itaro*.'

'Exactly,' said Bernini. 'You have obviously done your homework. You know I am often at the Caffè La Strada, since I am part-owner. You know I have money. You know I am likely to be willing to pay to get the statuettes back. I think we may take it for granted that the bizarrely dressed person who approached my shop-manager—'

'Hold it,' Penny said. 'Nothing bizarre about Issey Miyake except the prices.'

'—was in fact yourself. Very well, Miss Wanawake. Name your price.'

Somewhere off-stage, a telephone rang. The boy came in and plugged a pale green handset into the floor by Bernini's foot. Last time Penny had seen someone do that, it'd been to Truman Capote at '21'. It had looked pretty nifty then. It looked pretty nifty now.

Bernini started being cute into the receiver. '*Cara*,' he said. He sounded like he was pouring maple syrup out of a warm jar. '*Cara mia*.' While he spoke, his silvery eyes looked deep into Penny's.

Whoever was on the other end was mad about something. She was clearly audible. Not just to Penny on the other side of the table but probably to the Pope on the other side of the city. Whoever it was suspected that Bernini was having lunch with a woman that very minute. She didn't like it one bit. She kept on saying so. Bernini denied it. He tried to stall. He pouted reproachfully into the receiver. '*Tonia*,' he said. '*Tonia*.'

Tonia didn't buy the soft soap. She kept on nagging. Bernini finally gave in. He said she was right. He *was* having lunch with another woman but it wasn't what she thought. Tonia made one of the noises Giula was so good at. Bernini said the only reason he hadn't told her was because she was so jealous—so flatteringly jealous, man of his age and all. He kept looking at Penny. She could tell he loved it, the big political honcho being bawled out by a woman.

He moved smoothly into falsehood. The woman he was lunching with was a reporter, an American, actually, doing a feature for *Newsweek* on the coalition Government. She must have heard of *Newsweek*, it was one of those American news magazines, like *L'Espresso*. No, the reporter was not very beautiful, not nearly as beautiful as she was, quite ugly, in fact. His eyes apologised.

It sounded good. It sounded believable. Penny almost believed it herself. After a while, Tonia did too. Bernini looked at his watch. He said the reporter had a plane to catch and he'd have to go. Yes, he'd pick her up that evening at 7:30. Yes, he'd booked a table. Yes, of course at the Ristorante Reale, where else? Yes, yes, he absolutely adored her.

'My fiancée,' he said, as he put down the phone. His face had gone soft. Penny guessed the fiancée was probably young enough to be his daughter.

The houseboy came and took away the phone. He came back and took away the empty dishes. When he leaned across Penny, she could smell flowers. She wondered why he kept a knife in his waistband. Above the hills, two small planes were making smoke trails. One crossed the other's path, leaving an X drawn against the sky. She'd have taken it for a sign if she could have figured out whether it was a kiss or a cross. It hung there for a while before it began to drift and dissolve, the arms wavering as they moved away from each other.

In the roof garden the greenery was perfectly still,

leaves exhausted by the hot afternoon sun. She became aware that someone with the fixed intensity of a bird-dog pointing at a pheasant was staring at her through them. It wasn't a place you expected to find an intruder. Not nineteen storeys up. Unless it was Spiderman.

'If you are reasonable in your demands, I am content to go along with them,' Bernini said, as though there had been no gap in the conversation.

'Hold your water,' Penny said. 'What demands?'

'I am only thankful that the figures have not yet left the country.'

'I told you, I don't know squat about them.'

'And I told you I don't believe you.'

'Boy, are you ever making a mistake.'

'I have built a political career out of not making mistakes,' Bernini said. 'Of any kind. In Italian politics, there are very few who can say the same. I am an ambitious man, and Cossiga cannot last forever. The *Achille Lauro* business isn't just going to be swept under the carpet. When he goes, as he will eventually have to, I intend to be among the contenders for his job.'

'Show a little respect, Bernini. I'm not one of your morons can't brush their teeth without an illustrated manual. I got a college degree, man. Matter of fact, I got two.'

'So?'

'So I'm trying to tell you I'm not stupid. If I really had the figurines, would I just walk in here like this, leave myself vulnerable to any attack you might care to make?'

'With the elections coming up, it will be a tremendous coup for me if I can recover the statuettes,' Bernini said. 'Particularly since I was the minister responsible for having the Commission of Enquiry set up in the first place. I personally recommended Ferlinghetti to head it. Can you imagine what a laughing-stock his absconding with the

179

statuettes makes me appear, not only to my fellow ministers, but in the eyes of the voters?'

'Vividly.'

'If I can get them back and turn them over to the Belle Arti people, I shall not only retrieve my reputation, but also be seen as a man who gets things done. Italy has great need of such a man.'

'You might also be seen as a man with the Mafia riding in his passenger seat.'

'I think not. Now, how much do you want for the statuettes?'

'I already told you I don't know anything about them,' Penny said. 'Ask me, instead of wasting your time giving me lunch, you should be out pricing hearing-aids.'

'Miss Wanawake, please.'

'The only reason I ever got into this whole mess is because I'm trying to locate Bruno Ferlinghetti.'

'The statuettes—'

'I haven't got them. I've never seen them. I don't know where they are,' Penny said.

Bernini tapped on the glass window. Outside, the leaves moved as though a predator lurked. She stood up. On the other side of the glass, so did Bernini's muscleman. Dryadic, he surged from among the greenery in a track-suit of red Banlon with white stripes down the thigh. He'd pushed the ribbed cuffs of the top up above his elbows. He looked very businesslike. Penny hoped his business wasn't with her.

The houseboy came in and started watering the philodendrons from a long-spouted watering-can. He'd taken off his white gloves. The gorilla shouldered in through the terrace doors.

'I just hope this isn't what it looks like,' she said.

'What does it look like?' Bernini said.

'A threat. Two of them, actually.'

'It would be incredibly foolish of me to threaten you,' Bernini said.

'I'll say. I can tear up telephone directories with my bare hands.'

'I'm inclined to believe you.'

'You better.'

'The elections take place at the end of the week,' Bernini said. 'I need the publicity before then if it's going to be of any benefit to me.'

'You're an asshole, Bernini.'

Bernini threw another smile ceilingward. 'You are not the first to think so,' he said.

'That I can imagine.'

'But I am a rich asshole and I am, as I say, prepared to pay for the statuettes.'

Talk about a fixation. It was useless trying to communicate with the guy. 'I'll have to talk with my—uh—principal,' she said. It was one way of getting out of there. She backed away across the hairy white rug. Her heels kept catching in it. She reckoned that although she could give the muscleman a hundred kilos or so, most of them were fat. If she remembered the leg kick she'd learned a couple of months back at her T'ai Chi Ch'uan class, she'd be fine. It was the houseboy she was worried about. Him and his knife. Just because he smelled of flowers and looked like a cherub didn't mean he'd behave like one.

'You could telephone him,' Bernini said. He snapped his fingers. The houseboy jumped, dropping a small bulbous bottle that rolled round in a circle on the floor. Bambino Bio, if her eyes were not deceived.

'Jesus Christ, Bernini. Do you behave like this in Parliament?' she said. 'Not listening to a thing anyone says?

181

I'm just as interested in finding the damn figurines as you are.'

Bernini puffed amused air down his nostrils. 'Tell me your terms.'

'How about thirty years' hard, with no time off for good behaviour?'

'Guido,' Bernini said. The word cracked out of his mouth like a snapped towel.

The big man pushed forward. The little toe of his right foot peeked in and out of a hole in his sneakers. Close to, Penny could see white hairs in his black eyebrows, and a spatter of pock marks on his cheekbones. Someone had once taken his face apart and not bothered too much about putting it back together again.

He grabbed hold of her upper arm and pushed her into the waist of the grand piano. He loomed. Faster than a speeding bullet, Penny picked up the photograph of Bernini's daughter and smashed it down. The glass shattered. She grabbed the biggest piece and gouged it down the polished case of the instrument. The muscleman gaped.

'Stop,' screamed Bernini. 'What are you doing?'

Penny grinned. She'd figured him correctly. A material man. She seized the celadon vase and held it above her head.

'My God,' moaned Bernini. 'That vase is two thousand years old.'

'It's not going to make two thousand and one, 'less you call off the heat.'

The muscleman lunged forward.

'No,' Bernini shrieked. 'Don't touch her.'

'Listen to me, Pietro,' Penny said. 'And listen good.' She'd always wanted to say that to someone. 'I haven't got your statuettes. I don't know where they are. I don't *care*

182

where they are. I am only interested in Bruno Ferlinghetti. Have you got that?'

The doorbell rang.

The houseboy looked at Bernini. Bernini was ready to spit. He nodded.

The boy let two men into the flat. They didn't have white gauntlets and slouch hats, but Penny wasn't about to quibble. Who cared how the cavalry dressed, as long as they got there in the last reel. One wore a turquoise silk tie with a grey silk suit that gleamed where it caught the light. He had dark eyes set in brown pouches, and thick grey hair, although he couldn't have been much over thirty.

The other man was natty in navy, with a white shirt. A gold bar joined his collar ends under a tie featuring preppy red and blue stripes. He was black. Eddie Murphy on Wall Street, but better looking. Only thing that spoiled the image was the airline bag on his shoulder. When he saw Penny, the corner of his mouth lifted. He ran the back of his thumbnail over his top lip.

It took the man in grey a short second to reconnoitre most of Penny. He looked like he'd come back later for a more detailed inspection. He flashed some ID.

'Good afternoon, Inspector,' Bernini said. He started being suave with one of his grey cigarettes.

The man with grey hair said that there were a couple of matters he'd like to discuss with Signor Bernini. If, of course, Signor Bernini didn't object. Signor Bernini didn't seem to have a whole lot of choice.

'I am naturally always delighted to co-operate with the police,' he said, cold as a Puritan witch-hunter.

'Well, listen,' Penny said. 'I won't hang around, Mr Bernini, embarrass you when you got business to discuss I bet. Thank you so much for lunch. It was quite delicious. We must do it again some time.'

Bernini didn't answer. She walked towards the front door of the flat. The houseboy drew his lovely brows together as she passed him. He looked stricken. He looked as though he'd dropped his trumpet while the heavenly choirs were in the middle of a quiet bit. He'd probably been told to wade in if she got away from the big guy. She hoped he wouldn't be beaten to death once the police had gone.

Kimbell came after. 'Sorry we were a bit late,' he said. 'Did we do good?'

'The best,' said Penny.

'Did he pull something like you thought?'

'Exactly like.'

'I'm glad we got here in time. Way you were looking at the guy last night, no one was ever gonna believe rape.'

Penny laughed. 'Give your friend a great big kiss from me, won't you.'

'People might talk,' said Kimbell.

18

THE LAST FINGERNAIL OF SUN DROPPED ABRUPTLY BE-
hind a hill. No time was wasted on twilight. Immediately it
was dark. Not pitch black, but enough to be confusing,
unless you were a cat. Or a bat. Here and there among the
box hedges, pale lamps hiccuped into life, giving light but
not illumination.

Penny ground along the gravel path that ran through the
campus of the Hands Across the Sea School. All the buildings looked alike in the dark. Glass and stucco with dark
wood trim. Which one housed Dunlap's office? She
stopped beside a window that began two inches above her
head. Standing on tip-toe, she could see book-stacks and
the heads of girls. Some were chewing gum.

'You filthy pervert,' someone said behind her. A hand
locked on to her shoulder and swung her round.

'To the perverted, all things are perverted,' Penny said.

The hand dropped away. 'Jesus,' it said. 'You're a
woman.'

'Check.'

'Is there some way I can help you?'

'Just show me Antony Dunlap's office. Home-room. Whatever.'

'He's not here at the moment.'

Which was exactly why she was there. 'That's okay,' she said. 'It's just I think I left a book in his room when I was visiting him the other day. He said it'd be all right for me to go look for it.'

'Follow me.'

The man led her across grass and around a brick-edged fountain which dripped half-heartedly into a dank pond. She could scarcely see him. From an open window somewhere, a transistor poured Madonna into the night.

The man pulled open a glass door. On the inner side it said EMERGENCY EXIT ONLY. 'Up there,' he said.

In the light from a upstairs hallway, she watched him take her in. White beaded braids, pure cotton dress, pearl earstuds. He started doing rakish things with his eyebrow and lids. Lifting one of the former. Letting the latter sag halfway down his eyes. Not just unsubtle, but unsuitable, too, considering he wore a soutane.

'I'm the school chaplain,' he said, holding out his hand. 'Father O'Brien.' He couldn't have been more than twenty-eight.

'Penny Wanawake.' She squeezed frost into her tone. It didn't do to encourage this sort of thing. Not in a celibate.

'Ah, Penny. You're a fine-looking girl.' O'Brien held her hand both longer and tighter than was necessary. Not for the first time she wondered about the ethics of a religion that required young men to renounce something before they had much idea what they were renouncing.

'I presume you're talking in the spiritual sense,' she said coldly.

'I hadn't got that far,' O'Brien said. 'I find I get better

results if I deal with matters temporal before matters spiritual.'

Penny wrested her hands from his. '*The Thorn Birds* didn't do a thing for the Church's rep,' she said. 'You certainly aren't helping.'

'Can you blame me?'

'Not really.' Penny showed him her dimples.

He glinted bright blue eyes back at her. 'I'm most terribly sorry for calling you a pervert,' he said.

'God may forgive you, but I never can.'

'Now I get a proper look, there's nothing perverted about you.'

'Would you please show me Dunlap's room,' Penny said.

'You'll have to come to mine first.'

'Why?'

'Because I'm the one that has the keeping of his keys.'

They began to climb some stairs made of mottled grey vinyl. Through the treads, Penny could see along cream-painted corridors to other rooms. Nobody was about. Except for the light in the upper passage, the place was dark. O'Brien's skirts swished softly with every step. The leather belt round his waist creaked.

He stopped outside a door made of imitation wood, grained to look like rosewood. 'Could I tempt you to a glass of wine?' he said.

'No.'

'Or something a little stronger?'

'No.'

'Shall I read to you from the Bible, maybe?'

'Just give me the keys, O'Brien, if you don't mind.'

'You'd be doing a Christian act.'

'I'm a Buddhist.'

'Ah well.' O'Brien opened the door, using a key from a

bunch at his waist. 'Tell me,' he said, turning to her. 'How come a slob of the likes of Dunlap has a guest like yourself, while I, a decent Godfearing man, am visited only by bobbysoxers with fearsome teeth and the sex appeal of an abcess?'

'Sounds like one for God,' Penny said.

'I keep hoping that one day he'll invite me in to take a drink or two with him. But the man is so mean, he wouldn't pay a nickel to see Christ himself ride by on a steamroller.'

'That is *mean*,' Penny said.

'I am aware,' O'Brien said, 'of his circumstances. But considering the booze I've poured down his throat in the past, you'd think in all decency he would occasionally pour some down mine.'

'Broke, is he?'

'Chronically. Mind you, there is the wife to pay off. Perhaps that explains it.'

'I didn't realise he was divorced. But then I wouldn't have believed he was married.'

'Love moves in a mysterious way.'

'Doesn't it just.'

'It's a fairly recent divorce, I believe,' O'Brien said. 'And probably part of the reason he came to work over here. Personally, I think he must spend all his spare money on food. Have you seen the way he eats?'

'Unfortunately, yes.'

'Enough for five. Enough for fifty, even. In these days of worldwide starvation, it is truly obscene. I've told him so often enough but he merely offers me some rudeness and orders another piece of Boston Cream Pie.'

'The key, please,' Penny said. She recognised a gossip when she saw one.

188

'It's an uncharitable vicious-tongued creature you'll be thinking me,' O'Brien said.

'Never.'

'I fear I am often less kind about my fellow men than I should be.'

'Let me into Dunlap's place and we'll say no more about it.'

Overhead strip-lighting made blue-rimmed shadows in the corners of Dunlap's room. The place still smelled of wood glue. A translation of the Countess Tolstoy's diaries lay on the desk. Leo had been an autocratic old bastard, no doubt about that. But women like Sonia, whingeing and suffering from premenstrual cramps, always bring out the worst in bullies. Maybe that's why they so often seem to marry them, so they've got an excuse to complain for the rest of their lives.

The three dead flies on the window-sill had been joined by a fourth. A fresh pile of term-papers stood beside them. There was another on the shelf. Penny lifted it down. It was the same one Dunlap had taken away from her before she could look through it. She did so now. Nothing except a lot of secondhand thoughts about Jane Austen. Anne-Marie Huizinger's essay still lay on top. She'd got a B for it. Most of the girls had trouble spelling 'prejudice'. The pages of squared paper in Bruno's handwriting weren't among them. She hadn't really expected they would be.

Where would you hide them? She felt behind the rows of books in the bookcase and went through the desk drawers. Again nothing. The filing cabinet in dull grey steel stood behind the door. Locked. Penny got out her manicure set, the one that cunningly concealed a set of equipment designed to facilitate breaking and entering. She'd never fully mastered most of the tools it held, despite coaching from an old cellmate of Barnaby's, but so far she hadn't let Barnaby know. For the cellmate's sake. However, she could handle the lock-pick fairly competently. She did so now. She fiddled around. Inside the circular lock set into the top left-hand corner of the cabinet, things moved about and rattled. She probed as delicately as a dentist. She was hopeless at this sort of thing. Was it manual dexterity she lacked, or the true criminal urge?

Although it was far from the work of a moment, eventually the top drawer slid open, releasing the lock on the lower drawer as well. She went through all the files. When she'd finished, she wondered why she'd bothered. She'd found nothing germane. Plenty of data about the students. Report cards, copies of aptitude tests, recommendations from their US colleges. But no squared paper covered in brown writing.

Dunlap's in-tray held three letters, all unopened. One from the Bank of Virginia. One from an archaeological society. One from a Mrs Jean Dunlap, with an address in Seattle. The fact that there was no steam kettle around saved Penny from any dilemma on the morality involved in opening someone else's private mail. Even she drew the line at simply tearing open the envelopes. In the out-tray was a paper on the dig at Toscana al Vesuvio plus an accompanying letter to the Royal Archaeological Society in London, both horribly typed, with a covering note to the typist to do them again. Penny picked the paper up and read it. She found it very interesting indeed. She realised the chances of ever seeing Bruno's missing pages again was nil.

Dunlap came into the room. Octagonal rimless glasses sure didn't add much to the friendliness in a guy's face. Nor did a gun in a guy's fist. Seeing it, Penny found it hard to repress a shiver of something she hated to acknowledge as fear. She played it cool. Flicked her braids around some. Gave him plenty of eye-contact.

'Looking for something?' he said.

'Yeah.'

'What?'

'Actually I was hoping to stumble across an ampoule of a subtle but deadly poison distilled from the venom-sac of a spider found only on the northern slopes of the Andes.'

'Any luck?'

'Not so far.' As she spoke, Penny folded the papers and put them into her bag. He didn't appear to notice.

'You've got five seconds to tell me what the hell you think you're doing,' Dunlap said. He moved around and put one massive buttock on the edge of his desk.

'I presume you have a licence for that thing,' Penny said. Pure bravado. They both recognised it.

'What are you going to do about it if I haven't?' said Dunlap. 'One.' The desk shifted and creaked under his weight. His little white teeth gleamed with what she took to be amusement. Eye-contact was proving to be a big flop.

'Um,' she said. She reminded herself that Father O'Brien was just down the hall. That there were girls studying in the library. The only a madman would try to get away with cold-blooded murder. This whole thing was ridiculous. English teachers just didn't go round shooting people in their offices. Did they? Fact or fiction she couldn't recall a single case.

She tried not to think of Bruno. Suppose Dunlap had forced him at gunpoint to some remote place and murdered him there. Or was keeping him there after sending a ransom note with dire threats if the police were informed. Which might explain Palma Ferlinghetti's nervousness. Suppose he was about to try the same trick on her. She wondered how much his ex-wife was stinging him for alimony payments.

'Two,' Dunlap said.

'Forgive me for asking, but is that a .38 Smith and Wesson you're pointing at me?' said Penny.

'Yes,' he said. 'Three.'

Penny nodded. 'Thought so.'

'Forgive *me* for asking, but how the fuck did you get into my locked office?' Dunlap said.

'Nigger charm.' Penny grinned like a golliwog.

'Hmm,' Dunlap said. 'The nigger bit's fairly obvious. The charm rather escapes me.'

At least he was talking, not counting. 'Funny,' said Penny. 'I was saying the exact same thing about you not ten minutes back. About the charm, I mean.'

'Who to?'

'Tut,' said Penny. 'And you call yourself an English teacher.'

'Can the smart-mouth,' Dunlap said. He jerked the gun at her. 'To whom?'

'Father O'Brien is to whom.'

A savage look crossed the steppes of Dunlap's broad pink face. 'Damn him,' he said. 'He's supposed to be at a meeting of the Little Flowers of St. Francis.'

'Maybe they'd all faded by the time he got there,' said Penny. 'I hope you don't think you can get away with anything here.'

'I was on my way to my car when I saw the light go on in my office,' Dunlap said. 'Naturally I wanted to check it out.'

'Are you seriously going to shoot me?' Penny said. There was nothing more frightening than a man with a gun in his hand and an expression that didn't change.

'You're trespassing,' said Dunlap. 'Trespassers will be prosecuted.'

'The rule of law may be breaking down all over, but there's a difference between prosecuted and executed.'

'I shall probably fire in self-defence.'

'Father O'Brien will testify I only stopped by to pick up a book.'

'Fuck Father O'Brien.'

'He was complaining that no one ever does,' Penny said.

'Besides, you're a friend of Bruno Ferlinghetti's, art thief extraordinaire.' Since Dunlap had stopped counting, Penny figured she had a sporting chance of kicking the gun out of his hand, if she could get two feet closer. Otherwise she didn't think she had a sporting chance of anything.

'Bruno wasn't the only person on-site when those figurines disappeared,' Penny said.

'At the time they went, I was lying in my excessively uncomfortable bed in what Meg is pleased to call an hotel down in Toscana,' Dunlap said. 'Tossing and turning, a martyr to indigestion. Anybody will vouch for me.'

'Did they check up on you?'

'As it happens—'

'So you could be lying about how ill you were.'

'My dear girl, I was throwing up all over the place. In no sort of condition to be breaking into the safe.'

'Listen, Dunlap,' Penny said. 'I'm going to do you a favour.' She stared at the darkness beyond the windows as if she couldn't care less. She shuffled her feet about. She moved six inches closer to Dunlap. He probably wasn't serious about using it. On the other hand, she wasn't taking any chances.

'What's that?'

'Going to give you the name of my dietician. You lose a

couple of pounds you could start a whole alternative career modelling tyres.'

'Is that supposed to be funny?'

No, you clunk. It's supposed to take your mind off the fact that I'm gradually edging nearer in order to have a shot at disarming you. 'It's pretty obvious you had something to do with Bruno going missing,' Penny said.

'Obvious? Why?'

'Man waving a gun about's certainly got something to hide. And if you know where Bruno's at, you probably know where those statuettes are, too.'

'If I knew where the frigging stat—'

'Pull the other one, Dunlap.'

'I told you, I've never even seen the damn things. Let alone stolen them. Nobody has. Except Meg.'

'And Riordan.'

'No. She wouldn't even let him see them.'

Behind him, the door opened suddenly. O'Brien came in.

'I hope I'm not interrupting anything,' he said. 'If the mountain won't come to Mahomet . . .' He had a bottle in one hand and three plastic beakers in the other. Dunlap blinked. Behind the glasses his eyes moved. Penny did too. With a noise like a wet facecloth hitting the bathroom tiles, her foot connected with Dunlap's arm. He screamed, grabbing at his sleeve with his other hand and dropping the gun.

'Jesus Christ,' he said.

'Thou shalt not take the name of the Lord thy God in vain,' said O'Brien.

'Will you keep your goddamned nose out of it,' said Dunlap. 'She's broken my arm.'

'Teach you to tangle with a trained killer,' Penny said. She picked up the gun and put it in her bag.

'You can't take that,' Dunlap said. 'I need it. Rome's getting as bad as New York.'

'All these guys with guns, you mean?'

'Mothera God,' said O'Brien. 'Was that a gun, for chrissakes?'

'Okay,' Penny said. 'A couple of questions, Mr Dunlap. Where was this dig where Professor Tarrance was suspected of getting rid of finds to the black market?'

'In Egypt, near Saqqara.'

'When was this?'

'A couple of summers ago,' Dunlap said sulkily.

'Who else was there, who was also at Toscana this summer?'

'All of us,' Dunlap said. 'We spent about a week there before going on to the symposium the Egyptologists had arranged with Cairo University. We all went. Along with several hundred others.' He cradled his arm against his chest. 'Do you realise how much this hurts?'

'We'll call in the medical team in a second,' said Penny. 'Just spell this out for me. When you say all, who do you mean?'

'Us,' Dunlap said. 'Meg, Bruno, Drusilla, Riordan, me. All of us.'

'And who went to the conference at the University of Virginia last summer?'

'All of us. Except Drusilla, of course. She spent the time in Rome. With her boy-friend, I should imagine.'

'I thought she and Meg were a couple.'

Dunlap produced a sardonic expression, then winced. 'That's what Meg thinks too. Naturally Drusilla keeps him strictly away from Toscana. But I see too many girls on heat in this place not to know it when I see it.'

Very interesting indeed.

Drusilla Ross was proving to be more enigmatic by the minute.

Definitely a lady worth watching.

19

WHOEVER DESIGNED THE RISTORANTE REALE HADN'T tried too hard for intimacy. There'd have been more of that in the middle of Grand Central Station. You might have wondered why anyone would want to eat there unless you caught the crowd of *paparazzi* outside the door. Then you knew. To rate among Rome's glitterati, you had to eat at the Ristorante Reale, and get photographed either arriving to do it or leaving having done it. If you wanted to see your face in the gossip columns the next day, it was probably worth enduring the draughts which whistled across the huge marbled room and tugged at the swags of gold velvet curtain lining the walls.

Penny sat at a table near a screen which fielded some of the wind. She thought a person could get very tired of eating out all the time. It might be kind of nice to be home with a person's loved one, once in a while.

'What does divorce mean to you?' she said.

'Means I'd be free to marry you,' said Kimbell.

'Means alimony, is what it means,' Penny said. A waiter rocketed past, carrying fifty different dishes under silver lids. She watched Kimbell dip an asparagus spear into hot butter and then his mouth. 'If Dunlap's already in debt and there's the ex-wife and kids at home to maintain, where does he get the dough?'

'He doesn't sound like he's cute enough to make it turning tricks,' Kimbell said.

'But he *does* spend his spare time digging up treasures from the past. What's to stop him slipping the odd one into his pocket and passing it along to the bad guys?'

'You think *he's* the one took the statues you're after?'

'It's Bruno I'm after,' Penny said. 'The statues are incidental.'

'They're also solid gold.'

'According to Meg Tarrance.'

Kimbell wiped butter off his chin. 'Sounds like one of those meaningful remarks supposed to make my ears prick up,' he said.

'Isn't it rather odd that no one seems to have had any hands-on experience of these statues except Meg?'

Kimbell wiped his fingers. 'Yeah, well,' he said. He shuffled his feet under the table.

'Solid gold means pure gold, doesn't it?' said Penny.

'Guess so.'

'And back in the olden days, they didn't know too much about alloys, right?'

'Didn't know too much about anything, ask me.'

'There's something not quite jake about Meg's story of finding the statuettes in those boat-chambers,' Penny said.

Water glistened on the ends of Kimbell's praline-coloured fingers as he held them above the fingerbowl beside his plate. 'How do you mean?' he said. He sounded wary, as though afraid she was about to launch a small explosive device in his direction.

'If the place's been done over by everybody from

Genghis Khan on down, how come the figurines're just lying there?'

'What're you saying?'

'Be a doll and let me see inside your airline bag's what I'm saying.'

Kimbell looked around. No one was staring in their direction, even though they were the only blacks in the place. 'You want me to wash my dirty linen in public?' he said. He sounded incredulous.

'Who said anything about washing?'

'What's the interest in my used jockey shorts, anyway?'

'If you've got laundry in there, I'll eat it,' Penny said. 'Show me.'

'Couldn't do that.'

'Go on, Kimbell. Bet you could.'

'Not even for you, sweet stuff.' Kimbell touched his upper lip.

'Not even if I do that cute trick with my dimples?'

'Sorry.'

Penny's attention was suddenly attracted by someone on the other side of the room. 'Hey,' she said. 'Isn't that Sophia Loren just came in?'

Kimbell turned round. 'Where?'

'With the older guy in the tux. Wow. She really is some kind of a woman, isn't she? Just look at that figure.' As she spoke, Penny got her foot under the strap of Kimbell's bag and hoicked it towards her. She bent down and unzipped it.

'Which older guy?' said Kimbell.

'Over by the pillar,' Penny said. 'Look. In that slinky black creation.'

'*Her?*' said Kimbell, still staring over his shoulder. 'She's about as much like Loren as you're like Monroe.'

'Boop-boop-a-doop,' said Penny. 'Folks get me and Marilyn mixed up all the time.'

'Sophia Loren, for gosh-sakes. You need your eyes tested.'

Penny rootled around in the bag. She smiled. 'Well, now,' she said. 'I heard of Jackie O wearing mink panties, but a PI in gold jockey shorts is a new one on me. That the latest fashion idea over there in Washington, DC?'

Kimbell turned round so fast you could hear the air splinter. 'Leave my stuff alone,' he said quietly. It was the kind of quietly that had sensible people reaching for their hats and leaving. A dangerous kind of quietly. So what. Penny felt kind of dangerous herself. Not to mention pissed off.

'I think I'm beginning to understand a thing or two here,' she said.

Kimbell reached under the table and pulled the bag back to the side of his chair. 'So?'

'I think I'm beginning to wonder about this whole ball of wax. Like how come you're supposed to be bodyguarding Mr Riordan but you're never with him. Like why's Riordan come back to Italy anyway, and what's he planning on doing, now he's here?'

'You got no right,' said Kimbell. 'Poking about in my stuff like that. Anyway, I'm not minding Riordan.'

'Just his stuff?'

'He's down in Toscana. Went down there straight from the airport.'

'Looks like you been holding out on me, Aaron.'

Kimbell glared. She crunched a breadstick as aggressively as she knew how and glared back. 'No right,' he said.

'Goddamned cheating nigger.'

Kimbell sighed. 'It's always a mistake trying to mix business with pleasure.'

'Especially when it's my business and your pleasure.'

'You saying you don't like it with me?'

'I trusted you, Aaron. Dammitall,' Penny said.

On the far wall, a gust of wind stirred the yellow velvet curtains. She seethed. Boy, she was really mad now. Really getting twisted. She saw a lot of hair hanging off some woman's head. Lucia Torella's. No mistaking that cascade. The hair was bouncing about being animated. The man she was with stared at it, the way a suggestible patient might stare at a hypnotist's watch. He wore heavy glasses and a couple of chins. Maybe he liked Lucia's hair because he had so little of his own. He wasn't anyone's idea of blond beefcake. Penny couldn't help wondering why Lucia would let herself be seen in a place like this with such a geek. Maybe he was something big in industrial plumbing and Lucia was feeling him up for a fat contract.

'Minute I noticed that reinforced leather strap, those fancy brass edgings, I should have realised that wasn't no ordinary flight bag,' Penny said. 'I'm surprised you don't handcuff yourself to it at night.'

'I do,' said Kimbell. 'Less I got company. I told you, Mr Riordan hired me as a safe-deposit box. I meant it, too. I'm here to look after these things for him. Nobody goin' suspect a jig like me is carrying round all this valuable stuff.'

'What did he bring them over for?' asked Penny.

'He didn't say. But he's got an export licence for them. It's all strictly by the book.'

'Is that so?' Penny knew it couldn't be. Something wasn't right. What it boiled down to, was Kimbell stringing her along, or was Riordan stringing Kimbell along?

'Did you find out about the phone calls?'

'Yes,' Kimbell said. 'There was four long-distance telephonic communications in the two days preceding my arrival at Mr Riordan's establishment. Them's the butler's words.'

'I guessed they weren't yours.'

'Two was incoming, one outgoing. Guess where to and where from.'

'Italy.'

'Right.'

It was eight o'clock. Just about time for the floorshow. Right on cue, the door of the restaurant opened and Bernini came in. He started a heavy number with the headwaiter, who immediately went into a display of headwaiter-type shit. Snapping fingers, smirking, inclining from the shoulders with servile dignity. What a nawz. Penny hated that kind of stuff.

Behind Bernini came the fiancée. She looked as though she'd been heaped into her backless sequins with the aid of a forcing bag. Hair was piled up on top of her head. Diamond earrings hung down into her cleavage.

Penny recognised her. But only just.

So Bernini had been lying.

'How do you like that guy?' Penny said. She shook her head. The perfidy of man.

Kimbell took hold of the strap of his airline bag. Then he turned round. 'Prefer the chick,' he said after a moment. 'Any day.'

'He's been blowing smoke in my eyes.'

'You turn over *his* private stuff same way you turn over mine, I'm not too goddamned surprised,' Kimbell said.

Just about every male in the place watched as a waiter showed the fiancée's cute little behind to a reserved table right in the centre of the room. Bernini liked them watching. He sat down and leaned across to plant a kiss on the fiancée's shoulder.

Penny got up. ' 'Scuse me,' she said. She pushed be-

tween the crowded diners to Bernini's table. 'I know neither of us believes in coincidences,' she said. 'But isn't this
just the darnedest thing?'

Bernini looked up from the menu. If she'd hoped to see
an expression of pleasure on his face, she lucked out.
'What is?' he said.

'Why, the two of us choosing the same place to dine in.'

'What do you want?' There wasn't any Bernini charm
being flung around tonight. Not in Penny's direction, at
any rate.

'Hoping you'd introduce me to your lovely fiancée,'
said Penny.

The lovely fiancée put out her hand. 'I'm Tonia Rossi,'
she said. She spoke very clearly, the way an ESN teacher
might when trying to impress on her pupils where the lavatory was. Just so Penny wouldn't get any weird ideas. Like
that she was someone else entirely. Like that she was Drusilla Ross.

'Tonia's short for Antonia, is it?' Penny said.

'It is.' Drusilla reached for a bit of hair to chew and then
remembered where it was.

'Account number OXY two six three seven eight O two,
if I remember correctly.'

The sudden chill on Drusilla's face would have turned
the Dead Sea into ice-cubes in a matter of seconds. 'It
sounds very much as if you do,' she said.

'Mind telling me what the name of this particular game
is?'

Drusilla looked across at Bernini and smiled. It wasn't
one of those sights that had you reaching for the palette and
brushes to capture for all time. Something like a cold slug
inched between the roots of Penny's braids.

'Catching up,' Drusilla said. 'Evening things out.'

'What are you two talking about?' asked Bernini. 'I do

not understand. What is this account number? This catching up?'

'The elections take place in a couple of days,' Drusilla said very fast, in English. Looking up at Penny. Although it didn't sound like a request, Penny knew it was.

'I'm only interested in finding Bruno,' she said.

'This has nothing to do with him,' said Drusilla. 'Believe me. Nothing.'

Penny did.

Bernini banged a fist on the table. Glass rattled. The people nearby turned to watch. 'Why do you think my fiancée has anything to do with your criminal enterprises?' he said loudly, making political hay. 'With the crimes you and he have committed against the Italian State?' A murmur arose. More people looked. 'You know my position. Please leave my fiancée alone.'

'Which one have you really got the hots for?' Penny said to Drusilla. 'Professor Tarrance? Or him?' She jerked her head at Bernini. She didn't think much of Drusilla's choice of boy-friend.

Again Drusilla smiled. It wasn't any prettier than it had been first time around. 'Hots?' she said. 'I don't know what you mean. I'm just a nice Catholic girl.'

'Do nice Catholic girls wash their hands before meals?' Penny said.

'Always,' said Drusilla.

Was Drusilla kicking with both feet, or just pretending to? Did Bernini know that Tonia Rossi was also Drusilla Ross? If not, what exactly was going on? And why was Drusilla one moment living in that squalid room in Cambridge and the next swanning round Rome in sequins?

On the way back to her table, she passed a square-headed man with a growth on his neck. He had his right hand flat on the table, holding down a wine-glass. The gold ring on his finger had jewels of some kind on it. He was smoking a cigar. When he saw her, he nodded. She nodded back. Good grief. They'd be kissing next.

She felt sorry for Meg Tarrance. She even felt sorry for Bernini. Not desperately, but a bit. Someone was being conned. Either Meg, or Bernini. Or both. Maybe even Penelope Wanawake, private dickette. The big black girl with an eyeful of smoke.

A few minutes later, Drusilla stood up. The whole room noticed. She touched Bernini on the shoulder and headed towards the washroom.

Penny headed after her.

20

'I HATE HIM,' DRUSILLA SAID. FIERCENESS TWISTED HER lips out of kilter.

'I agree there are probably nicer guys right now on Death Row,' Penny said.

'Loathe him.'

'Is that why you're planning to marry him?' Penny sat on the edge of a white porcelain basin decorated with a thin gold line to match the taps.

'Marry him,' spat Drusilla. 'I'd die first.'

Penny didn't say anything. Just looked at the diamond-surrounded sapphire on Drusilla's finger. It might not be big enough to play golf with, but you wouldn't want it stuck in your throat.

'For heaven's sake,' Drusilla said. 'You can't imagine I'd go through with it.' She narrowed her phlegm-coloured eyes. 'Or is it possible that in spite of all your nosey-parkering you haven't discovered what's going on?'

It was one of those questions demanding the answer no. 'No,' Penny said. 'I don't believe I have. Not all of it.'

'He's my father,' Drusilla said.

'Your *father?*'

'My father.'

It was beginning to sound like a quintet from *The Marriage of Figaro*. 'You'll probably think I'm a real dumbo,' Penny said, 'but last time I glanced through the Thirty-Nine Articles, they came out pretty strong against a girl getting hitched to her father.'

'Yes.' Drusilla stared at her reflection in the glass which lined three walls of the washroom. 'A quick run-down on the life of Drusilla Antonia Rossi,' she said. Her face twisted. The words came out fast. She didn't look at Penny.

'Twenty-five years ago, my mother came over to Italy as an au pair. She wanted to get fluent in Italian before she went to university to read modern languages. Pietro Bernini was a young lawyer then, with a baby daughter. It was his family my mother went to. Bernini seduced her. When she told him she was pregnant, he kicked her out, so she went back to England. Instead of taking up her university place, she had me. And kept me, although it was in the days when being an unmarried mother was a lot less acceptable than it is now. Without proper qualifications, she never got a decent job or a decent wage. She spent her whole life doing the most degrading work you can imagine.'

'Couldn't Bernini have helped?'

'Of course he could. My mother wrote to him many times but he never answered. We lived in the most appalling conditions for most of my childhood. When I came over here for the first time and saw the way *he* lived...' Drusilla gave another of her grim and ghastly smiles. 'Middle-class poverty is a double-edged knife. Not only are there the grinding conditions to cope with, there's also the comparison with what life used to be like, the expectations unfulfilled, the niggling feeling that things have to get better even though they never do.'

'What about your mother's family?'

'My grandfather was one of those Bible-reading bigots who think when it talks about charity and doing unto others, it doesn't mean them. After I was born, he never spoke to my mother again, never let my grandmother do so, either. Cut her completely out of his will. The first she knew of his death was reading about it in the paper quite by chance. By then it was too late.'

Fierce little flashes from the diamond earrings sparked off Drusilla's dress every time she finished a sentence.

'Why?'

'Out of desperation my mother had remarried.'

'Uh-huh.' Penny knew this was going to be tough.

'My step-father was a psychopath and a drunk,' said Drusilla. 'You read about families like ours in the newspapers. It was really happening to my mother and me. The murderous beatings, the abuse, the cruelty.'

'Why didn't she leave him?'

'By the time she realised he wasn't going to change, she was too terrified. Anyway, she knew he'd just come after her. Being beaten half to death at least twice a week for years does that to you—it breaks your spirit. God, how I hated him. And her too, sometimes, for putting up with him.' Drusilla stared into the mirrors above the basins and tucked in a stray piece of hair. 'I lost my shoes once, at school, and he got hold of my puppy and strangled it very slowly in front of me, while I screamed and sobbed and pleaded with him.'

Penny had seen children all over Africa with swollen bellies and fly-thick lips. She'd seen families with nothing except the rags that covered them, nothing except the slow torment of starvation. She'd seen sickness and poverty and death. The one thing she had never seen, out there in the refugee camps, in the filth and the stench, was an adult ill-treating a child.

Drusilla was sick, no doubt about it. It was easy to see why. But private dicks can't afford to get involved. Even amateur ones. Penny's the name and finding Bruno's the game, she told herself sternly. Sometimes it worked.

'If Bernini's your father, and you don't plan on marrying him, how come you're engaged to him?' she said.

Drusilla gave a bitter little laugh. Like her earlier smiles, it was not a thing of beauty. 'What do you think the smear of incest is going to do to his career?' she said. 'Or the story of the abandoned au pair girl, left to bring up her child alone? Even though that bastard out there is one of the richest men in Italy, he never paid one penny towards my upbringing. Well, he's going to pay now.'

'What about his—'

'He's always presented himself as the moral standard-bearer, staunchly Catholic, staunchly pro-home and family,' said Drusilla. She was working herself up now. 'The man they couldn't dig up any dirt on. Well, they've got plenty of dirt now. Believe me, in a couple of days this whole edifice he's built up around himself is going to come tumbling around his ears.'

'Poor old Pietro.'

'Poor? *Poor?*' Bits of Drusilla's hair had tendrilled away from the main mass. She kept pushing at them. Her teeth clenched. 'Two years ago, my mother died in a public ward from cancer of the throat. I wrote and told him she was dying. I asked him at least to come and see her. I explained that she'd always loved him, always made excuses for him. I said the one thing in the world she wanted was to see him again. The bastard didn't bother to reply. But he'll pay for that. He'll pay for every bruise my mother's husband gave her. So will his daughter. Living in the lap of luxury while my mother and I starved. Riding lessons . . .' The thought seemed to choke Drusilla.

Shiver. 'Is your step-father going to pay too?' asked Penny.

'He can't,' said Drusilla. 'He's dead.'

'Oh?'

'He hanged himself. When my mother finally decided to leave him. After she'd discovered that he'd been sexually assaulting me for years.' Under the bright lights reflecting off mirror-glass and porcelain, Drusilla's face was very pale. 'Everyone thought I must have suffered the most dreadful shock, finding him like that, hanging from the banisters. But I didn't.' She looked at Penny for the first time. 'It was the happiest day of my whole life. You know how they talk about people jumping for joy? That's exactly what I did. I saw him hanging there, with his eyes bulging and his tongue sticking out, and I literally jumped for joy in front of him.'

Penny could hardly believe she was hearing this.

'And there was absolutely nothing he could do about it,' Drusilla said.

'I can see where he might have felt kind of powerless,' said Penny. 'Dead and all.'

'Oh, but he wasn't,' said Drusilla. Her eyes looked as if they'd been sprayed with Perrier water. 'He knew when I came home from school. He'd timed it so that my mother and I would arrive just as he jumped. He'd done it before, but we'd always managed to get him down. He hadn't realised that my mother was going to be late that day. And of course, I didn't have the strength to get him down on my own.'

'Couldn't you have got someone else to help you?'

'Yes,' Drusilla said. 'But I didn't. I just sat on the stairs and watched him die.'

Jesus. Time to bring out the straitjackets. You could see why the primitive cultures used to hand over captives to be dealt with by the women.

Penny tried to speak, found her throat clogged up, cleared it carefully. 'And Bernini?' she said.

'I'm going to tell him tonight who I really am. I shall inform the press tomorrow. That'll be the end of him. It'll be all over the papers. Pictures of him kissing me, pictures of my ring, pictures of us on his yacht and in Corfu and skiing together at St Moritz. This has been going on for a while, you know. You don't get engaged to one of Italy's top politicians just overnight.'

'Isn't Bernini much too experienced a hand to let your accusations get to him? Couldn't he pass it off as the delusions of some poor female with a grievance?'

'I've set this whole thing up very carefully,' said Drusilla. 'Politicians are more sensitive to adverse publicity than almost anyone.'

'I hadn't got Baby Doc figured for a sensitive guy,' Penny said.

'He was running a dictatorship. But even in England, fooling around with your secretary can damage your career. Over here, where they're still trying to pretend there's no divide between Church and State, it's much worse.'

Damn. If Drusilla was telling the truth, another promising theory had just blown. The one that had Drusilla stealing the figurines and selling them to *galleria itaro*, then informing the police. Oh well. At least she'd been right about a connection between Drusilla and Bernini.

'I just hope you know what you're doing,' she said.

'Don't worry.'

It was beginning to feel as though the oxygen supply

had run out. Penny moved towards the door. 'Where does Bruno come into all this?' she said.

'He doesn't.' Hatred had squeezed the mascara off Drusilla's eye-lashes and on to her cheeks. She took a tissue from her bag and dabbed at it.

'Who's been paying you two hundred pounds a month?' Penny asked.

'That's my business.'

'Could be mine too.'

Looking at her in the mirror, Drusilla made a decision. She turned. 'Paying for a flat in Rome and maintaining the kind of wardrobe that goes with being the fiancée of what might have been the next Prime Minister of Italy takes a lot more than I can earn in Cambridge,' she said. 'I had to make up the shortfall somehow.'

There was a knock at the door. *'Cara?'* It was Bernini. Drusilla cooed something saccharine at him.

'Blackmail?' Penny said. 'That's one good way of overcoming shortfalls. So is stealing. Especially if you have a good friend like Meg Tarrance to root for you. Maybe even take the blame for you.'

'I'm sorry about Meg,' Drusilla said. Her skin grew pink. 'But I couldn't see any other way.'

'Hasn't it occurred to you that you might be in real trouble?' Penny said. 'For one thing, Bernini's not going to take this lying down. And I know you've got the Mob on your back. That guy who spoke to you in Toscana, the one with the growth on his neck. He gave you an ultimatum, didn't he?'

'A week,' Drusilla said. She seemed very unfazed.

'When's that up?'

'At midnight tonight.'

'You know he's sitting out there in the restaurant, don't you?'

212

'Yes. But he's not with the Mafia.'

'People like that are killers,' insisted Penny.

'I can handle him.'

How could she ever have thought Drusilla was limp?

'Cara.' Knuckles rapped at the other side of the door.

'How do you know?'

Drusilla smiled. 'I've done it before,' she said. She went out.

Kimbell was surrounded by breadstick wrappers when Penny got back to the table. 'Where have you been, girl?' he said.

'Talking.'

'Spelling the letters out on your hand, or what?' grumbled Kimbell. 'Just hope it was worth it, time you were gone. I already turned down three offers, waiting for you.'

'Why didn't you take one of them up?' said Penny.

'They was all from guys.' He bent across and took Penny's wrist between thumb and forefinger. 'Learn anything?'

'Nothing that's going to find Bruno.'

'Ever occur to you maybe Bruno don't want to be found?'

Penny nodded. For a while now it had occurred to her. All the evidence pointed to Bruno taking the figurines. After that, had he simply skipped off with Miss Sandy Leon? Had he decided after all to cut his losses where Giulia was concerned, and start again?

As they drove back to Kimbell's hotel, bells were ringing in the dusty night.

She wondered what the hell for.

21

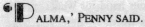

'PALMA,' PENNY SAID.

'I beg your goddamned pardon.'

'Palma.'

'That does it.' Kimbell lay back on his side of the big hotel bed. 'Jesus Christ. Guy spends hours giving it to some chick, uses all his skill and ingenuity, not to mention *rigid* self-control so he don't get there 'fore she do, and then she calls him a ham.'

'Palma's hiding him,' Penny said. 'Or at least she knows where he's at.'

'Okay,' said Kimbell. He punched the big linen bolsters set against the headboard. 'Think you gone tempt me into bed wit' you again, give you the benefit of three years' Government-funded research into the delights of the mysterious East courtesy the Kennedy and Johnson administrations, you can think again.'

'All that redecorating crap,' Penny said. She moved her hand along the smooth line of his muscled arm. 'Décor's the last thing Bruno would have had on his mind.'

'Tell you what I got on mine,' Kimbell said. He turned over fast. He slid an arm under Penny's back.

214

'What if I said I have a headache?'

'Might be forced to slip on down to Room 156 and see what ol' Nancy's got on offer.'

'That desperate, Aaron?'

'Been that way ever since you went away, babe.'

Later, Penny pushed back the covers and got out of bed. Through the shutters across the window, bars of light threw tiger-stripes across her skin. Kimbell watched her. Long, slim body, brown on the curves, black in the hollows. In at the waist, full on the hips. Small breasts below straight shoulders. She stood in the half-light, flicking her braids up and down on the back of her neck. Nothing special about her. Except that he loved her.

'I just wish people didn't waste so much time in bed,' she said.

'Let me tell you, wasn't nothing wasteful about the time *I* just spent in bed,' said Kimbell.

'Lookit. Six thirty and nobody in the world is up except me.'

'And me. Come back here and I'll show you.'

'Geez. I heard about you black brothers,' Penny said.

'And every word is true.' Kimbell sat up and closed his eyes. He pressed three fingers against his temples. 'Wow. What was that stuff we drank last night? Said wine on the menu. Feels more like gelignite.'

'Château di-ethylene,' said Penny. 'At least your bladder won't freeze up this winter.'

Kimbell popped a couple of Maalox out of their cellophane blisters and chewed them. 'Orange flavour,' he said. 'Yecch.'

'What'll you do today?' Penny said.

'Supposed to meet my buddy Manzi for lunch.'

Penny stared at him thoughtfully. 'I can see where Rior-

215

dan's gold might be safer with you than with him. But why's he brought it over here in the first place?'

'Case you hadn't heard,' Kimbell said, 'there's a symposium on in Florence. End of the week. All us archaeological types gonna be there.'

'And Riordan's chairing a Show 'n' Tell session, I suppose.'

'I suppose.' The blankness of Kimbell's gaze was blinding. 'You gonna meet me and Manzi for lunch, or not?'

'Where you going to be?'

He told her. Then he said, 'Hey. Since I'm not cooking yet this morning, how's about you come back here and get me on the boil again?'

Penny looked at her watch. 'Right,' she said.

She banged on the door of Palma Ferlinghetti's flat. Nothing happened. 'Open up,' she called. 'I know you're in there.' She pressed the doorbell and kept on pressing. After a while, someone spoke in a tiny voice. *'Chè?'*

'Penny. Penny Wanawake.'

Keys turned on the other side of the door. Bolts were drawn. Palma Ferlinghetti appeared in the crack the chain allowed. 'Penelope,' she said. 'What in the world?'

'Let me in,' Penny said.

'At this hour of the morning?'

'We have to talk, Mrs Ferlinghetti.'

'Palma.'

'Whatever.'

'What do we have to talk about?'

Penny had the definite impression that Palma wasn't glad to see her. 'About Bruno,' she said. She nodded importantly. She was good at important nods. More than enough to impress Palma.

216

'Oh my lord,' Palma said. Her little hands fluttered at the neck of her housecoat.

'Come on, now,' said Penny.

The door closed. She heard the chain come off, then it was opened again and Palma let her into the hall. She wore a wrap-around with a portrait of the sphinx hand-blocked on the back. Two palm trees curving up each side of it emphasised her tiny waist.

The decorations were even more aggressively dynastic than last time Penny had visited. All available spaces seemed to be cluttered with figures in bronze or gilt or stone. Slim ladies with their knees together held up dishes. Bulls and falcons stared impassively atop seated human bodies. Bewigged men sat on stone thrones.

Palma put a knuckle to her mouth. Her eyes were wide with what could only be called mute appeal. She shrank back, a frail figure, against a Ramessid tomb. It was easy to see why she'd never made it big in movies.

'Don't give me that startled fawn shit,' Penny said. 'I'm not Erich von Stroheim, offering you a comeback.'

'Dear Erich,' Palma said distractedly.

'What, did you meet him at a séance?' Penny said, deliberately cruel.

Palma straightened. She retied the belt on her robe. 'If you want Bruno, you've come to the wrong place,' she said. Her voice was steely. The authentic sound of Pittsburgh. After all the Scarlett O'Hara years, it was a miracle she remembered how.

'Where's the right place?'

'What makes you think I might know? I'm only his mother.'

'I saw him the night before last,' Penny said.

'What else did you see? A couple of fan-dancing aardvarks?' Palma said. 'A pink elephant?'

'I didn't realise at first who it was.'

'Whoever it was, it can't have been Bruno.'

'I suppose he's been here all along.'

'I tell you he has not.'

'Is that why he suggested you redecorate? So he'd have somewhere to hide the gold?' Penny tapped her nose with her finger, as though she knew a lot more than she was saying. 'And I notice his car's gone from outside.'

'It has?' Palma seemed puzzled. 'Are you sure?'

'Look out the window and you can see for yourself.'

'Having problems, Mrs Ferlinghetti?' It was Alex. He'd obviously put in some overtime on eliminating his Italian accent since there was no longer any trace of it. He was in turquoise cotton today, so tight over his behind she could see the line of his G-string briefs. And very nice too.

'Nothing I can't handle, thanks.' Palma sidestepped past Penny and walked quickly across the room. The movement of her body made the sphinx on her wrapper look as if it were chewing gum. She pulled the cords that opened the curtains and looked out into the street. Alex joined her.

'Penelope,' she said, 'I understand your position. Giulia is worried about Bruno, I know that. I'm anxious too. But I honestly haven't seen Bruno for weeks.'

'I know you're lying,' Penny said. 'How could Bruno tell you he loved the new décor if you only started it a week ago?'

Palma turned so Penny could see the facelift scars behind her ears. 'You must believe me, Penny.'

'I'll probably hate myself for it later,' Penny said, 'but I don't.'

Palma shrugged. 'How can I persuade you I'm telling the truth?'

'You can't. I suppose he lifted the figurines and drove straight up here with them. Did he tell you why?'

'Miz Ferlinghetti said we started redecorating a week ago,' Alex said. 'According to my records, it was more like a month. You know how it is.' He ran his tongue over his lips and jerked the lower half of his body about. Too distracting.

'Wouldn't it be truer to say it was last Thursday?' Penny said. 'The day Professor Meg Tarrance uncovered the figurines?'

The doorbell rang. Palma looked at Alex. She turned very pale, blood moving out of her face and down her neck. The bell rang again. 'Who's that?' she said.

'The postman always rings twice,' Penny said.

Alex went out of the room.

'Bruno had some odd phone calls after he'd been asked to serve on that Commission of Enquiry,' Palma said. 'Perhaps one of them frightened him into leaving town for a while.'

It didn't sound like Bruno. Before Penny could say so, Alex came back, followed by Oscare who stopped short when he saw her. Behind him was a policeman.

'Penelope,' he said. He threw out his arms like an actor meeting his past on *This Is Your Life* and pretending to love it. All the time he spoke, his eyes flicked over the room. Panning for gold. She'd done the same thing herself. Like her, he wasn't having any luck. If the Royal Pair had ever been there, they weren't there now.

'Hi, Oscare,' Penny said. 'What's going down?' Something was wrong. She'd always lined up alongside Bruno and Giulia. That automatically put her on the other side to Oscare. So why the big hello?

Oscare's smoothness gave way to melancholy. 'Ah, such terrible news,' he said. He hefted his shoulders as though each had a glass of full cream dairy milk balanced on top of the pads.

219

'Don't tell me you're going to be a father,' Penny said.

Oscare smiled. 'They have found Bruno's car.'

'They have?' Palma said. 'Where?'

'Abandoned at the airport, Viscontessa.'

'What's the difference between abandoned and just straight parked?' asked Penny.

'I do not think this was simply parked.'

'Why?' Alex said.

'There was a body in the trunk.' Oscare couldn't have been happier if he'd just been voted Millionaire of the Year.

'A dead person,' confirmed the policeman, reaching into his pocket. He brought out a toothpick. Putting his head on one side, he began to pick his teeth.

'*Lord*,' screamed Palma. 'Who, for heaven's sake?'

'Not . . . not . . .' Penny couldn't say it. Please, God. Not Bruno.

'No,' Oscare said. 'Not Bruno.'

'Who then?'

'We don't know,' said Oscare.

'There was no identification,' the policeman said. 'Impossible to tell who she was.'

'She?' Penny said.

'In Bruno's car?' said Palma. 'Oh, my *God*.'

'Do not worry, *cara cugina*,' Oscare said, smooth as a plastic-siding salesman.

'*Cugina*? I'm not your cousin, you schmuck,' said Palma. 'And don't you ever forget it.' Pure southside.

Smiling slightly, Oscare said, 'Bruno will have to come forward now, if only to clear his name. If, that is, he is not guilty.'

'You know damn well he's not,' Palma said. 'Creep.'

'Signore Torella has agreed to come down and make a statement,' said the policeman. He dug around in a bicuspid for a moment. 'It might be helpful if you would come too, Viscontessa. Perhaps you may know this unfortunate dead woman found in your son's car.'

'Screw that,' said Palma. 'No way am I going to look at bodies this early in the morning.' She turned on Oscare. 'And just how the heck did you get to hear about this before I did, anyway? What business is it of yours?'

'When Bruno first disappeared, I naturally made myself available to the police,' said Oscare. 'It occurred to me that I might save you some distress if the police dealt directly with me. After all, I am family.'

'Not mine,' Palma said.

'I'll come down with you to the police station, if you like,' Penny said. 'Since I'm involved and all.' Was she going to meet Sandy Leon at last? Better dead than never.

'If you wish,' Oscare said. He looked at the *carabinieri*, who nodded.

'Uh. Any indications as to when she died?' Penny asked.

The *carabinieri* shrugged. 'Yesterday, maybe. I don't know.'

The police car outside the Ferlinghetti flat was barnacled with small boys. The *carabinieri* made roaring noises through his teeth at them and they shouted insults back. Oscare stared suspiciously at them as though they were undercover assassins. As the car pulled away from the kerb, he turned to watch out of the back window.

Having made sure they weren't being followed, he shifted round to face Penny. There didn't seem to be enough room on the back seat for both of them.

'I believe my wife asked you to find Bruno,' he said.

'Right.'

'What does he have that I have not?' said Oscare suddenly.

221

Giulia's love was the main thing. Penny didn't want to say that.

'I love her,' Oscare said. 'She has never loved me. Some day she might. If she is given a chance. If Bruno will give her one.'

'Yeah,' she said.

'It is a sad thing, Penelope, to love someone who does not love you.'

'Yeah.'

'I am helpless about Giulia. I would do anything for her. I would even find Bruno for her if I could. But I will not give her up.'

He sounded sad. For the first time she saw him as a suffering human being. She wished life was other than it was. She wished that the pangs of love were less acute, that Oscare was someone else. The messes other people made of their lives were no less sad and seemingly insoluble than the mess you made of your own.

She put her hand on his knee. 'Life's tough,' she said quietly. Poor Oscare. Just because you were a crumb didn't mean your heart wasn't as tender as anyone else's.

'Perhaps now she will see that the man she has worshipped for so long is nothing more than a murderer and a thief,' Oscare said.

Penny took her hand away quickly. She preferred Oscare the Jerk to Oscare the Bleeding Heart. At least there wasn't a conflict of interests. 'Can you seriously imagine Bruno killing someone?' she said.

Much as he wanted, Oscare couldn't. 'My wife seems to think I am responsible for Bruno's disappearance,' he said.

'Are you?'

'Would I tell you if I was?'

'It's obviously not Bruno who killed this girl,' Penny

222

said. 'What could he possibly have to gain by murdering her and leaving her body in his own car? After all, he's managed to stay hidden for over a week. Why would he suddenly want to draw attention to himself?'

'Who knows how the mind of such a man works,' Oscare said.

'It seems to me that whoever *did* off her and try to set Bruno up has to be really dumb. Don't you agree?'

Oscare sneered like Beau Brummel catching the Prince Regent in the wrong waistcoat. 'A man who has just killed cannot be considered entirely rational. In panic, he might well do something that on mature consideration he could see would be a stupid move.'

'Bruno is not a stupid-move kind of guy,' said Penny.

Rome moved past them. Towers. Spires. Fountains. Squares full of strong black shadows. The people seemed twice as alive as Londoners. They passed the Forum. Pearl-grey light straddled by arches still crowing over vanquished peoples. Paving stones trodden by Caesar's sandal, stained with Caesar's blood. This kind of historical continuity made Virginia's look pretty callow.

'What's your real connection with Bernini?' she demanded suddenly. Catching people off guard sometimes worked. Not often. But it was worth a try.

'Only that some of his business interests interlock with some of mine. We've never actually met.' Oscare began chuckling to himself. He pulled a small leather bag from the pocket of his waistcoat. From it he took the gold box that Penny had been looking at in the *galleria itaro* a few days earlier. In the dim light of the car, the gold seemed duller, the features of the goddess less clear. 'Look what I bought from Bernini just yesterday,' he said.

'I thought the Instituto Ferlinghetti was going to buy that.'

'So did they,' Oscare said, 'but in the end, as you see, it was sold to someone else.'

'To you.'

'To me.'

From his expression, it was clear that the purchase had been made out of spite. Penny wondered how many other items the Instituto had lost because Oscare couldn't cope with the fact that his wife loved another man. No wonder the place was gradually going downhill again. She looked at his fleshy profile. In spite of the momentary empathy between them, she hated him. 'If they squeezed the shit out of you, Oscare,' she said, 'they could bury you in a soap-dish.'

She thought how much better Giulia's life would be if Oscare wasn't part of it, and then wished she hadn't. It made him seem suddenly vulnerable.

She stared out of the window for the rest of the ride.

The police station looked like a Fellini set for *Gomorrah Nights*. Monumental ladies with half-veiled breasts held up the walls. Frescoes involving semi-naked shepherds sprawled across the ceiling. A group of hookers swapped insults with a couple of guys in expensive suiting. Difficult to know if they were the girls' pimps or their lawyers. People sat about on long benches. Some looked poor, some as if they'd dropped by to audition for the orgy scene. A fat lady wept into a handkerchief, stopping sometimes to slap one of the children who surrounded her. Somewhere out of sight, a drunk called monotonously upon St Jude to get him out of there. Three small English tourists explained apologetically to a man reading *Il Corriere* how their passports had been stolen. The whole place stank of stale booze and staler sweat.

The policeman led Penny and Oscare through to the back. A considerable update had taken place here. Electronic gadgetry flashed numerals up on green monitors. Well-tempered voices spoke from amplified phones. Screens shimmered with enough vital statistics to cover a Miss Galaxy contest.

The policeman took them over to another, who was sitting at a cluttered desk. He looked up and winked at Penny. He motioned to her to sit down. The first policeman took Oscare away. The second one winked some more. Maybe he'd got a mote in his eye. He took a statement from her about her friendship with Bruno and got her to sign it. He went away. After a while he came back and asked her to follow him. She asked where to and he winked again.

They went downstairs and into the morgue. It was an old morgue, the freezing-plant of second-rate efficiency. The smell was as strong as a stun gun. The policeman called over a little old woman in a grey overall and spoke to her in a low voice, glancing at Penny as he did so. They followed her to another room lined with small refrigerator doors. The old woman pulled one open.

'This is the girl found in Dr Ferlinghetti's car,' the policeman said.

'One thing,' Penny said, putting off the moment. 'How did you know to look for her?'

'A tip-off,' the policeman said. He winked.

'Was it a man or a woman?' asked Penny.

'A man. Phoned in early this morning. Told us where to find the car, and what would be in it. I should tell you that Signor Torella was unable to identify her.'

Penny looked down. She didn't say anything.

'Do you recognise her?' the policeman said. 'Ever seen her before?'

Penny had.

Even though someone had pulled a sharpened knife-blade across her throat so deeply that the head was almost

225

severed. Even though at least five of the eight or nine pints of blood her body once contained had leaked out. Penny breathed in through her mouth, feeling the anger that death's irrevocability always roused in her.

Forgiveness makes you better than your enemy, she wanted to say. Revenge just makes you his equal. Drusilla had gone for equality. It was her choice. We all die in the end, one way or another. Some ways were better than others. She hoped Drusilla's revenge had been sweet. She hadn't enjoyed it for long.

22

T HE POLICE DIDN'T KEEP HER. THEY TOLD HER DEATH was provisionally placed at four o'clock that morning. She gave them only the minimal information. They could ferret the rest out for themselves. She said that Drusilla lived in England and was working on the dig at Toscana al Vesuvio. She added that she had seen her the night before at the Ristorante Reale with a man called Pietro Bernini. That caused a certain amount of excitement. Bernini would have been gratified.

The way Penny saw it, Drusilla had diced with death and lost. If Bernini was responsible, there was no reason why she should let him off the hook. Sooner or later the police would have been on to him anyway.

She found the café where Kimbell was meeting his friend. The friend turned out to be the guy with the prematurely grey hair who'd showed up at Bernini's place. They were sitting at a table outside on the pavement. Both of them were laughing. When he saw Penny, the friend stopped laughing and took her hand in both of his. She loved the serious way Italian men approached women.

'Hi,' she said. 'I'm Penny Wanawake.'

He repeated the name twice and filed it away in some mental cabinet.

'I am Enrico Manzi,' he said.

They sat down. Manzi ordered coffee and ice-cream.

'I'm most grateful for being rescued yesterday,' Penny said.

'It was a pleasure.'

'What exactly did you have on Bernini?'

'Nothing,' Manzi said.

'How about this?' She told him everything Drusilla had told her the night before.

Manzi nodded. 'That could be very useful information,' he said. 'We have never found anything to pin on him, although the big man who protects him is known to the police. Has been for many years. Guido Cavalari. He hires himself out as a bodyguard, though for a long time he worked as an enforcer with the—uh . . .' He gestured delicately. 'You know who I mean, I think.'

'Does Bernini know that?'

'An interesting question.' Manzi leaned back and considered it, a spoon halfway to his mouth. 'I am inclined to think not, despite the poor reputation that surrounds Italian politics. But it is a mistake for a man with Signor Bernini's ambitions to employ such a type.'

Uh-oh. Looked like Bernini goofed. And if he killed Drusilla, he goofed badly. One mistake might be regarded as a misfortune. Two, surely, looked like carelessness. Using Bruno's car to draw attention away from himself— that was something else. That was bandwagon-jumping. Bruno already stood condemned of grand theft. Bernini might well have reasoned that the public would be that much more likely to swallow him as a murderer as well.

But if a man would murder for gold, how much more so would he murder if his future were suddenly threatened? If he'd spent years in committee-sitting, in attending dull functions, in speeches and letters and favour-doing, only to have someone try to take the prize away just when it was in his sights?

'Bernini thought I knew where Dr Ferlinghetti was,' Penny said. 'He had some wild idea that we were working together, trying to sell the missing figurines to the highest bidder.'

'Ah yes,' Manzi said. 'The missing figurines. But of course you were not.'

Penny reminded herself that he was a policeman. Policemen were suspicious of everything. 'Of course not,' she said. 'I only wish we were. Then at least I'd know where he is.'

'Yes,' Manzi said. 'That would be useful. I feel that he is in danger.'

'You do?' Kimbell said. 'Why?'

'That car of his, found early this morning at the airport after an anonymous tip-off?' With a long-handled spoon Manzi pushed aside the whipped cream that covered his cassata, and excavated the interior. 'Mmm,' he said. 'They marinade the fruit for the *tutti frutti* in brandy.' He spooned some ice-cream into his mouth and closed his eyes. 'Simply delicious.'

'What about the car?' Kimbell said.

'It has been examined for fingerprints, naturally,' said Manzi. He bent towards them. 'You understand that, although I have followed this case, I am not personally handling it. I looked at the files only because you, Kimbell, my friend, asked me to as a great personal favour.'

'Aw, Aaron,' Penny said.

Kimbell looked as demure as a first Communion candidate.

'What about the fingerprints?' asked Penny.

'There weren't any.' Manzi licked thoughtfully at the ice-cream on his spoon. 'These people are perfectionists. That is why I brought you here. They steep the vanilla beans in cream before they make the *gelati*.'

'None at all?' said Penny.

'A couple of partial latents on the back of the passenger seat, Signorina Penny. And one under the lid of the boot. Otherwise it was clean.'

'That's marvellous.'

'Yes.' Manzi tapped the side of Penny's dish. 'Eat, signorina, before it melts.'

'Of course,' said Kimbell, 'Ferlinghetti wouldn't need to hide his dabs. In his own car, there'd be no point.'

'Precisely.'

'So someone else parked it at the airport,' Kimbell said.

'Having first wiped it everywhere he could think of,' said Penny.

'Forgetting that anyone turning to speak to someone in the back would be quite likely to leave prints on the back of the passenger seat.'

'Same with the one under the boot,' said Penny.

'Which is why I think Dr Ferlinghetti should take extremely good care of himself,' Manzi said. He winked at Kimbell. 'You have told me a lot about this signorina, but you did not tell me she was related to Sherlock Holmes.' He pronounced it Holl-mez.

'This is a fox you won't see too many like, my man,' Kimbell said. 'Didn't I say that, huh?'

Manzi laughed. 'Many, many times.'

Kimbell stood up. 'It's been nice visiting with you folks,' he said, 'but some of us hired on to work. I got to go up to Florence this afternoon. Check out security arrangements for this symposium. Won't be back until tomorrow.' He looked at Penny. 'Hear that, lady?'

'I hear.'

'Keep in touch.' He hefted his airline bag on to his shoulder.

'You bet.'

'Well, I gotta roll.'

He did so. Penny and Manzi watched him in silence until he turned the corner of the street. A tabby cat sleeping in the roots of a big tree growing out of the pavement got up and wandered after him.

'Only one thing,' Penny said. 'Can you sit on what I just told you for a couple of days? I already gave your colleagues enough to be going on with. It's just that someone on the force seems to think Oscare Torella should be informed of everything that goes down.'

'Like I said, it's not my case,' Manzi said.

'Any clues as to where she was killed?'

'When I left for lunch, the forensic people hadn't yet come up with anything.'

'I can't understand why the press haven't pursued this one harder,' Penny said. 'It's got all the ingredients of a first-class society scandal. Gold statues and a noble name. What more do they want?'

'Someone killed it at top level,' Manzi said.

'Why? Who?'

'Who I don't know. I should imagine the reason is to give the—uh, you know who I mean—a chance to come in on it at leisure.'

'The Mafia,' Penny said.

Manzi winced. 'We have files on all those known to have affiliations, though we seldom have a chance to use them. Despite rumours about corruption and incompetence, the police force in this country is in fact extremely efficient.'

'I'm sure it is.' Penny worked her dimples. 'And I'll bet

231

you have files on all foreign residents, too, don't you? Especially the ones who work or have worked at Toscana al Vesuvio.'

'How perceptive you are.'

'Is there any way a girl like me could get a look at them?'

'Of course,' Manzi said.

'Oh?'

'A girl like you would simply have to agree to have dinner with a man like me, and the particular files would be opened at once for her inspection.'

'I see,' said Penny.

'Good,' Manzi said.

23

S HE CALLED ROOM SERVICE TO ORDER A JACK DANIEL'S on the rocks and a newspaper. She was packing an overnight bag when the bedside telephone rang.

'I'm returning your call,' Barnaby said, cold as a death sentence. She could hear his heart beating. 'Did you have anything special to say?'

'Hang on, will you?'

'Why?'

'Want to put my fur coat on,' said Penny. 'Don't know whether it's the air-conditioning in here or what it is, but I'm about to freeze to death.'

Barnaby brought his voice up to just above zero. 'Have you found Bruno yet?'

'No. But I found a couple of other things.'

'Such as?'

'A ring.'

'A ring?' Barnaby said.

'Yeah.'

'As in smuggling?'

'As in heavy and gold. The band made of twisted gold

and silver wires. The top formed into the head of Anubis with some kind of stone for the eyes. Amethysts, I think.'

It was probably her imagination that Barnaby's heart-beat suddenly sounded faster. 'Anubis,' he said carefully.

'Yeah,' said Penny. 'The dog-headed god of ancient Egypt. Protector of the Dead. Probably a lot of other things too.'

'I know who Anubis is.'

'Thought you might.'

'With amethyst eyes?'

'Yeah.'

'It sounds like the Ring of Hatshepsut,' Barnaby said. He sounded as if he had just swallowed an avocado stone.

'Could very well be,' said Penny. 'Who's Hatshepsut?'

'An eighteenth-dynasty queen,' Barnaby said. 'Probably the first feminist.' He laughed.

'Sounds like a stitch and a half.'

'She thought she had as much right to the throne as the male claimant, a kid called Tuthmosis. Owing to the weird marriage arrangements they had in Egypt in those days, he was her nephew and her step-son.'

'Most marriage arrangements are kind of weird, if you ask me.'

'Good thing not everyone agrees with you,' said Barnaby. 'Do you want me to put the phone down, or shall I go on telling you about this very strong-minded Egyptian lady?'

'Go on.'

'Just in case the kid got any ideas about who was really king, she not only assumed male titles and used the masculine pronoun on her inscriptions, she also went round dressed as a man. Even had herself shown in masculine dress on her monuments and statues. You'll have noticed that ring's not particularly feminine. Much more suitable for a king than a queen.'

'Wasn't there a piece about it in *Hermes* a while back?'

'Probably. It was stolen from Christie's strong room a year or so ago, just before a major auction of Egyptian antiquities. Nobody's seen it since.'

'Except me.'

'Where did you see it?'

'Lying on a table.'

'What?'

'On somebody's finger.'

'Tell me about the somebody.'

Penny did.

'I knew it,' Barnaby said, on an indraw of breath. 'Fazal. Everyone suspected him, but no one could prove it.'

'Isn't he pushing his luck a bit, wearing a stolen ring?'

'Probably banking on not many people recognising it. And if anyone did accuse him of stealing it, it would give him a chance to air his views on what he calls national theft. It's his theory that if it once belonged to Egypt, it still belongs to Egypt. Wonder why he's hanging around Bruno's place.'

Fazal. Not a Mafia man at all. Not even an Italian. 'Didn't you say he was a gold freak, like Riordan?'

'Yes.'

'What's his money from?'

'You know these rich guys,' Barnaby said. 'They like to diversify.'

'I'll bet anything you like that Fazal is into mass communication. Either newspapers or radio stations. Something like that. I also bet he's a paid-up member of the Egyptian equivalent of the National Front.'

'Easy to find out.'

'Tell you what else I bet. That he specialises in Egyptian gold.'

'I think you're right,' Barnaby said. 'That's not the only stuff he's supposed to have lifted, by any means.'

'I'm on my way to Toscana,' Penny said. 'I think I just about got this thing sewed up.'

'If Fazal's involved, you want to be careful. From what I've heard about him . . .'

'I'll be careful.'

'Good.'

'Barnaby.'

'Yeah?'

'How's the languishing going?'

'To tell you the truth, I'm getting somewhat tired of it.'

'Come back.'

'I might do that.'

'It'd be so much easier to discuss things face to face.'

'As it were.'

'In the privacy of our own home.'

'Right.'

'Though I don't want you to think I've altered my views.'

'I haven't altered mine either,' Barnaby said.

'I love you, Barnaby.' It wasn't something she said very often. She heard him smile. ' 'Bye.'

She phoned Dr Lunghi at the Instituto Ferlinghetti. And Palma Ferlinghetti at home. Both confirmed that there had been attempted break-ins in the past week.

In the middle of her conversation with Palma, room service arrived. The Jack Daniel's came in a miniature. The rocks came in the glass. She smiled a thank you and gave him a tip. Room service gave her the newspaper and a smouldering glance. She jerked her head at the door. Move it, buster. Wasn't a person safe anywhere these days?

As soon as she put the phone down it rang again.

'Where the hell have you been?' Meg Tarrance in sunny mood. Her deep voice made no concession to manners. 'I've been trying to contact you for hours.'

'What's up?' Penny said.

'I saw her yesterday lunchtime.'

'Who?'

There was some impatient tutting at the other end of the line. 'Cindy Leon, of course.'

'Sandy.'

'Whatever the blasted girl's called.'

'Are you sure it was her?'

'Absolutely certain.'

'What did she say?'

'I didn't speak to her. She strode off as soon as she saw me coming, the way she always does. But it was unmistakably her.'

'How do you know?'

'Well . . . how does one know these things? I recognised her hair. The way she was dressed. The way she walked. Good God, what else is there?'

'How was she dressed?'

'Dungarees. One of those Greenpeace sweat-shirts. It was definitely her.'

'What was she doing?'

'Poking round at the far end of the site.'

'With a stick, do you mean?'

'For God's sake, woman. Of course not. She was in the no-go area. You remember. I showed you.'

'Where those doorways are boarded up?'

'Yes.'

'Any idea why?'

Pause. 'Not really,' Meg said. Another pause. Then she

said diffidently, 'Though it did occur to me that maybe she and Bruno hid the figurines right here on-site.'

'Why would they do that?'

There was a shrugging noise. Diffidence wasn't natural to Meg. 'How the hell do I know? They could be planning to pick them up later, when the heat's off.'

'Does that mean you no longer think Bruno's taken them abroad?'

'I can't imagine what the Leon woman was after otherwise.'

'What were *you* wearing, Professor Tarrance?'

'When?'

'Yesterday lunchtime.'

'Why do you want to know?'

'I'm planning a new wardrobe and want to model it on yours.'

'My usual things,' Meg said. 'Shorts. A T-shirt. It's too hot down here for anything else.'

'Especially at that time of day.'

Yet Sandy Leon was wearing a sweat-shirt. Was that significant? Sweat-shirts have long sleeves. Long sleeves hide things. Such as distinguishing marks. Briefly she wondered if Sandy Leon were hideously disfigured or covered in tattoos. Maybe she was a drug addict and wanted to conceal the track-marks. Nah. Bruno wouldn't be going around with a druggie. If going around with the girl was in fact what he was doing.

'Also,' Meg said, 'I found Bruno's missing log-book. It had fallen behind the filing cabinet in his office.'

'All right,' said Penny. 'I might come down tomorrow.' She didn't say she had already planned to drive down that day. A Meg Tarrance taken by surprise might be quite different from a Meg Tarrance prepared.

Prepared for what? It was over a week since the Royal

Pair had gone, and Bruno along with them. It was time he surfaced again. Surfaced. That was some kind of a word. She'd been imagining Bruno, unshaven, handcuffed, locked away somewhere in some dirty shack. Now she thought of him held at Toscana, thrown into an underground room, tied up in one of those boat-chambers with the earth heaving all round him.

If Meg had heard about Drusilla's murder, she was covering up her emotions fairly successfully. If she hadn't, Penny wasn't about to tell her. Not over the telephone.

'Good,' Meg said. 'See you then.' She put the phone down.

Penny looked at the ceiling. She closed her eyes. Fill the mind with a ceiling and you had a nice clean space on which to set out some questions that badly needed answering. For instance, had she really seen Bruno outside the Casa Ferlinghetti the other night? Just because Palma denied it, there was no reason to suspect she was telling the truth. And now Sandy Leon had reappeared. Why would the girl show up at Toscana and yet avoid talking to anyone there? What could she have been looking for? Penny recycled the conversation she'd just had with Meg. All along, Sandy Leon had avoided the other archaeologists at Toscana. Lunghi, at the Instituto Ferlinghetti, claimed that he'd never heard of her. And when Bruno disappeared, so did she. Why? If she was walking about, showing up at the site, then she was presumably a free agent. So where was she now? With Bruno?

She opened the newspaper. Bernini's resignation from the opposition party made all the headlines. There was a picture of him looking earnest and distressed, talking about other commitments. There was a picture of his daughter holding a handbag in front of her face. There was a picture of him addressing a group of anti-PLO demonstrators a couple of months earlier. A leader inside spoke of the grave loss to Italian politics and hinted at scandalous revelations to come. Would Drusilla lie easy now?

On another page, there was a picture of the Pope blessing a large crowd at St Peter's. He was quoted as saying that the age of miracles was by no means over. He referred to someone called Father Vicente de Paolo. He explained why. He certainly convinced Penny. She took a closer look at his photograph.

She called Giulia's parents. Giulia was out. Penny left a message to say she would be out of touch as she was driving down to Toscana. She drank the bourbon quickly. It was time she got going.

24

ONE WAS A TORPEDO-COLOURED MERCEDES, ONE AN orange Fiat 500 some wit had painted with large black spots. Otherwise, the road outside the Villa Ferlinghetti was empty. There was a lot of fine dust about, lying like talc on the fringe of rough grass along the verge and powdering the matt-black bumpers of the Merc.

Through its dark-tinted windows she could see two men. The one in front could have been carved out of bog-oak. The one in the back had a scarf wrapped round the lower part of his face. With temperatures in the high 80s, you couldn't help but wonder why. Penny thought about driving right on by or doing a fast three-point turn and heading back to town. The only sorts of men who sat around outside someone else's place in cars with tinted glass were bad ones.

She parked and walked over to the Merc. Miss Valiant-for-Truth, with a flaring boil of fear in the middle of her chest and a heart beating louder than a pneumatic drill. She bent her knees and peered in through the open back window.

'Hi, guys,' she said. 'Looking for something?'

Neither of the men answered. There was a gun lying on

the passenger seat in front. She could feel the cold shivers hanging about her spine, ready to run up it. Or down. She wished she couldn't.

The man behind the wheel of the Fiat got out. He came over and stood much too close behind her. Very menacing. Also very stupid. Stand that close and you make yourself vulnerable to surprise attack from the front. The heel of a Bally sandal might not be much good for getting pickles out of a jar but it could do all sorts of damage if the wearer kicked up hard behind. Other things being equal. But they weren't, not with a gun within a split second's reach of a man more than ready to use it.

The man in the back had both his hands on the seat. The scarf didn't hide the swelling behind his ear. She nodded at him. He nodded back. Saving the kisses for next time.

'Hey, I'm real glad we caught up with each other like this,' she said.

He didn't reply.

'I've been wanting to ask you. What's between you and Drusilla Ross?'

'Who?' he said.

'Drusilla Ross.'

'I know no one of that name,' he said. His voice was muffled by the scarf.

'Come on, Mr Fazal,' she said. 'Your secret is safe with me.'

He stared at her. Then he reached for a button and hit it. Penny was already leaning down hard. Instead of closing, the window stayed open. Fazal looked at the button, then at her. He touched it again.

It was tough, using sheer brute force to keep the window from closing, but she still had something to say.

'Pietro Bernini,' she said quickly. She watched for a flicker of recognition. There wasn't one. Instead, Fazal said something to the man at the wheel, keeping his mouth very small and tight while he spoke. An obvious anal retentive. A man who wouldn't let go of something if he thought it belonged to him. Even if it didn't. She didn't understand what he said.

The man at the wheel obviously did. He touched the horn. Three short bleeps, one long. Twice. Beethoven's fifth. It sounded like a signal. Probably to some piece of Italian crud turning over Bruno's house right that minute.

She stood up. She could feel a painful groove all along the underside of her arm, but she wasn't going to rub it in front of Fazal.

'One thing about it,' she said. 'When I see you, I know you still haven't got the figurines. Guess you need to talk to Bruno Ferlinghetti.'

'If I could find him, I would,' Fazal said.

'Stick with me, baby. I'm going to find him if it kills me.' She turned round. The man who'd been behind her was holding a gun. *Jee*-sus. She hadn't realised that. Suppose she *had* kicked up. That thing would have gone off, torn a hole right through her chest, *ruined* her silk shirt.

She felt sick.

It was one thing with the bossmen, quite another with the trigger-happy punks. They were always a problem. The bossmen at least had some sense. Like, if you come up with a goose that might lay a golden egg, you don't go shooting it. Blow away the golden goose and you don't get any golden eggs. Likewise, waste the kid who just might know where Bruno Ferlinghetti was, and you could whistle for the statuettes. The bossmen knew that. The punks didn't. Which is why they were punks and not bosses. Why they drove the Mercedes instead of being driven.

She took off her Ray-Ban Olympians. She gave him the

150-watt smile. He stepped back. Behind her, Fazal said something small and hard. The gun dropped.

She still felt sick.

The air floating across Bruno's herb garden smelled of bouquet garni. The cicadas hummed like haymakers. She closed her eyes. Wished she'd brought a hat. The last thing she wanted right now was a sunstroke. Though with a complexion like hers, that was the last thing she was likely to get.

She walked back to her car. Her spine felt precarious. Even the cold shivers were scared. The horn sounded again. After a count of four, the front door of the villa opened. A thin man in black trousers came out, shielding his eyes against the sun. He shook his head. Turned his thumbs down. Took in Penny and the white Lamborghini as his vision cleared. He shouted hoarsely and came running towards them. At the gates, he hesitated, then started to climb them. The keys were right there in Penny's bag, but she didn't see why she should make things easier for them.

The thin guy fell over the top of the gates. The man in the road picked him up and hustled him into the Fiat. Fazal spoke again, not moving his lips. Creamy smooth, the Merc started up and moved off. The Fiat trundled along behind.

Penny opened the gates. She started breathing again. Powder-purple butterflies rose from the lavender bushes as she drove the Lamborghini between them. The shadow of the villa's roof was black across the gravel in front of the house. The thin man had left the front door open. She didn't want to go inside. She picked a leaf of scented geranium and chewed it. Remembered Bruno telling her once that Roman matrons used it mixed with mint and honey to mask the smell of wine on their breath. Roman matrons were supposed to stick to light drinks. Wine was reserved for men and gods.

It's difficult to turn a house upside down when there's nothing much to turn. The punk had tried, but Bruno's minimalist furnishings hadn't made it easy. Once he'd checked out the cushions of the seating unit with his knife, there wasn't much place else in the main room to look. He'd opened the egg-shaped television housing. Even turned the set on. A swarthy man was on-screen, having a coronary beside a giant packet of detergent while several housewives holding items of male underclothing looked on.

Penny's legs were weak. So was her stomach. It wasn't so much that she was scared of two-bit jerks. Just that she hated the guns they always waved about. Guns brought her out in a cold sweat. Guns were intimations of mortality. She didn't need reminding that in the midst of life we are in death. She'd killed a man once. She'd lived through every second of his dying. She knew how a bullet in the gut felt. She *hated* guns.

The television switched to the news. Anti-apartheid protest meeting broken up in Durban. Shots of men in army fatigues smashing black heads in. Student demonstrations against foreigners in Cairo University. Shots of square-haired young men waving placards. Forthcoming elections in Rome. Shots of candidates looking electable. Shots of Bernini looking grieved and responsible.

Penny switched off.

She went out to the pool. There were no signs of recent police activity. No flowers for Lavette. A sprinkle of dead insects floated like oregano on the surface of the water. Brown petals had gathered in the corners, rocking gently when the air moved. Through the glitter of chlorinated water, she could see the corpse of a worm sprawled on the bottom, bleached as string. Someone had removed Lavette's gun. The filtering system had removed his blood. She stripped off, jumped in, started swimming lengths.

Housemartins sat in a line on the gutters and watched her. Though she didn't look directly up beyond the umbrella pines to where the olives were, she soon picked up the guy on watch. Smaller than Lavette and better. He was sitting salamander-still behind the crumble of stone wall. She knocked off fifty and climbed out. Wet footprints followed her into Bruno's study. The punk had done better in here. There were papers everywhere. The skull had rolled into a corner. All the file drawers had been forced open. She tidied a little, but not much. Better to wait until Bruno got back to sort it out. If . . .

She piled letters and carbons and lecture notes together, picked up index cards and agenda. Bruno didn't use his wastepaper-basket as often as he might. She found a scatter of old conference timetables and tried to put them into some kind of order. The most recent had been the previous summer at the University of Virginia. Papers delivered by doctors and professors, including Meg Tarrance and Bruno Ferlinghetti. Symposia chaired by household names. Sessions on the accuracy of carbon dating techniques. Talks on the lost tombs at Saqqara and King Naymlap of Peru. In the credits at the back, Safe & Sound was listed as being responsible for security.

Which meant any one of the Toscana archaeologists could have met Littel at the conference. Or seen his name in the programme. Any one of them, therefore, could have hired him to spy on Bruno.

Bruno's bedroom looked a mess. Pillows were flung about, the mattress shoved off the bed, stuff from the wardrobe strewn over the floor. So were the contents of Bruno's drawers. Socks, shirts, sweaters. A spill of handkerchiefs and cufflinks. A fancy garter. A snapshot of Giulia taken last summer, her hair round her face. On the back, *To my darling*, *for ever*. Sad eyes, sad mouth. Although you couldn't see it, you could guess at the sad heart that went with them. Penny picked up the best she could.

She put on one of Bruno's shirts, white, with a faint pink stripe. It made her feel like a stick of rock, even when she cinched it with a red tie. Down in the study she found a felt-tip and some paper. Wrote COFFEE? in big letters. Went out to the pool and propped it up on the arms of a folding chair. The watcher should be able to read that.

He was. By the time she'd set hot water on to boil, he was on the patio.

25

'HI,' SHE SAID. 'I'M PENNY WANAWAKE.'

'Wanawake,' he said. 'You're already on my list.'

'But we only just met.'

He grinned. 'Forewarned is forearmed.' He was a lot younger than Lavette. Younger than Penny, too.

'Four arms could come in useful,' Penny said.

'Depends what you're using them for.' He grinned some more. 'Like, take you, for example. Need four arms, just to get a hold.'

'You're pretty mouthy for a kid, aren't you?' Penny said.

'Yo, grandma.'

He was shortish, with strong muscled legs and a heavy tan under short fair hair. He wore sneakers without socks. His shorts and T-shirt were the colour of the hillside shale. He told her his name was Jeff Hurtz.

Penny brought a tray out to the side of the pool. Coffee for him. A tisane for her. According to Bruno, it would calm the nerves. Maybe he was right. It did zilch for the tastebuds. Under the trellis, the air was cooler. Where the sun broke through the vine leaves, it burned as though focused through a glass.

'Are you Lavette's replacement?' Penny said.

'Who?' The kid stared at her.

'The guy who was here before you.' Perhaps Littel had forgotten to tell him that Lavette had wound up face down in the pool with a bullet through his head.

'Oh, him,' Jeff said. 'I never did learn his name. How did you know?'

'We make it our business to know,' Penny said.

'We?' Jeff's eyes were as big as LPs. Penny wondered which pre-school playgroup Littel had pulled him out of. He glanced around, as though someone might be eavesdropping in the pool, and lowered his voice. 'What're you? CIA?'

'Is the Ayatollah crazy?' Penny said. 'Do onions make you cry? Does the road wind uphill all the way?' Draw your own conclusions, kid.

The kid did. He took a deep breath. 'Wow,' he said.

'Keep it under your hat,' said Penny. She tried to indicate without words that there were matters too sensitive to come right out with. That national security could be involved.

'Oh, I will,' Jeff said. He nodded.

Penny never felt much reluctance to tamper with truth. Especially not if it served her ends. But this kid was something else. Pin a diaper on him and he'd win Best Baby in Show, no question. Could she really steal his candy?

Sure she could.

'What's Littel's angle, anyway?' she said.

'Whose?'

'Steve Littel's. Man who runs Safe & Sound.'

'Is that his name?' said Jeff. 'I didn't speak directly to him.'

'So you don't know who's behind this surveillance?'

'I wasn't told. Just that I'm to keep an eye out. Log who comes and goes. Take registrations. Like that.'

Darn it. Looked like there was no candy to steal.

'Anyone come yet?'

'One or two, while I've been here. You, for instance.'

'You spotted that, did you?'

'And those guys outside the gate. I didn't know whether to log them, until one of them climbed over the gate. How'd you get rid of them, anyway?'

'You learn to handle situations in our game,' Penny said. She sipped her tisane. Horrible. Infused pennyroyal tasted even worse than infused fennel.

'Guess you guys don't miss much,' Jeff said.

'You're pretty good yourself,' said Penny.

'I am?'

'You've had your hair cut, but you sure had me fooled,' said Penny. 'When you were staking out the Ferlinghetti place in Rome the other day. I'd have bet any money you were just a kid on vacation, back-packing round Europe.'

'I didn't see you,' Jeff said. He sounded chagrined. She guessed he wasn't too thrilled at being spotted so easily. Or at not spotting her spotting him.

'That trick with the Listerine is dynamite,' she said.

'Listerine?' Jeff wrinkled his brow. 'Oh yeah. Right. It's just I got this fungal infection in my gums. Pyorrhoea, they said, down at the Salvatore Mundi hospital.' He pulled back his lower lip with his index finger. 'Look.'

'Think I'll raincheck that one,' said Penny. She poured him some more coffee. Jeez. Asking people to look at your gums was even worse than asking them to listen to your dreams.

'This list,' she said. 'Who else is on it?'

Jeff put down his coffee. He felt in the back pocket of

his shorts and pulled out a piece of paper. It was typewritten, like Lavette's. Probably standard issue. Also like Lavette's, it was greasy with tanning cream. He looked doubtful. 'Sure I should be telling you this stuff?' he said.

Penny shrugged. 'I expect it's the same as mine,' she said. 'Littel probably liaised with my people before he gave it to you.'

'Liaised,' Jeff said. 'Right.'

'It's up to you.'

'Guess it's okay, then.'

Penny smiled at him.

'Let's see here,' he said. 'There's a Lucia Formaggio, cousin, driving a red sports or maybe a blue Fiat. There's an Oscare Torella, ditto. A Palma Ferlinghetti, mother. A Giulia Torella, close friend, known to have keys. And then there's a Penelope Wanawake, which I guess is you . . .'

'Probably.'

'. . . on account she's a good friend of Ferlinghetti's and, it says here, the Giulia dame asked her to come out and look around, see if she could find out anything.' He looked up sharply. 'Thought you said you were CIA.' He folded the list up and put it away.

'Come on, Jeff. I didn't actually say so.' She winked.

'Oh. Right,' he said.

'Listen,' Penny said. She glanced around. 'Any idea what this is all about? I was just told to get down here. Head office doesn't bother filling us in on the details if they figure we don't need to know. Makes it kind of difficult sometimes.'

'Far's I know, the guy who lives here stole some gold statues,' Jeff said. 'The Holy Family, or something.'

'Royal Pair, do you mean?'

'Oh yeah, right,' Jeff said. 'And the guy who hired me wants to get them back.'

'That I knew,' Penny said.

''S all I've been told,' Jeff said. He was looking worried. His hazel eyes fixed on hers. 'Hey, listen. I don't want to mislead you or anything. Give the wrong impression. I'm strictly on surveillance. I'm not going to pretend I'm doing any hotshot investigating or like that.'

'Hard to believe, Jeff.'

'I mean, I don't want to get mixed up in nothing. I mean, I'm just a postgraduate student, you know? Doing a year in language school. I know how you guys work. If I ever wanted to go some place sensitive, El Salvador or Moscow or some place—not that I'm planning to right now—I don't want one of these buttondown Feds showing up, asking me to take on some kind of undercover-type assignment. Pass on letters. Waste somebody. I'm telling you right now I just won't do it. I don't want any part of that sort of thing.'

'Zero problemo,' Penny said.

'Looks like fun on film,' Jeff said. '*Spy Who Came In From the Cold* or whatever. But I'll bet it's no fun in real life. No, sir.'

'Just keep your nose clean,' said Penny.

'I always do.'

Penny thought of all the things you could do with a nose. Many of them involved getting it dirty. Like smelling other people's griefs. Like snuffing out truth from a mess of lies. A dirty nose was an occupational hazard in her line of business. Twenty-six, nearly twenty-seven, suddenly seemed infinitely older than this kid with his clean nose would ever be.

It looked as though Steve Littel, back there in Roanoke, had played it with Jeff the same way he'd played it with the liquor-loving Forrester. Close to the chest. What it boiled down to was that Jeff knew damn all about almost everything. Or did it?

Behind her, the doors leading out from the house to the patio slid open with a squeak of aluminum runners on aluminum track. Jeff stared. Penny turned round. She stared too. Lucia Formaggio in a white bikini would have made Homer stare. Whoever had designed the top half of it could have made a fortune in the packaging industry. Like many women of Mediterranean extraction, Lucia had more pubic hair than could be comfortably contained inside a bikini bottom. She wasn't worried about it.

'Penelope,' she said. 'I didn't expect to see you here again.'

'Long way to come for a swim,' Penny said.

'I was passing by—'

'My ass, you were.'

'—and suddenly thought how nice it would be to have a dip,' said Lucia. 'I let myself in and changed in one of the spare bedrooms.'

She adjusted the bottom half of her bikini. No question, she was in good shape. There was a gold slave chain round her waist and several more round her neck. The studs in her ears didn't look like glass. Poolside jewelry for the woman who had everything. Especially a dead husband with bucks.

'Oh please,' Penny said. 'Make yourself at home.'

'I must say, Penelope, that you seem to have left the house in something of a mess.'

'You know me. Miss Pigpen.'

Lucia walked past in a sniff of something expensive and dropped her big tapestry bag on to a chair. She smiled and dived neatly into the pool.

'Wow,' said Jeff.

253

'That's the Lucia Formaggio on your list,' Penny said, 'driving a red sports car. Or maybe a blue Fiat.'

'Oh, right,' said Jeff. 'It's the red sports. I saw her pull up outside the gates just before I came down here.' He put down his coffee cup. 'Guess I'd better get back up the hill. This isn't what Mr Littel is paying me for.'

'How long is the surveillance going on for?' Penny asked.

He shrugged. 'Until I'm pulled off the job.' His eyes followed Lucia up and down the pool. The high white heat of noon leaned on the landscape like a fire-blanket smothering sound.

'Nice chance to work on your tan,' Penny said.

'I got all the tan I want,' said Jeff. He examined the blond hairs on his arm.

'Better keep yourself oiled up,' said Penny. 'It gets really hot here.'

'Sun doesn't bother me,' Jeff said.

'Still. You should take care. Lavette looked like a charbroiled steak, last time I saw him.'

Jeff laughed. 'I've got a hide like an elephant.' He eased his behind against the slung canvas of his chair.

'Okay.'

Penny shrugged. She was thinking of other matters. For instance, the way Lucia had barely glanced at Jeff. Normally he'd have been the sort of thing to Lucia that flies are to wanton boys. For another, if Jeff had seen her car arriving before he came down to drink coffee, she'd been inside the house a lot longer than it took to shuck off a dress and shimmy into a bikini. Was that because she'd combined it with something else? Such as whipping through Bruno's papers to find whatever it was Penny had prevented her from finding last time? The weirdest thing of all was that she had smiled. Smiling did terrible things to your skin. It rucked it up. It wrinkled it. Lucia *never* smiled.

Penny looked up at the screened windows of the house, blank as a new diary, reflecting nothing, giving nothing away. Like just about everyone she'd come into contact with over the past week.

Like Lucia's bag. There was a leather wallet in it. A bottle of Joy. A gold fountain pen. Cosmetics. Keys. They rattled around in the bottom of the bag. They were all that was in it. No files taken from Bruno's study. No papers of any kind. Damn.

She put it back on the chair. Gave Jeff another CIA-type wink. Went away and made another tisane. It didn't taste any better than the first. When she came back, Lucia was climbing out of the pool. She wrapped herself in a big white towel. She shook her head about, at the same time twisting a finger round in one ear.

'So, Penelope,' she said, 'are you any nearer to finding Bruno?'

With a woman like Lucia, it didn't pay to give her a handle. And an admission of failure was quite a handle.

'Sure,' Penny said. 'I've just about worked the whole thing out now.'

'And the statuettes too?'

'Of course.'

'You have *found* them?' Lucia's prominent eyes were as round and hard as chestnuts.

'Let's say I have a good idea where they are,' lied Penny.

'You've found the Royal Family?' Jeff said. His eyes shone. 'Hey, that's great.'

'It is very good,' agreed Lucia. She took in Bruno's shirt, Penny's long legs, her own bag on the chair. 'It is excellent.' She leaned back and spread her arms behind her head. Looked casual. 'We must do all we can to shield him from the inevitable scandal. The family will support Bruno, of course. We might even be able to turn it to our advantage.' She hardly seemed to be talking to Penny.

'There you go again,' said Penny. 'Talking that family stuff.'

'You are a very cynical young woman, Penelope,' Lucia said. 'Naturally, since Bruno is my cousin, since we have even thought of marriage—'

'It was a fairly unilateral thought, wasn't it?'

'—I am concerned about him. Whatever he has done, it is up to us to minimise the danger to his career and reputation. And I, of course, will do anything, anything in the world to help.'

Lucia Formaggio as the Mother Teresa of the building trade took some getting used to. Cynical or not, Penny didn't think she was going to make it.

'Even if he did steal the gold things, he's not exactly going to end up in the condemned cell,' she said.

'I guess it would be kinda naive to ask you where the figurines are,' Jeff said, eager as Candide.

It really hurt to slap him down. ''Fraid it would,' Penny said. Besides, even if he asked, she couldn't answer.

Lucia was staring at the pool. She bit her lip. 'I'm older than you, Penelope,' she said. 'I know how seldom people get things right in their lives. Bruno has been done a wrong, a terrible wrong, and I should like to see it set right.'

'What kind of wrong?'

'If—*when* he comes back to us, you can tell him he will have my support.'

'Support? What're you—'

'I want you to know, Penelope, that I am intending to

marry again.' She flapped her left hand about so Penny could see the huge diamond on it.

'That's marvellous, Lucia. Who?'

'The gentleman you saw me with yesterday, at the Ristorante Reale.'

The bald-headed geek? It wasn't possible. Before she could ask any further questions, Lucia had gathered her things together, was walking back to the house, was gone. So was Jeff. He stood. He thanked her for the coffee. He went. Penny watched him push up through the olives and into the pines. Watched him settle himself with his back against the little wall. In his khaki shorts and T-shirt, he was nearly invisible up there.

Hmmm.

Food for thought.

Thought was in danger of being overfed that morning.

26

THE WATCHMAN'S STUBBLE HAD GROWN. OTHERWISE, Toscana al Vesuvio might have been trapped in amber since Penny's last visit. The sun was hanging low enough in the sky for every grassblade to have its own long shadow. The day's heat, fringed with the smell of sulphur, lingered close to walls, as though a narrow door to a kitchen in hell had been left open. Nothing moved.

The watchman was asleep with his feet up on the milk crate. They twitched a little each time he breathed in. Beyond him spread the site. From here, it was clear that, twelve years after its discovery, the greater part of it was still untouched, little more than some acres of grass hummocks studded with marker pegs. Days of heat had dried out the mud, leaving fissured potholes here and there. The guards in combat jackets were nowhere to be seen. Only the cicadas made any noise, hemstitching the hot silence from coarse clumps of grass.

There were three other cars in the car park. One was Meg's. Penny didn't recognize the others. She scrambled up a bank to the rudimentary road which ran around the site at present-day level. Cypresses speared the air between

Toscana and the volcano humped on the horizon. She looked down on a small clearance of narrow streets running deep between resurrected buildings, regular as a noughts-and-crosses grid. Some had four-squared orange roofs quartered in on hidden atria. The rest were empty to the sky. A ruined temple lay half hidden by buddleia, only the bases of its columns left. On the edge of town, an elliptical outline of cleared ground showed where the circus had once been.

On the far side of the site, a figure moved against the weed-covered slope of excavated soil. A generous figure. A figure whose shirt was dark under the armpits, whose waist, when it came to calories, had long stopped counting. Antony Dunlap. She could see the sweat on his chins. He was watching something down among the excavated buildings, his head turning slowly on its thick neck. He could have been there for centuries.

The corner of her eye caught a movement, no more than a flicker of something behind a colonnade holding up the remains of a pantiled roof. A bird? A swinging branch? Then Meg Tarrance came into view, walking slowly along a rutted street between raised pavements. Her head was bent. She carried a yellow plastic bucket.

Dunlap shouted to her. The sound lay on top of the heat for an infinitesimal fraction of time, then sank into the gulley between the houses where the black shadows slanted. Meg shuddered with the unexpectedness of hearing a human voice when she had thought herself alone. She looked quickly from side to side, as though expecting an S & D unit to leap from the silent doorways around her. Then she saw Dunlap, hieratic against the sky.

For a moment she was absolutely still. Then she waved at him. Pointed at the bucket. Beckoned. Neither of them saw Penny watching from across the site. Dunlap climbed down into the street, sliding along piles of dry earth. His face glistened like a dolphin's. Penny watched them walk carefully towards each other over the big limestone blocks which formed the road surface. Dust lay along Meg's collarbones and on the rims of her eyes. She seemed very tired. And years older than last time Penny had seen her. Whatever colour the shirt she wore had once been was just a memory now. She had the tails tied under her non-existent breasts, showing a triangle of firm, tanned stomach.

'What are you doing down here?' Penny heard her say. 'I thought you'd finished until next season.'

'Same here. I thought you'd gone back to Cambridge.'

'I'm just waiting for Drusilla to come back from Rome, so I can say goodbye. Then I'm off.'

'I see,' Dunlap said.

They came to an intersection where a crooked street crossed theirs at an acute angle. Meg looked carefully up and down before carrying on. She jerked her head over her shoulder in the direction she'd come from.

'We'll have to close all that off,' she said. 'A whole new lot of cracks.'

'More tremors?'

'It's bloody sickening,' Meg said. 'Some of them medium to severe.' She pointed to a fissure in the earth that ran out from under the foundations of a house. It followed the street for a few yards, skirting the limestone blocks, then slid beneath a blocked-up doorway. 'Do you realize that's more than half the bloody dig out of action?'

At her level, Penny saw the door of the museum open. Riordan came out in bermuda shorts of navy with a white seam stripe. He carried a bucket in his left hand and a long-handled spade in his right. He walked to the edge and looked down on the site. He probably couldn't see Meg from where he stood. The red-gold hair of his chest caught the deep yellow of the setting sun.

Meg and Dunlap walked through the black shadows. 'Some of the men working in the north-east corner found a horse this morning,' Meg said. 'And his rider. A soldier, we think, judging by the sword. Trying to control the panic, wouldn't you think?'

'More likely making a quick getaway,' said Dunlap. You knew that's what *he'd* have done. The hell with the women and children. He batted away a fly that had rejected a small pile of something nasty and decided to try its luck with a specialist in Russian literature.

'It must have been absolute chaos on the wharves,' said Meg, staring in the direction of the sea whose level she was below. 'What a terrible night.' They walked for a bit in silence. Then Meg said, 'We found some more coins this morning. Silver ones. And a silver mirror. Riordan's pleased.'

'Good,' Dunlap said. His tone was unpleasant. Taking off his glasses, he wiped his face with his arm.

'Don't be a bloody idiot, Tony,' Meg said. 'If he pulls his support out of this project we might as well forget it for years. I had a letter from the Ministry of Public Works people yesterday saying that they'll be cutting next season's grant by almost half, in view of the trouble at Pompeii.'

'What trouble?'

'Tourists. They're going to have to spend a lot more on protective measures. If this site's to remain viable, we need Riordan, whatever you say.'

'It just seems ridiculous that we all have to jump when that charlatan says. Just because he's rich.'

'Charlatan?'

'What else would you call him?'

261

'An amateur, Tony. Like yourself.'

'When is an amateur not an amateur? When he gets published in one of the archaelogical journals,' said Dunlap.

They skirted a curious humped block of pumice. Watching, head tucked below the level of the bank above them, Penny found it impossible not to wonder if perhaps once it had been living. If it was opened up, might there not be inside the perfectly preserved form of a child or a pet, caught forever in dying? Sitting here under the evening sky, it was all too easy to imagine the horror as the mountain vomited fire, as the roofs buckled under the weight of ash and lava, as the heat sucked the breath out of their throats. In Pompeii, she'd seen holes torn in the side of a house by those trapped inside. Their fear had screamed across the centuries. Whether it was San Francisco in 1906, or Mexico City in 1985, it was difficult to comprehend natural disasters on such a scale. They said Krakatoa could be heard halfway round the world.

'One thing about stopping work on the site,' Dunlap said. 'I don't have to talk to Riordan.'

'You will if you stay around. He's been here for the last three days,' said Meg.

'Why?'

'I'm not quite sure.'

'He didn't say he was coming over from the States again, did he?'

'Not as far as I remember.'

'Hell,' said Dunlap. 'I'll get straight back to Rome in that case. When he flies into one of his rages, the best place to be is out.'

Almost directly beneath Penny, unseen by Meg and Dunlap, Riordan walked carefully along a raised stone pavement, heading for the no-go area. He was going bald

262

on top, too. Someone should tell him it was time to get a toupee. She watched him. She was still watching when someone suddenly appeared behind him. Alex. Everybody's favorite interior decorator. What was he doing here? They both turned a corner, Riordan seemingly unaware that he was being tailed. Penny climbed down and joined the other two.

'Found the bastard yet?' Meg said. She'd obviously never read the book on how to win friends.

'Still working on it,' Penny said. 'If you mean Bruno.'

'Who else?'

'If you want bastards, there seem to have been an awful lot of them in Toscana last week.'

'Did you take something from my office?' Dunlap said.

'If you mean the gun,' said Penny. 'You want it back, you're going to have to drag the river.'

'Gun?' Meg said. 'Who's got a gun?'

'I didn't mean the gun,' said Dunlap.

'Finders keepers,' Penny said.

Dunlap didn't answer. They skirted a line of broken marble columns lying directly beneath the balconies of buildings built at twentieth-century level. They passed square, unwindowed houses as featureless as petrol stations, most exterior decoration long gone. Weeds flourished along rooflines and in the angle of ruined walls. A tangle-haired satyr of stone leered from above a doorway. Directly above his head, television antennae trembled. The culture shock was terrible.

The three of them went into the museum. Flat, wooden-treaded stairs led up past rooms full of red or black figure pottery painstakingly reassembled. There were amphorae and pieces of marble statuary and a few priapic bronzes. Dunlap found the stairs heavy going. His buttocks rubbed together under the loose seat of his trousers like giant mill-stones.

Meg showed them the horse. It didn't look much like a horse. It didn't look much like anything except a pile of bones drying on a wiremesh screen. 'We wash the bones first,' she told Penny, taking another out of her bucket. It was full of them, standing on end like sticks of dark celery. At the bottom were two empty softdrink cans. Tourist litter. 'We let them dry for a couple of days then we dip them into a solution of acrylic plastic. That hardens them. Stops any further deterioration. After that, we can begin to recon-struct them. Fascinating, isn't it?'

'Awesome.'

Meg showed her the long horse skull, the jawbones still stretched so wide you could almost hear the shriek of its death agony. Reluctantly she put it down. 'I'd better show you Bruno's things,' she said.

They went up another flight of stairs and Meg opened a blond-wood door with a key. A small, white room over-looking the site held shelves of box-files and a metal desk. On it was a hard-spined book with red corners. On a white label in the middle was the number IV. Outside, the shadows had almost obliterated Toscana Antiqua.

'Where did you find that?' Dunlap asked.

'I found it behind Bruno's filing cabinet,' said Meg. 'I had to move it when one of my papers slid underneath, and there was the book.'

'Gee whiz,' Penny said. 'Might have stayed hidden for years.' She looked at Dunlap.

'Not that there's anything in it,' Meg said. 'Someone seems to have torn the first few pages out.'

Penny picked up the book. 'I wonder who that could have been,' she said.

264

'Of course, I haven't the least idea what he'd written,' Meg said.

'I do,' said Penny.

She opened her bag. She took out several sheets of badly typed A4 paper and unfolded them. She made the most of it. A person didn't often get a chance to stand in for Nemesis. She cleared her throat and began to read aloud.

After the first three sentences, Dunlap started talking.

'You don't know what it's like,' he said. 'All the months I've spent slaving away in temperatures like a furnace, brushing earth away with a camel-hair brush for days on end. I don't mind the backbreaking effort and the discomfort. I don't mind the sand up my nose and the lousy food and the dust clogging my throat. But nobody ever takes you seriously. I've given years and years of my life, but to sneering know-alls like Bruno Ferlinghetti, I'm still just an amateur. If you don't lick their boots, you might just as well not exist. As for any chance of being trusted with anything important, fat fucking chance.'

'Yeah, we know. Life's a bitch,' Penny said.

'What the hell is the matter with you, Tony?' said Meg.

'I've got feelings,' Dunlap said.

'If you have tears, prepare to shed them now,' said Penny.

'For God's sake pull yourself together, man,' Meg said briskly.

Dunlap stared at her. His eyes were hurt and hating. '*Et tu, Brute*,' he said, in a voice that quivered. He walked out.

Pure carbolic soap opera. It only needed the opening titles.

'What was he talking about?' asked Meg.

'The day everyone left, who discovered Bruno wasn't here?' Penny said.

'Dunlap, as far as I remember. He told us he'd looked everywhere and Bruno wasn't around. Since Riordan had a plane to catch, we couldn't spend any more time looking.'

It figured. Dunlap panting into the office. Bruno gone. The log-book on the desk, open perhaps. Dunlap seizing the opportunist moment, tearing out the pages, and, since he could hardly walk out with Bruno's log-book, dropping it behind the filing cabinet. If anything had happened to Bruno, he had a chance at last, a passport to archaeological recognition. Or at least a visa. If Bruno reappeared, nothing was lost. Bruno was known to be absent-minded. He would probably think he'd torn out the pages himself.

Pathetic, really.

Alone with Meg, she didn't say anything about Dunlap. Instead, she told her about Drusilla's death. Meg listened, her face tightening. She brushed at some of the dirt on her arms, then knuckled the side of her forehead. 'I knew she was playing some kind of dangerous game,' she said. Her voice was husky with emotion. 'I told her she'd end up in a mortuary somewhere, and now she has. Do you know who's responsible?'

'I'm not sure. She'd been stealing things and selling them to the syndicate, hadn't she?'

'Yes. None of them very valuable. That's why I locked up the Royal Pair when I found them. I bailed her out once before, but I wasn't going to risk them going too. Especially not after I'd seen her talking to a couple of obvious crooks who'd been hanging round.'

Penny pulled out the morning's newspaper folded to the photograph of Bernini. 'Was this one of them?' she said.

'No.'

'Have you seen him before?'

'Who hasn't? Men like that are manipulators. Exploiters. They get to the top by treading on other people's balls. Especially women's.'

'Like the Press sisters.'

'They're corruptors, all of them. Degraders. I saw Drusilla with him last—last month. He'd changed her beyond all recognition. Turned her into a high-class bloody whore. She seemed quite besotted with him. Do you think he was the one . . . it was him who . . . who killed her?'

'I don't know,' said Penny.

Stumbling a little, Meg made for an upright chair against the wall. She sat. The frown-lines on her forehead came and went and came again. 'I don't know . . . what I'm . . . bloody well going to do without her,' she said. She held her hands to her face and closed her eyes. She pushed her fingers through her hair, leaving four runnels. The hair was blonde right the way through.

'There's something else you ought to know,' Penny said. She turned over the pages of the newspaper. 'Look.'

Meg did.

Her face grew very red. 'Oh, my God,' she said. 'The bastard.'

27

DOWN BELOW THEY HEARD VOICES. THEN FEET, RUN-
ning up the wooden treads of the stairs. Two pairs of them.
Giulia hurried into the room. She wore a hot pink silk
shirt. Her pleated linen trousers were pink, too, in a shade
dissimilar enough to make your eyes feel the way your
mouth did when you sucked a lime.

'I got your message, Penny,' she said. She looked over
her shoulder. 'Have you found him?'

'No, but I know where he is.'

Penny put the newspaper back in her bag. Beside her,
the brightness of Meg's blue eyes seemed to have dimmed.
Her shoulders slumped.

'Where?' Giulia said.

Oscare puffed into the room after her. 'I shall never let
you drive me anywhere again, Giulia,' he said. 'I have
aged thirty years.'

'I'm sorry, Oscare, but we had to get here as quickly as
possible,' Giulia said.

Outside, it was dark enough for the big window over-
looking the site to act as a mirror. The four of them were

reflected in the blackness, and, beyond it, close to the horizon, was the last white sky of the day.

'You know where Bruno is?' Meg said.

'I don't know exactly,' said Penny. 'Not *exactly*.'

'I do.' Reilly Riordan stepped into the room. One hundred and seventy-five pounds of aggression, aching for action. With him came a gun, stunted, black-metalled, vicious as a kick in the teeth. He pointed it at no one in particular, threatening them all. Nobody doubted for an instant that he was prepared to use it, whether or not it was necessary. All of them moved slowly away from him, fanning toward the walls. His navy shorts were dirty. He was bare-chested, the hairs of his torso lightly powdered with dust. Half-naked, he seemed to take up three-quarters of the available space. He smelled of sweat.

Penny was suddenly very afraid. There was a lot of white in Riordan's eyes. If they weren't all mighty careful, this scene could end with the curtain coming down on what the hospitals called a negative patient care outcome. Death, in other words. Anyone started firing in a room that small, if the bullets didn't get you then the ricochets would.

'Hey, that's great, Mr. Riordan,' she said.

'You wanna know where, huh?' Riordan said. Back home in Virginia, he hadn't been heavily into suave. Now he'd abandoned all hope in favour of some Dirty Harry based bad-guy image that was about as reassuring as a drunk plastic surgeon.

'I do,' said Giulia, 'very much.'

'What the hell are you playing at, Riordan?' Frowning at the gun, Meg wiped her hands on the sides of her shorts.

'Can it, bitch,' Riordan said. He looked harder at Giulia. 'You wouldn't be the little lady ol' Bruno's got the hots for, would you?'

'Guess you mean Sandy Leon,' Penny said quickly.

269

'Think I'm stupid or something?' asked Riordan. 'I already figured Sandy Leon.' Penny was sorry about that. She had too. 'No, I reckon this little girl might just be the key I been looking for. What's your name, honey?' He suddenly jabbed the gun into the soft part of Giulia's shoulder, below the muscle.

'She is my wife,' Oscare said. 'Signora Giulia Torella. How dare you speak to—'

'Giulia,' said Riordan. 'That's the name. I've heard Bruno sounding off about you.' He came up close to her. Without warning, he slammed his left fist into Giulia's stomach. The top half of her body bent forwards as she staggered back against the wall. Tears formed in her disbelieving eyes and moved slowly down her cheeks as she breathed in fast through her mouth.

No one in the room had ever seen a man hit a woman. Intellectually, they knew it happened. They'd read about it. To see it stunned them. For a moment none of them moved. Then Oscare surged forward.

"Bastardo!" he screamed. He stepped in front of Giulia, his arms waving. 'Keep your hands off my wife. American pig.'

Afterwards, Penny was never able to decide whether Riordan really had aimed his gun at Giulia, or Oscare merely thought he had. He raised his arm, the gun on the end of it, and Oscare jumped towards it. Riordan was surprised. He took a step backwards. His finger moved on the trigger. As the sound of the bullet exploded from the muzzle, Oscare was already crumpling. The force of the slug shoved him back, arms still raised in a gesture of surrender it was far too late for. Slowly he fell down the wall to sit crookedly on the floor. He leaned his head against his wife's knees.

She stared at Riordan. They all did. 'Oscare!' she said,

looking down at him. 'Oscare.' She knelt suddenly and put her arm around him.

Oscare turned to her. There was blood in his mouth. Behind it, he made a noise. Some of it spilled out, falling down his chin and on to his shirt, bright red and dangerous. It was obvious that something vital had been hit.

Giulia touched him. Her face was full of mourning, both for the past wasted years and for the present dying moment. 'Oh, Oscare,' she said. 'I'm sorry.'

He tried to lift his hand to hers but he didn't make it. It fell back on to his thigh. 'My own fault,' he said. 'I shouldn't have . . .' He turned into her shoulder.

'Jesus,' Meg whispered. 'Have you gone mad, Reilly?'

It wasn't the kind of question a sensible person expected an affirmative answer to.

'He probably always was,' Penny said. Perhaps anybody with a true obsession was. She looked away, not so much to avoid Oscare's face as not to see Giulia's. It was one of those situations, when you saw it on the television your heart didn't skip a single beat. Now it was for real, your heart skipped so many of them you thought it was on strike.

Riordan had grabbed Giulia by the shirt and was dragging her upwards. The movement straightened Oscare so he sat upright against the wall, his head hanging on his chest. Riordan lifted Giulia to her feet, his fist under her chin, forcing it up towards the ceiling.

'Okay, Signora Giulia Torella,' he said. It was clear he hadn't majored in language. 'Let's go.'

Giulia didn't hear. She was straining to look over her shoulder. 'Oscare,' she said. Her beautiful, husky voice was unsteady. You might not like your husband much, but it didn't mean you wanted some kook to come along and kill him.

271

'Uh, if it's not a rude question,' Penny said, swallowing what she could to get her throat working again, 'where are you taking her?'

'To see how long Ferlinghetti can stand watching his girl-friend knocked about without telling me where the figurines are hid.'

'There's something you ought to know,' Penny said.

'Look. I already know plenty. I know I spent almost a year setting up this operation,' said Riordan. 'I know I paid through the nose for those figurines and I still don't have them. I know that if Meg hadn't been stupid enough to give Bruno the keys to the safe, they'd be home with me in Virginia by now.' He turned the gun suddenly towards Meg. 'Didn't I tell you not to let anyone have the key?' he said. Meg didn't answer. She was too busy staring death in the eye. The room smelled of something sharp and dangerous.

'Didn't I?' Riordan screamed. 'Didn't I tell you, huh?'

'Yes,' Meg said. 'Yes, you did.'

Riordan jerked Giulia so she stumbled forwards. Her shirt was stained. Blood red and hot pink, the new fashion colours. 'Come on, honey, let's go see how long Bruno can hold out.'

Penny said, 'I know where those figurines are.'

'You do?'

'You quit waving that piece about, let go of Giulia, I'll show you.'

Riordan lowered his arm until the gun lay along his thigh. Penny opened her bag, holding it out so he could see that she wasn't about to produce a sub-machine gun and blow him away. She took out the newspaper, opened it, showed it to him.

For a moment, he stared at the picture of Father Vicente

de Paolo. He mouthed the first couple of words of the caption. 'What's it say?' he asked. Penny told him.

His chest began to flush. So did his face. If rage was a marketable commodity, you could have made a fortune out of him. 'Okay,' he said. 'If that's the way Ferlinghetti wants to play it, I'll go along. He takes my stuff, I'll take his.'

Behind him, Oscare suddenly fell to one side. His head hit the shiny composition floor with a bump. The movement forced a liquid burp from his throat. If he'd still been alive, he was now dead. There's no mistaking a body with the life gone from it or that terrifying apartness no faith nor love nor hope will ever gulf. Blood moved sluggishly out of his mouth. Oscare's demons, whatever they were, had finally caught up with him. Hysteria caught up with Giulia. She started screaming.

'Stop that,' Riordan said. His eyes were screwed up so small they had almost vanished.

She didn't. The noise, in that small room, was astonishing.

'Stop it,' yelled Riordan. He lifted his gun and aimed it straight at her face.

Helpless, Penny watched his finger tighten and the hammer lift. Then Riordan fell forwards on to one knee. The front of his chest opened like one of those paper umbrellas they stick into cute drinks in cute cocktail bars. Half turning, to see what had hit him, he pitched sideways. His gun reached the floor before he did.

Alex came in from the unlit passage outside. He was in baggy cotton trousers and a T-shirt with a rainbow on it. His bare arms were a living advertisement for Nautilus sports equipment.

'Hi,' Penny said.

He smiled.

Meg was staring. 'Who is that?' she said. 'I've seen him somewhere before.'

'Don't you love the trousers?' said Penny. 'Meet Alex. Or should I call you Sandy?'

'You can call me anytime you like,' Alex said.

'Sandy?' said Meg.

Penny walked over and put her arms around Giulia, who was sobbing, her face in her hands.

'Sandy *Leon*?' Meg said.

'Absolutely.' Alex pitched his voice high, moved his vowels about a little. Listening, you'd have sworn a woman had spoken. 'You might not believe it but I do a sizzling drag routine, working the local cabaret circuit. Ostrich plumes, garter belts, the works.'

'But why? What was the point in taking us all in like that?'

'Protection,' Penny said. 'Right?'

'Right,' said Alex. 'When Dr Ferlinghetti started getting threatening phone calls, he thought of us. Safe and Sound. He didn't trust any of the agencies here. Said there was too much networking between them and the Mob. Then, when he saw Dr Tarrance's find and realised what they were, we called Steve and had him send over a couple of extra guys. He didn't know who was responsible but he thought he might find out if he set a watch on his place and his mother's.'

So Bruno had hired Lavette and Jeff Hurtz. It was obvious when you thought about it.

'He's a smart guy,' she said.

'How did he know those figurines I found had been planted?' Meg said. 'God, I feel such a fool.'

'He's been making retreats up at the monastery for years,' Penny said. 'Naturally he'd have recognized part of the treasure. If he hadn't organised that expedition up there last summer, none of this would have happened. But once Riordan had seen the figurines, he decided, come hell or high water, he was going to have them.'

Something touched her feet. She looked down. Riordan had hooked one of his fingers over the edge of her shoe. His no-colour eyes were full of puzzlement and a pain that was much more than physical. She squatted beside him.

'Smart idea, Rile,' she said gently. 'Get someone to heist the figs, then bury them in the boat-chambers and make sure Meg discovered them. You knew she was so paranoid at losing anything that she'd keep them locked up tighter than the Crown Jewels. It was odds on that she wouldn't recognise the figurines as belonging to the monks. They weren't normally on show, and she hadn't been one of the sightseeing party last year. If she'd only obeyed you, if she'd resisted the impulse to show them off to Bruno, you'd have been fine. When you were ready, they'd have been stolen from the safe and you'd have taken them back to the States in one of those specially prepared flight bags of yours, right?'

He managed the smallest of nods.

'And I'd have been left to face the music again,' Meg said loudly. 'That would have been the end of my professional career. Do you realise that?'

'He realised,' Penny said. 'He was counting on it.'

'Bastard,' Meg said. Her voice shook. She went over and stood beside Giulia.

'Where've you been keeping Bruno, Reilly?' Penny said. 'The boat-chambers? One of the houses?'

This time Riordan shook his head. Did he mean no? Or did he mean he wasn't telling? Whichever, by the time the shake was finished, he was dead.

'Did he kill Drusilla?' Meg said.

'Like you said, she's been playing dangerous games,' Penny said. 'Someone else killed her.'

Fazal, the fanatically nationalistic newspaper proprietor, roaming the Western world in search of Egypt's plundered past? Or Bernini, not realising it was too late to stop the newspapers coming after him? Or one of the men of honour?

'I'll go and call the police,' Meg said. 'Jesus Christ. Look at this place.'

It wasn't an invitation that got a lot of takers. Blood and brains and dead guys all over. No thanks. Penny had better things to do.

'Bruno,' said Giulia. 'We must find him.' She stood up, stepping across Oscare's body, not looking at it.

'Yes,' Penny said. 'We must.'

28

WAS THIS THE HOUSE RIORDAN HAD STASHED BRUNO in? It was the only one where the iron sheeting was loose. Not very, but enough for someone to squeeze through if they really wanted to. Which she didn't. But if Bruno was down there, she had to locate him. She was mad with herself. Coming down here without a flashlight was the kind of dumb-fool thing only heroines in horror movies went in for.

Toscana was dark and still. Occasionally a sighing noise moved through the air, as deep as the heartbeat of the universe. Sometimes there were rat-like scurryings across the broken roofs and, after them, the small noise of loose soil trickling. She couldn't hear the others. Meg had gone to the boat-chambers. Alex was staying close to Giulia, searching the area nearer to the museum. She wished she could.

Rumble.

For several seconds the ground shook. The tremor vibrated up through her ankles and centred on her knees. Something somewhere close by crashed to the ground. She felt dust in her throat. Jeez. Suppose the ground ahead had split open, like a ripe tomato. Or the ground behind? Would she be able to get across the gap? She saw herself swallowed up, falling headlong into the red core of the earth. Down, down into hell. She pushed out a foot. The ground was still solid under it. She stretched the other forwards.

'Bruno,' she shouted, hoping.

There was no answer.

She pulled at the sheeting. Behind her, something shifted. She tensed. There was silence again. And another of the deep, long-drawn sighs.

'Bruno?'

Nothing.

Except a scraping noise.

She whipped round. Someone was following her. Someone was definitely following her, filling the air with hating, angry thoughts that pulsed across the divide of darkness between them. Who? Dunlap, riled and vengeful? Fazal, still hoping she'd lead him to the gold he felt rightfully belonged to Egypt? What about Lucia Formaggio or Bernini? Maybe one of them felt they had a beef with her. If it came right down to it, what about Henry Kissinger? Or Brooke Shields? Why should anyone be after her? The figurines were back where they came from. End of story.

Except someone obviously wanted to write an epilogue.

'If that's you, Dunlap,' she said into the darkness, 'this place isn't big enough for both of us.'

If it was Dunlap, he wasn't fool enough to answer. She remembered how fast he could move. He could be on her before she had time to think positive, let alone of how to get away.

'Mr Fazal?' she said.

She hadn't anything against the guy. As a matter of fact she had a sneaking sympathy for what he was trying to do.

When you thought about the colossal nerve, the arrogance with which earlier archaeologists and tomb-hunters assumed they had the right to cart away as much of someone else's history as they liked. Fazal was only trying to set things right.

Movement stirred the air. She smelled decay. Damp. Something faintly clinical. She heard the sound of a softly-taken breath. The movement of clothes, fabric rubbing against fabric. Something hit the corrugated sheeting beside her. Sharp and sudden, it sounded like a stone. She knew it wasn't. Throwing herself to one side, she heard another ping, and the small thunder of vibrating corrugated iron. Someone was firing at her from the opposite building. She looked up. Across the street, leaves waved gently against the sky. Between the remains of second-floor walls was the shape of a head. There was a flash and a sound like a cork being pulled from a bottle. By then, she had scuttled across the road in a Quasimodo crouch. She squatted up against the foot of the house from which the shots had come. Her heart was jumping at the back of her throat.

A demented cicada started up. She heard a shoe drag across the crumbling brickwork above her head. A dislodged stone dropped into the roadway. She breathed in through her mouth, listening. What exactly was going on? Okay, so she'd never publicly called for an end to prostitution, never came out strong against spiritous liquors. Never claimed to be Snow White. Just because she didn't see why men had all the fun, was that a reason to put a bullet through her heart?

The answer had to be no. Therefore there had to be another reason why some maniac was stalking her, trying to get off a shot that would put her permanently out of action.

She forced herself to think. The figurines had been returned to the monks. That particular wrong had been righted. But there were other sins. And other sinners. Which one of them might want her dead? Think.

It couldn't be Dunlap. He'd come back to Toscana hoping to trash the last piece of evidence to show he'd lifted Bruno's notes, only to find out it was too late. Supersleuth Wanawake was wise to him. For him, the game was over. He'd have to find another way to wow the archaeological world. Wonderful human being he might not be, and anyone who carried a gun was no Mr Clean, but he had sense enough to see that there'd be no point offing her. Besides, fast mover or not, nobody his size was going to horse around on the top of derelict walls. Not if they wanted to live.

She thought of Meg. Meg had understood what had been done to her as soon as she saw the newspaper photograph. Father Vicente de Paolo beaming, the figurines on his outheld palms, behind him the mountains and the high-perched monastery. She'd seen at once that her figurines were gone, and with them, her chance of further funding. She was back to square one. So not Meg.

Fazal? He had a quarrel but it wasn't with her.

Who, then? Lucia? There was no earthly reason why Lucia would risk her precious skin to stumble about Toscana in the dark. Maybe she'd been trying to help Oscare in some way, but again, with the figurines returned to their keepers, she could retire gracefully.

Reluctantly she thought of Giulia. All over the world there were women who wanted to offload their husbands, but even for Catholics there had to be easier ways than murder. Was this whole thing an elaborate set-up? She considered it. She told herself to get a grip. Giulia couldn't have known that Riordan would shoot Oscare. Nor assumed that Oscare would defend her to the death. Or could she? All along, Giulia had called the shots. Giulia had got her into this in the first place. Giulia had come haring over to Rome when Penny appeared to be on the track of something. Giulia had insisted on that pointless trip to the States to see Riordan. If Alex hadn't come in when he did, would Riordan really have fired at Giulia, or was it just window-dressing? Even if it was, why come after Penny?

What had she seen or heard that made her a danger to someone still?

Damned if she knew.

Whoever was on the wall above her jumped down on the other side. Only a thickness of brick separated them. Her throat was dry but not with dust. She heard the scrape of a body. The chink of metal. Very slowly she stood up, spreading her arms along the walls on either side to keep her balance as she pressed in close. Ten yards away was a crossway. If she ran for the corner. . .

Bernini? Long ago he'd cast his bread upon the waters, never expecting to see it again, and lo, it had come back to him poisoned. His career was a wash. His private life would be spicing up breakfasts for months to come. But that wasn't any reason for him to be stalking Penny Wanawake. Or was it? If he'd murdered Drusilla, perhaps she herself held some vital clue that could put him behind bars. She tried to think what vital clue she held. Couldn't.

It kept coming back to Drusilla. All things to all men. At Toscana, drab as a week-old sandwich. Kingfisher-bright in Rome. What would you feel, expecting the first and seeing the second? Meg must have had quite a shock, seeing the metamorphosis, realising to what extent she'd been used, just how much of a fool Drusilla had made of her. It must have been a killer.

Penny took off for the corner. Every micro-second before she reached it was choked with imagined pain, with splintered bone and gushing blood. With death.

She made it.

Meg. It had to be Meg. Meg had laid her professional reputation on the line for Drusilla last summer. She was emotionally hooked to the girl. After seeing her with Bernini, she must have followed the girl home and, out of jealousy and betrayed love, killed her. Easy enough, afterwards, to link the death with Bruno. She knew his car was outside his flat. She only had to dump it at the airport, with Drusilla's body inside, and take a bus back to Rome. Maybe even tip the police off. That deep voice of hers could easily be a man's.

And she, Penelope Wanawake, was the only one who knew where Meg had been yesterday evening. She'd started to say last night, and changed it to last month. She must have known Penny would recall that slip of the tongue and realise what it meant. But with Penny gone, why should anyone suspect Meg of murder?

Penny stayed close to the corner. She was trembling. Darn it. She might as well *be* a heroine in a horror movie. She stared at the angle of the wall. Whichever came round it first, the gun or Meg, she'd be on to it like a handcuff. She kept staring at the corner. Pinpricks of light danced in front of her eyes. The strain of listening was making her ears ring.

Something scraped along the wall. The gun. There was a small cracking noise as a loose stone turned. Where would Meg get a gun from? The soft pad of a shoe sole on dirt. Her shoulder muscles ached with the strain of hanging in there. Her lungs needed filling. Only millimetres away was a killer. Was the Holy Family really worth all this? The Royal Pair. Whatever.

The barrel of the shotgun slid out from the end of the wall. Thank God no one had yet invented a gun that could shoot round corners. She grabbed it, pushing it down and at the same time whipping every inch of her six feet forwards and sideways into the person who held it. There was a puff of long-held air knocked out of rigid lungs. A thud as a body hit the ground. A grunt as she fell on top of it, jamming the gun hard across its throat. If this was what people meant when they talked of having their bones jumped, she hoped no one ever did it to her. Even the one doing the jumping got hurt. She pressed down, feeling cartilegal resistance. Hands scrabbled at her hands. The body beneath her bucked and heaved. She went with it like a rodeo star. Ride 'im, cowboy. At the same time she leaned on the gun barrel. She hoped it hurt. She *knew* it hurt. She thought of Jack Lavette. And Drusilla. In the distance, she heard voices calling.

Something smashed into either side of her face. Probably no more than two halves of a Roman brick, but it felt like most of a Roman wall. Jesus, that hurt. She drew breath in sharply through her teeth. If there was one thing she hated, it was pain. Too bad. She got a whole lot more. The two bricks crashed together like cymbals with her head between them. She could hear bloodvessels breaking. Skulls fracturing. There was blood in her ears. Things flashed in front of her eyes. She knew they weren't falling stars.

She was losing the strength to keep the gun pressed down. Under her, the body twisted madly, trying to wrest itself free. Ugly words in combinations she'd never even dreamed of hissed into her face.

'Hey, man,' she said. 'Knew you were in language

school. Didn't realise what kind of language they were teaching you.'

There was a worse pain, crashing down on top of her head. Her eyes closed. She forced them open. Then somebody stopped the world, and she got off.

29

'IT'S A MISTAKE TO THINK THAT ACTIONS TAKING PLACE subsequent to a particular event are in fact generated by that event,' Bruno said. He smiled round at them byronically, beginning with Giulia. Ending with her too. One of his arms was around her shoulders, keeping her close. Safely back at the Villa Ferlinghetti, he'd been smiling a lot over the past few hours. In one hand, he held a glass of something greenish made out of leaves freshly plucked from his herb garden. Coltsfoot, it might have been. Or lungwort.

Penny was drinking wine. Faster than she ought, considering the heat. But at the back of her throat she could still taste Toscana-flavoured dust. Beside her, the pool scintillated like a vast diamond.

'Like Lucia,' she said.

Bruno nodded. The shadows on his face were green-tinted in the light filtering through the vine leaves.

'Who didn't give a damn about any statues, only about the love letters she sent you,' Penny said.

'Lucia has some very strange ideas,' said Bruno.

'Like thinking that you'd use those letters against her if the opportunity ever arose.'

'As if he would,' said Giulia.

'Lucia would,' said Penny. 'Naturally she assumed Bruno had dropped out of the same mould. When she heard he'd disappeared, it seemed a good opportunity to get them back. She was terrified he'd show up dead and his files—including those love letters—would be made public. And with her new husband some kind of politico, she decided she'd have to get them back. I *knew* that tapestry bag wasn't really her style.'

'I had a love letter once,' Kimbell said.

'It wasn't from me,' said Penny.

'That's why I remember it so vividly.'

'She drove down and took all Bruno's letter-files away before I got there,' Penny said. She noticed for the first time that the pool-side tiles were the same colour as the unshaded hills. 'Trouble started when she tried to put them back.'

'Every time she stops by, there's this foxy black lady laying around,' said Kimbell.

'Right. And when she saw Lavette watching the place, she got it into her head that he'd been hired by her future husband to check up on the family he was marrying into.'

'Lucia's *fidanzato* is a powerful man,' Bruno said.

'He the guy we saw in the restaurant?' Kimbell said. 'The old dude?'

'Love is blind,' said Penny.

'Bald too.'

'With Pietro Bernini gone, he will become an even more important man,' said Bruno. 'Lucia might have been justified in what she feared.'

'The whole family is paranoid,' said Giulia. 'Oscare always . . .' She stopped. Fiddling with the comb that kept her hair off her face gave her an excuse to remove her hand from Bruno's.

Oscare had died trying to save her. The wife who would never love him. The wife, it now turned out, he'd been cheating on before they even got to the altar. Stark in bereaved black, Lucia had sobbed it all out. How the letter from the American Consul in Kabul had arrived while Palma was visiting the States. How, happening to be checking the Ferlinghetti flat for her, Lucia had found it, and given it to Oscare. How Oscare had concealed from Giulia the fact that Bruno was alive.

Penny sighed. She twirled her glass on its stem, watching the light diffuse redly through. Red is the colour of my true love's blood. Oscare's still streaked the wall of Bruno's office in Toscana. She could see, with sad clarity, how Oscare would lean from the grave to cast a cold shadow over Bruno and Giulia.

'Why didn't the papers pick up the story about the statuettes being returned?' Kimbell asked Bruno. 'I mean, you got them back to the monastery only a few days after you first recognised them at Toscana.'

Around them, the hills blazed. The shale threw heat down on them. There were no shadows. No clouds. They could smell the pines.

'This is hard for me to say,' said Bruno, 'but the truth is, I was afraid. Not just of the Mafia. I was afraid that the dig at Toscana would close down if Meg was removed from her position. Perhaps I wasn't thinking very clearly, but it seemed obvious to me that she must be the one who had stolen the Holy Family of Montbella from the monastery and planted them at Toscana. It was only later that I realised how unlikely this was. But for this reason, I asked Father Vicente to keep quiet about the return of his figurines until I could decide what would be best.'

287

'So that Nefertiti act of your mother's was just a blind?' said Penny.

'Indeed. I hoped that if any of the gentlemen who had followed or threatened me should hear of the disappearance of the figurines and send someone to ransack my apartment, they would be confused by so many other Egyptian statuettes of a similar kind. My mother was very accommodating about it.'

'Besides, she was probably sick to death of cabbage roses,' Penny said.

'But you can imagine how surprised I was when I returned to Toscana,' Bruno said. 'Reilly Riordan refused to believe I had already returned the statuettes to the monks.' His tanned forehead showed his bewilderment. Penny wondered when he'd started to go grey. 'Why should he think I would lie to my friend?'

'Not everyone is as honest as you are, *caro*,' said Giulia. Guiltily she squeezed his hand and then put her own back on her lap.

'And then to point a gun at me,' said Bruno. 'To march me into the House of the Breadmaker—that is what Meg and I had provisionally called it—to march me there and throw me down into the cellars. I did not understand what was wrong with the man. I thought he must have gone mad.'

'Back in eighteen forty-nine they called it gold-fever,' said Penny.

'I was afraid I might be down there until I died,' Bruno said.

'I should have found you,' said Giulia. He looked at her and smiled. Giulia smiled back. For a moment you could tell they wouldn't have noticed an earthquake. Then Giulia stopped smiling. It's not something nice girls do when their husbands have just been murdered. Penny thought Giulia wasn't going to be able to forget that for quite a while.

'You were right about the boy,' Kimbell said.

'Some boy.'

'My friend Manzi had a look at the files. Back home, he had a record as long as your leg.'

Penny stretched one of hers out and looked at it. Added the other one. 'Pretty long,' she said.

'No wonder the girl's parents sent her over to school in Italy to get away from him. Turns out he only followed her because he couldn't think of anything better to do with himself last summer. Same reason he tagged along when your fat pal Dunlap took her down to Toscana to keep an eye on her for her pop.'

'This is all my fault,' Bruno said. 'I should not have taken so many people to the monastery.'

'I wish you could have called,' Giulia said softly.

'How could I do that, and put you in danger?' Bruno said, handsome as a film star and twenty times more human. 'I thought that perhaps Os . . . Oscare was behind the theft. And I knew that the Mafia was angry about my involvement with the Commission. I was so afraid the telephone might have been tapped. By calling, I could have endangered your life.'

Giulia looked down at her hands. She was still wearing her wedding ring. She twisted it round on her finger. Penny knew she was thinking that by not calling, Bruno had endangered Oscare's life. She knew the thought would linger.

It hadn't taken Jeff Hurtz long to suss out Drusilla. She was a woman waiting. For him. He moved in on her and told her so. After one night together, she decided he was right. She would have waited indefinitely. It was easy for Jeff to muscle in on her little deals with the Mafia. Far as Drusilla was concerned, he could muscle in on anything of hers he liked. He got ambitious. With her connections and his expertise, he thought they ought to move into the big time. Was it the psychopath's sensitivity to weakness in others that put him on to Riordan? Or was he just dazzled by the gold-lust burning in Riordan's eyes when, as a special favour to Bruno Ferlinghetti, the innocent treasurer of Montbella showed them the figurines?

Whatever, he persuaded Riordan to fork out big money to have him steal them. He suggested putting them where Meg would discover them. He'd already unearthed the scandal of last summer, and knew Meg would guard the statuettes with her life. The idea was that Drusilla would liberate them when the time was right. Riordan would then take them back to the States in his super-special flight bag, along with some other gold pieces for which he already had valid permits. All very neat. Except Bruno got in first.

'What beats me is why someone like Drusilla would fall for a jerk like Hurtz,' Kimbell said. As if it didn't matter at all, he picked up Penny's hand and kissed the palm. Penny had always found that heat made people randy.

'He was a class act,' said Penny. 'No question. Almost fell for him myself. Cute college kid, all innocent eyes and naivety. After the turkeys Drusilla was used to, that untouched-by-human-hand look must have been a terrific turn-on.'

'Maybe he appealed to her maternal instincts,' Kimbell said.

'They'd jail any mother with instincts like that,' said Penny.

She felt responsible for Oscare's death, knowing she should have been on to Jeff Hurtz sooner. For instance, when he told her he didn't use sun-oil, after she'd noticed oily fingerprints on the list of names he'd taken from Lavette. Or when he referred to the figurines as the Holy

Family. It was only Meg, ignoring the swaddled child, who'd called them the Royal Pair. Jeff had stolen the Holy Family of Montbella, and that was the name he knew them by.

He was the one who'd tried to warn Penny off by calling her at her hotel. That hadn't worked. Hearing her tell Lucia that she knew where the figurines were, he'd followed her down to Toscana. By then, he'd also realised that, with Drusilla dead, Penny was the only person apart from Riordan who could link him with Ferlinghetti. Riordan wouldn't talk. She would. She had to be eliminated. He'd stalked her through the streets of Toscana Antiqua, like a leopard after an antelope, waiting for a chance to go in for the kill.

'I ask myself if the evil ones, such as this young man, are born that way or turned towards it by circumstance,' said Bruno.

'Don't think they've come up with an answer to that one,' Penny said. It was a long-standing debate. Nature versus nurture. Environment versus genes. Nobody knew the answer.

'I can never figure the effort the bad guys put into being bad guys,' Kimbell said. 'If they worked that way at something legit, they'd be up there with the Rockefellers and the Vanderbilts. No sweat.'

'No risks,' said Penny.

'It's the risks they are after,' Bruno said.

'Or they just like being bad guys,' said Giulia.

'Yeah.' Penny wouldn't quickly forget Jeff Hurtz sitting on a chair in Bruno's office at Toscana with his hands tied behind him. His hair had been boyishly rumpled. His smile had been the kind they call infectious, except nobody wanted to catch anything he'd got. He'd been reading the titles on the spines of Bruno's books. The two bodies still lay where they had fallen. They and Jeff had been waiting for the police.

'Hey,' he said. '*The Golden Bough*. I read that in high school. It's good stuff.'

He'd looked as if he'd swap his mother's cows for a handful of beans any day. When Alex had asked him if he'd shot Jack Lavette, he had been surprised.

'What else was I supposed to do?' he'd said. 'He was in my way, man.' He'd grinned. 'Got him right between the eyes, from halfway up that hill. Didn't think I was that good.'

Later, one of the policemen sent down to escort him back to Rome had asked him if he had also killed Drusilla. He'd shrugged. 'Yeah,' he said.

When the policeman asked why, his hazel eyes had widened, ingenuous as an angel's. 'Come on, guys, you know how it is,' he'd said. 'She bitched the whole deal up. After all the sweat I put in on the job, she let that Ferlinghetti guy get clean away with the figurines.'

The two policemen, serious family men, had looked down at him, not knowing how it was at all, only knowing that sometimes they got one like this, a bad guy who didn't give a damn how much he spoiled things for the good guys. They had been reluctant to touch him, as though he might rub off on them.

'Why that particular night?' Penny had said.

'Listen,' said Jeff. 'Do you have any idea how long it took me to fix up that heist from the monastery?'

'No,' Penny had said.

'Nearly a year is how long,' said Jeff. 'You wouldn't believe the planning that took. Plus breaking in. Jeez. Talk about *Where Eagles Dare*. Way I heard, those religious guys're supposed to be more interested in God than Mammon, right? Says so in the Bible. Well, that crowd up at

Montbella sure aren't giving anything away. The stuff I had to organise. And then that dozy broad—'

'Drusilla,' Penny said.

'—yeah, right. Then Drusilla ups and tells me she just happens to've cleared up some kind of personal business, never did tell me what, and whyn't we forget the figurines and go off somewhere together? I wasn't having that, not after what I'd gone though. And she wasn't even what I'd call a looker. She just kept on and on about it until I could have murdered her.' He'd looked round at them. 'Well, gee. I guess I kind of did that anyway, didn't I?' He'd laughed. Alone.

Remembering, out there by the glittering pool, away from the shadows, Penny hunched her shoulders. She thought how like death evil was. How solid and immutable. How unrelenting. Up on the hills, the silver olives shivered.

'It was Jeff, of course, who broke into the house the night I arrived,' she said. 'Hoping Bruno might have stashed the figurines there. He wasn't too happy at finding Lavette already on stake-out duty. For the same reason, he'd tried to break into the Instituto Ferlinghetti and Palma's flat. Unsuccessfully in both cases.'

She felt tired. Sometimes a person wanted to be held close. Just that. If only a person didn't have to accept conditions, make commitments, before she got to be held close.

Tomorrow she'd call Barnaby. He'd ask her again to marry him. She was afraid she already knew what answer she'd give.

About the Author

Susan Moody was born in Oxford, where her father was an English don. After leaving school, she spent two years in France as personal assistant to that country's top orchid grower. While living there she met and married an American biologist and spent ten years in Tennessee.

She now lives in Bedford, England, with her three sons and is working on future Penny Wanawake books.